BELLA'S DANCE HALL

(MATT BANNISTER WESTERN 3)

KEN PRATT

Bella's Dance Hall
Ken Pratt

CKN Christian Publishing
An Imprint of Wolfpack Publishing
6032 Wheat Penny Avenue
Las Vegas, NV 89122

Paperback Edition

Paperback ISBN 978-1-64119-504-1
eBook ISBN 978-1-64119-503-4

Library of Congress Control Number: 2019932996

I grew up thinking I knew what being tough was, but I never knew true toughness until I met my wife, Cathy. She's been battling Early Onset Alzheimer's for seven years now. She was diagnosed in 2012 and given between five and ten years to live. Her Alzheimer's isn't genetic, it's caused from repeated blows to her head while being physically abused for ten years in her first marriage. Cathy decided early on to fight this disease and she has every step of the way. She is still fighting with the heart of a champion and refuses to be defeated easily. Time means everything when this wicked disease comes along, and we cherish every day with her. She is an example of courage, strength, a fighter's heart and endurance. And Praise the Lord, she isn't done fighting yet. If there is any one thing she has that keeps her going, it's hope. And that's ultimately what this story is about...Hope. This book is dedicated to my wife, Cathy.

"For we walk by faith, not by sight." 2 Corinthians 5:7

ACKNOWLEDGMENTS

I must acknowledge my son, Keith Pratt for his wisdom. This story was originally a sub plot within a larger novel. With Keith's insight, it was removed from the original story and expanded to become its own book. This book wouldn't exist without Keith's suggesting it. Keith is always the first to read, edit and always the first to be the most critical and honest. His critical thinking brings up some great points to ponder and quite often his ideas make their way onto the pages. Thank you, Keith, you're a very big part of my small writing circle, buddy!

I want to thank my friend, Andrew Worley for listening to the countless hours I spent talking, explaining, over-emphasizing and frustrated venting while writing this story. He listened and took an interest in the story and to my appreciation made himself available for sudden emergency phone calls after midnight to hear me say, *"Hey, I'm stuck. What do you think about...."* A friend like that is rare, but one willing to talk about the characters in a book is far rarer. I appreciate you so much Andrew. Thank you.

Finely, I want to thank Mike Bray and Lauren Bridges and the rest of the folks at CKN Christian Publishing for doing all the hard work to make this book and others possible. I thank you all.

AUTHOR'S NOTE

First and foremost, I want to take a moment to explain that Sweethome, Bella's Dance Hall and the next book in the series titled, The Wolves of Windsor Ridge, all take place at the same time at three different locations. There is a reason for this, but I won't go into it right now. So, as you read this story, keep in mind, Matt Bannister is in Sweethome trailing Truet Davis. This story is what happens in Branson while he is gone.

BELLA'S DANCE HALL

PROLOGUE

Branson, Oregon, July 1883

WALTER LEARD WAS one of the best-known names in Northern California and had brought a large herd of his horses north. He intended to sell them at a few special auctions along the way to Boise, Idaho, where the remainder of his herd would be sold to the Army. Although the Army would buy mixed stock, his Flying L Ranch-brand quarter horses were hard to come by in Oregon, and they were the reason many people would attend the auctions. The horses were higher-priced than others, but they were Walter Leard bred, broke, and trained, and reputed to be some of the best in the West. Not everyone could afford the price for his trained animals, but few would miss the chance to bid on a horse of such quality.

Annie Lenning wouldn't miss the opportunity to be at the auction, but she was more excited to meet Walter Leard over breakfast at the Monarch Hotel's restaurant with her brother, Lee Bannister. The three of them sat in a quiet corner and talked about ranching, cattle, marketing, and other relevant details of the trade. When Walter spoke about making the transition from cattle to his passion for breeding and training horses, she listened avidly. To raise and work with horses was exactly what she had always wanted to do. She had grown up on the Big Z Ranch, and working cattle was their business, but it was her dream to raise horses and build the kind of reputation and business Walter Leard had.

"Tell me, Mister Leard..." Annie spoke seriously. She was dressed in a tan dress and had her hair tied back in a low bun. Her sincere curiosity showed clearly on her attractive face. "How do you manage the ranch and all the responsibilities and the business side of it and have time to work with the horses? If I were to attempt that much, our business would fail. It was my Uncle Charlie's ranch, and cattle is his business, but he is retiring. He still is hands-on right now, but in a limited capacity. It is my ranch, Mister Leard, but I don't have much help at the moment. We are so busy simply keeping up that I have no time for breaking horses. I know that if I want my dreams to come true, I need to make some drastic changes, but I fear changing our bread and butter for horses may do us in. We're cattle ranchers."

"How many cowhands do you have?" Walter asked.

"Altogether, if we called in our local teenage help, maybe ten. But we don't have any experienced cowboys working for us."

Walter Leard was an older man with gray hair and a short, well-kept gray beard. His aged stern blue eyes showed wisdom acquired from years of tough living, yet also revealed gentleness. He approved of Annie's character. "Your simple answer is that you need more help. If you don't mind me asking, why isn't your husband here? Lee mentioned he would be at this meeting, and it seems odd that he isn't here to discuss the future of his ranch. It's a man's duty to be here to talk business."

Annie took a deep breath and sighed with frustration. "I'm afraid my husband is not...very involved in the ranch, Mister Leard. And I thought he would be here too, but I have not seen him since last night when we arrived. He has friends in town and has disappeared with them again, I am embarrassed to say. However, it is *my* ranch and *my* business, Mister Leard. Not his." Her displeasure was clear in her expression.

Walter shook his head slightly. "I am sorry to hear that, Annie. It's none of my business, of course, but what the hell is his problem? You're too beautiful a young lady to run a ranch alone. A man's duty is to his family and his livelihood. Real men don't run off like a child on a school recess, which it sounds like he's doing. You'll want good, reliable men to start a horse company, Annie. Unreliable men are a hazard to themselves, your family, and your business. Any cowboy who is loyal to you would knock him on his ass and toss him off the ranch for good. Half-assed labor won't do what you need done, just so you know."

Annie's face reddened, her embarrassment making itself visible. "I...won't make excuses for him. He used to be more passionate about the work and learned fast, but recently, he...well, he quit coming to church with us, and his attitude went down from there. Our church's Reverend came one Sunday afternoon and condemned his drinking and gambling after he'd come home hungover after a weekend here with his friends. Kyle was offended and has never gone back to church. He's still mad at Reverend Ash. That was about three months ago now, and he's become more bitter since then."

"Sounds like he needs to grow up and lay the bottle down. Anyway, let's get back to you and start with the basics. Do you have a bunkhouse and cookhouse for your cowhands?"

She shook her head. "No. The ranch has always been small and makes a decent living, but Uncle Charlie has never wanted too many hands living there. He hired for drives, roundups, and things like that, but always on a temporary basis, and only men he knew. My uncle's name is Charlie Ziegler, and he was a bounty hunter of some significance way back when. As a result, he never wanted too many people around him and his family. After the Dobson Gang came to Willow Falls from Texas to kill him, strangers were no longer welcome on the ranch. And yes, you may have heard that when the Dobson Gang came looking for Uncle Charlie, my brother Matt killed them all. Lee was driving cattle with Charlie when that happened."

Walter turned to the other man. "So you're no stranger to the ranching game?"

Lee shook his head. "No. I grew up working on the ranch, and both my father and grandfather were ranchers, so I know the business and the investment costs involved. I prefer my line of work, though. It's somewhat cleaner," he said with a small smile.

"I have heard of your uncle. He was a force to be reckoned with back in the day. Your brother as well." Walter paused for a moment before continuing, "Okay, if you want to build your ranch into a horse company, you'll need men who know what they are doing. Professional cowboys who can break a wild stallion, and are tough enough to do it every day. You'll need a handful of them, because a small horse breeder may break a few horses a month, but a successful horse company breaks a lot more and has them

4

ready to sell. You will never make your payroll by selling a few without keeping and preferably expanding your cattle business.

"Look, when I started, I had the bunkhouses and a large herd of beeves, but I was successful enough to give the cattle business to my little brother to manage. That relieved me of all that responsibility, and I put my attention on the horse trade. You need to decide if you want to expand your ranch first, and that means men living on your land full-time in a bunkhouse and close to your family. If you do decide to expand, you'll need to build the facilities to bunk, feed, and care for some good men who will make you money with their trade. I will warn you, cowboys can get ornery on their weekends off, so prepare your little town," he said with a smile. "But if you choose to go forward, I will sell you a good herd of a dozen unbranded horses to get started with. Hand-chosen by me."

"You could talk to Adam about managing the cattle," Lee mentioned to Annie. "Perhaps the Big Z could merge with him, and that would free you up?"

She looked emotionally torn as she agonized over giving Walter Leard an answer. While she wanted to jump on the opportunity, one thought made her hesitate. "I have to talk to Uncle Charlie about it first. He is not one for change."

"Oh, I know," Lee agreed.

Annie looked at Walter. "Mister Leard, I have a dream, exactly like you had. But I don't have the luxury you did. I can afford to offer the hands a decent living, but I think it may take some time to get the ranch ready. Rest assured, I *will* own a horse company and I *will* make this work, but I have things to put in place first. It isn't only the financial cost of new buildings, but also where to put them. There's a lot to consider and plan for if I'm serious about this. We have more than enough to do to simply maintain the ranch as it is right now, but I will work to prepare it to start a horse company. When I am ready, can I write to you about finding some good men to help me get started? I can break a horse myself, but as you said, I will need help."

Walter smiled slightly, admiring the ambition that glowed in Annie's eyes. "I didn't realize you were so hands-on," he commented with real awe in his expression. The dark-haired, beautiful young lady before him became more impressive by the moment. Knowing it was more satisfying to be a horseman than a cattleman, he understood her longing and spent another hour giving her all the advice he could. He also answered every question she or Lee had. In addition, he made them a deal on twenty horses as foundation stock for her business when she was able to make a start.

When the breakfast meeting was over, Lee encouraged her to take advantage of the situation and go for her dream, and even offered her a loan to upgrade the ranch. He had mentioned the idea of consolidating Adam's ranch with the Big Z and having two businesses as Walter did—the cattle and the horse company. There was more than enough land for both. They merely needed more facilities and manpower. It would have to be discussed in further detail and be approved by Uncle Charlie, and that thought raised a degree of anxiety. It was, in fact, asking the man to surrender and give away everything he had spent his life building and trust her to care for.

She had gone to the auction at noon, and again, her husband Kyle had failed to show up. Annie had already discussed buying a few of Walter's best quarter horses for a reduced price, which she did. However, her friend Rory Jackson had fallen in love with a beautiful tan buckskin mare at first sight, and paid a high price to ride away on the beauty she named Princess. For Rory, her mare was worth every cent.

When the auction was over, Annie had three horses to take back to Willow Falls. She was satisfied with her purchase and excited about the potential for her future. However, she was furious that her husband hadn't shown up for breakfast or the auction. The auction was the reason they had come to Branson to begin with. They had left their children to visit with Kyle's parents, while Kyle and Annie were supposed to stay in the Monarch Hotel and spend some time together without their children for once.

It hadn't worked out that way. He had left on Friday evening to say hi to his old friends Paul and Sam for a minute, and she had not seen him since. She knew where he was. He was with his friends, drinking and gambling like he did at every opportunity he had to come to Branson. Annie was sick of it, and this was the straw that broke the proverbial camel's back.

She didn't know where his friends lived, but she knew they rented a small cottage from Lee. Over the years, her brother had bought land, knowing the city would expand. With Branson growing the way it was, he still bought and developed rows of small houses that he called cottages. They were basic, simple homes with one, two, and a few three-bedroom options that were made for larger families moving to town. They all looked identical, except for the occasional one painted a different color. Most all were simply light gray with white trim. The only thing different about every one of them was the number painted on the door jamb.

Annie was only interested in the one where Paul and Sam lived. Lee didn't have to look at his rental contracts. He already knew they rented number seventeen on Lexington Lane—a private alley that cut through the center of a city block filled with his cottages. The two young men reminded him that they were friends with Kyle every time they paid their monthly rent at his office.

She asked her brother Matt Bannister to go with her, and he obliged happily. He spoke as they walked toward Lexington Lane off Fourth Street. "I stood outside my office and saw three ladies in very nice dresses walking toward me. One of them—her name is Christine, I discovered—was so beautiful that I could not keep my eyes off her. I don't know that I have ever experienced that before. I mean, I literally couldn't take my eyes off her. It was weird."

"Did you say hi at least, or did you stand there like an idiot with your mouth hanging open?" she asked, glad to hear that he had finally noticed the ladies in Branson after moving there in January.

"I said hi, but some hee-haw of a sheriff from Loveland interrupted the moment and wouldn't shut up until after the ladies had passed by."

"How do you know her name, then?"

Matt frowned and shook his head in embarrassment. "Um...that sheriff made a stupid comment to them, and one of her friends called back, 'Christine likes the marshal.' I assume that means me, right? Oh, and then that beautiful girl pushed her friend like it embarrassed her."

"Did she look back at you?" Annie asked, and paused in the street to hear the answer.

Matt nodded. "In fact, she did."

She shrugged. "It sounds like she's interested. Remember this, Matt: interested girls will always look back if they're walking away, and will watch you if you're walking away. Do I have to teach you everything about women?"

"Probably. It wouldn't hurt, anyway," he said with a shrug.

She resumed walking. "Then I'll have to if we ever expect you to get married. Who is she, anyway?"

"I really have no idea! I have never seen her or her friends before. Right then, Adam and William arrived, and William said they were dancers at the new dance hall on Rose Street. Which would be too bad, because that Christine girl really was quite beautiful, and there was something about her, like I said, that...I don't know, captivated me. I have never experienced anything like that before. I mean, I literally could not take my eyes off her. But I'm not interested in prostitutes, no matter how beautiful they are. It's too bad, though. She was stunning."

"And how do you know she is a prostitute? Some dancers are simply dancers, you know. You shouldn't judge a person too quickly, Matt. You of all people should know that," Annie said as they reached cottage number seventeen. "Now, let's see why Kyle missed the auction."

"I'm not judging her, but you have to admit it isn't a very wholesome environment."

Annie looked severely at her brother as she reached the door. "Neither is being a marshal. In my opinion, you should go down there tonight and check it out." She knocked loudly on the door. When no one answered, she banged louder.

"Hold on!" a voice shouted impatiently from the other side. A moment later, the door was opened by Sam, a blond-haired man of short stature. He looked as if he had just woken up and didn't feel as good as he normally would. He shielded his eyes against the sun. "What do you want? Oh..." He changed his tone when he recognized the visitors.

"Where's Kyle?" she asked, making no effort to hide her frustration.

Sam turned to his right and pointed at the davenport. Kyle Lenning laid across it on his stomach with a cooking pot beside him on the floor, obviously for vomit. The room was dim and smelled of liquor, body odor, and bile.

Annie didn't wait to be invited inside. She stepped forward and spoke loudly. "It looks like you had a great time, Kyle. It's a lot of fun puking in someone else's cook pot at three in the afternoon, isn't it? It's absolutely ridiculous. Now, get your ass up, and let's go! Come on, Kyle."

"I'm sick," he said weakly.

"Oh, I know! But unfortunately for you, I don't give a damn. Now get up and let's go. I bought three horses at the auction, so you don't have any more drinking or gambling money to waste, along with your day. Listen to me, you drunkard. My father lost his family and his ranch because of drinking and gambling. I won't do it, and I won't let you bury the Big Z in drink and laziness either."

Kyle looked at her, leaned over, and vomited into the cook pot with a long, forceful stomach contraction that must have hurt. Air and a long line of thick drool were the only things that came up. His stomach contracted again in another long dry-heave.

Annie looked at Sam and Paul, who'd now emerged from his bedroom. He leaned on the doorjamb. "I'm really not happy with you all," she said.

Sam shrugged helplessly. "He wouldn't quit drinking until the sun was up."

"So, you bought some horses, huh?" Paul rubbed his eyes. "Want to sell me one? I wouldn't mind having a pony of my own. Hey, Matt, how are you doing?"

Matt nodded. "Better than you, by the looks of it."

"Undoubtedly," Sam agreed. "Well, I'm going back to bed. Kyle, get up and get moving. I'll see you later, bud. Annie, it's always a pleasure. Come back anytime, but I have to get to sleep."

"No," Annie said irritably. "Kyle, stay here and drink and puke your brains out because tonight's the last night you get to do this. No more, Kyle. Have fun, because after tonight, these days are over!" She looked at Matt, "Let's go. I'm leaving the drunkard here to puke his guts up. I'm not cleaning up after him."

"I guess I'll talk to Kyle about buying a horse," Paul said as Annie walked out of their house.

She turned quickly and spoke sharply. "Kyle can't sell you anything except what I say he can, and the only thing he will sell you is a wheelbarrow-load of muck from the pigpens."

Paul laughed lightly. "Love you, too, Annie."

Once outside, Matt asked his sister, "Are you doing okay?"

She shook her head in frustration, and anger burned in her eyes. "Matt, I am so disgusted right now, I could puke! The man has a family to take care of, and he'd rather get drunk with his friends than spend time alone with me. I'm his wife! You'd think he should at least love me enough to want to spend time with me. We left the kids with his parents and had the weekend to ourselves in the Monarch Hotel." She sighed and shook her head. "He left yesterday after we got to the hotel, saying he'd be back, and I haven't seen him until now. If he shows up at the hotel this evening, I will kick him out. He can go back to his friends' house. I have no desire to see him until we go home tomorrow. He chose them over me, Matt," she said sadly, her voice faltering.

He put his arm around his sister as they walked. "I'm sorry, sis. When he sobers up, maybe he'll understand what a fool he's been. I hope so, anyway. But look on the bright side. At least you get to hang out with your brothers tonight without any children to pull on your sleeves."

She smiled. "Yeah, I suppose you're right. Except, you have a date, don't you?"

Matt frowned, "No."

"Dance hall girl? Christine? Go meet her. She might be more than you think. She will never be as perfect for you as Rory is, but go find out for yourself."

CHRISTINE KNAPP SMILED with excitement as she took a ticket from a paying customer to dance for a few minutes to the music the band played. She took him by the hand and led him out onto the dancefloor. Facing one another, they began to dance respectfully, and her partner looked more enamored with Christine than Matt Bannister had ever seen a young man look before. He was twenty at most, with dark hair and a short goatee. He was dressed in his Sunday best, no doubt. His joy in Christine's presence was infectious. Matt smiled as he watched her glide around the dancefloor with the lucky man.

The marshal hadn't visited the new dance hall before and was impressed by the size, the beauty of the decorations, and the cleanliness. He had not bought any dance tickets or walked too far into the main dance hall. Instead, he remained close to the exit door and tried not to draw attention to himself as he enjoyed his second look at Christine. She was beautiful—the most beautiful girl he had ever seen—and he watched her with possibly the same expression in his eyes as the young man who danced with her. In short, he was enamored by the beauty and grace of a young woman who appeared almost angelic.

"Matt Bannister, what are you doing here?" Travis McKnight asked, suddenly at his side.

"Oh, Travis, hi. I am looking around. You?"

"The same. I was curious what this place was all about. Some of my employees keep talking about it. Thought I'd come down and see for myself."

"How's the family?"

"Good. How's yours?"

Matt nodded and pointed casually at Christine and the young man. He explained, "It looks like he really likes her. She walked by my office today, and I wondered who she was. Her name's Christine, I think."

Travis nodded, and a serious expression settled on his face. "Yeah, well, he had better be careful with her. Remember those employees I told you about? Well, one of them was diagnosed with syphilis, and the other two are running scared after being with her. She has a beautiful face, but she carries a lethal dose of poison in that smile of hers. I'd stay away from her, Matt, if you're smart. You know what I mean?"

"She's a prostitute?" His question sounded more like a statement than a question. Either way, he sounded very disappointed.

Travis shrugged. "My employee didn't get syphilis from dancing with her, Matt. She cost him five dollars, which is darn near two days' work for the poor guy, and she gave him something to remember her by. Don't be fooled by her pretty face. She's as much of a polluted whore as any used-up scrap of a woman you'll ever find."

"Well, we'd better tell that young man before he ruins

his life," Matt said.

"I know him. That's Brent Boyle, Deuce McKenna's nephew. I'll talk to him later."

"Hmm. I suppose I'll head home, then. It's too bad she has to resort to that kind of lifestyle. She is absolutely beautiful. You'd think she could find a decent man to marry rather than do that, huh?"

Travis turned toward Matt and pointed at Christine, who was still dancing. "Do you see her dress? She makes a fortune dancing and singing, so she whores for fun and pure evilness, I'd guess. Remember, Satan was the most beautiful angel God created, but it didn't make him loving or kind. Some women are the same way."

Matt looked at Christine one last time. He looked away when her eyes locked onto his, and she smiled. "I'll see you later, Travis," he said, and turned to walk out without looking back.

"All right, Matt. Have a good night." Travis watched Matt walk out of the dance hall, looked at Christine, and smiled. He walked across to her and handed her a ticket. "Hello, beautiful, how are you tonight?"

"I am well. Hey, was that Matt Bannister you were talking to?" she asked with interest.

Travis grimaced. "Yeah, it was, but you don't want to get involved with him. He's a mess. He was under the impression this was a brothel. I had to tell him it wasn't. He's going up the street to buy some loving, if you know what I mean."

"I didn't think he was like that. That's not the kind of man I heard he was," she stated, disappointment in her voice.

Travis shrugged. "There's the daylight Marshal Bannister everyone sees, and then there's the hidden in-the-dark, prostitute-hungry Matt Bannister, except from us men who know him. He likes to keep his reputation clean, but we all know he is infected with syphilis and spreads it around in pure hatred of women. I'd stay away from him if I were you, Christine. Sometimes, he doesn't take no for an answer, and I'd hate to see you hurt by the likes of him. I like you far too much to want to see you hurt."

"Well, thank you. I thought he was a Christian man, is all," she said with a disappointed shrug.

Travis laughed lightly as they danced. "Remember, even Satan knows and quotes scripture, but it doesn't make him a Christian. He merely acts like it until the sun goes down."

She frowned. "That's unfortunate. Everyone around here thinks he is one, but that matter will be settled between him and God someday. So, would you be interested in staying after we close to visit? You'd have to sit down here and mind the rules, but we could talk for a while longer."

Travis smiled. "I'd love to. I haven't had the opportunity to sit and talk to a beautiful young lady since my wife died, and that's been a year ago like I told you."

"I haven't wanted to talk to another man since my husband died, so I really do understand."

Travis smiled slightly as he stared into her eyes. "I know where you're coming from. I have to say, I hate how we both got here, but I'm glad I had the chance to meet you."

"What about getting to know me?" she asked with a slight laugh.

"Of course. I am very thankful to get to know you. I never thought I could talk as easily to another lady as I find I can to you. It must be fate, huh?"

Christine smiled. "Maybe. But I won't rush into anything, okay?"

"All I have is time, Christina. All the time in the world to wait for you."

1

Willow Falls, Oregon
   July 1883

KYLE LENNING CURSED IN IRRITATION. It was a Friday after-noon, and instead of closing a shop to enjoy a relaxing weekend like his parents always did on Fridays in Branson, Kyle stood in a hayfield under the hot sun. He waited for Darius Jackson to bring one of the wagons back from the barn so they could load it with loose, dusty hay again.

The field was devoid of shade, and it was in the mid-nineties. He wore a straw hat to shade his face and a sweat-drenched, gray long-sleeved shirt under the suspenders that held up his dark cotton pants. A good pair of cowhide gloves from the Natoma Glove Company in the next town over was necessary, but they made his hands itch and sweat. He was miserable, hot, and covered with layers of dust, and he had run out of water to drink. All this had put him in a foul mood that grew worse by the minute. He was tired and thirsty, and had no desire whatsoever to work until dark like they had done all week.

The Big Z was owned by Charlie Ziegler and his wife Mary. The spread was twenty-five hundred acres, with a thousand head of cattle scattered across the ranch and additional open range as well. Charlie once had long-standing contracts with the government to provide cattle to two Indian reservations but had recently lost them to ranchers more local to those areas. He sold beeves to various meat markets when the price went up, and he supplied beeves to the local butcher shops around Branson and the other little towns. Unfortunately, the days of having government contracts to depend on were coming to an end for the Big Z.

Charlie had worked the ranch for many years with his nephews and hired hands that came and went, but his one constant for over thirty years had been his friend Darius Jackson. Together, they had made the Big Z Ranch a success. He was not a cattle king by any means, but for a small family-run ranch, it had prospered well enough year after year—until the recent loss of his two main contracts.

Kyle never understood why Charlie didn't hire experienced cowhands and expand his ranch into a cattle dynasty, but the old man had never wanted a big spread or many hired hands. He was content to do the work himself, and keep it just large enough to manage himself and live comfortably. Now, the two old-timers were both in their mid-sixties and growing older, and the physical labor had become too much for them. They worked hard, but they weren't as productive as they had been, and it showed.

The ranch had never been less productive than it was now, and Charlie still didn't want to hire any full-time hands to help catch up on the work that needed to be done. The workload thus became a matter of priorities that Kyle, as

Annie's husband, was expected to attend to. Oddly enough, he had never wanted to work on a ranch. He had been raised in Branson and had worked at his parent's hardware store. It was a regular job, serving customers during regular hours and giving him regular days off to enjoy life. He enjoyed staying clean, being indoors, and talking to customers.

While he was comfortable with the urban life of a merchant, unlike his father, Kyle had dreamed of owning a saloon and making it the liveliest and most fun place in Branson. He wanted to make a living doing what he loved to do, and that was having fun. He knew he could make a fortune if he could do it his way, and he would enjoy every minute of it.

If he had fallen in love with any other young lady in the world, he could have remained in Branson and be living his dream by now, but he had fallen in love with Annie Bannister. She was Charlie and Mary Ziegler's niece, whom they had raised on the Big Z. Kyle had known when he asked for her hand in marriage that she would never leave the ranch, and that he would have to change his life to share his with hers. It was the sacrifice he would make to love the most hard-headed, hardest-working, and most beautiful lady he'd ever known.

Unfortunately, the years had gone by, and he had come to resent the life he now lived. He wasn't a cowboy, and he was tired of acting like one. Annie was the only reason he sat under the hot sun in the middle of a field and waited to throw hay onto a wagon. Unfortunately, that single reason was losing its influence on him.

He heard the squeak of the wagon's wheels and stood as Darius Jackson drove the wagon toward him. He retrieved his hayfork and looked curiously at the other man as he pulled to a halt beside the stack of hay Kyle had leaned against. "Where are the boys?" he asked irritably.

The two teenage boys who had helped load the wagon all day had ridden back to the barn with Darius on the last trip because the boss wanted to talk to them. They had not returned, which meant more work for the two remaining men.

His companion shrugged. "Charlie sent them all home for the weekend. He paid them and told them to come back Monday morning. I guess he's getting soft in his old age. He never gave me time off," Darius said, his smile constant as he stepped off the wagon.

Kyle scoffed in disgust. "So we have to load this ourselves?"

"You betcha! We can do it, though. A couple of cowboys like us shouldn't be put off by a day's work, isn't that right?" Darius said optimistically as he handed a full canteen of water to Kyle.

He opened it and took a long drink, and lowered it to breathe before taking another long drink. When he finished, he wiped his mouth and replaced the cap. "I'm not working until dark. I've had enough. I'll help you load this wagon, and then I'm done. If Charlie sent those boys home, I'll go home too."

The other man looked oddly at him as he pulled his hayfork out the back of the wagon. "Them kids have worked as hard as we have for two weeks without complaining, but they're only hired help. You're a part-owner of this ranch now, and if you don't mind me saying so, if there's work to do, you need to get it done. We'd all like to call it a day, but we can't."

Kyle couldn't hide his annoyance. "When I *do* run things

here, I'll sit on the porch and hire this job out to others. I won't ever get dirty again."

Darius laughed. "It's good to dream, but those hired cowboys cost money. The more you pay for the work you could do yourself is that much less in those deep pockets of yours."

He liked the old man, but he resented the fact that he was a hired hand with more authority and higher wages than he had himself. It was true that Kyle would own the ranch eventually, but he had no desire to work it. What he did know was that when he cut the aging hand's wages someday soon, he could afford an experienced cowboy to run the ranch for him.

Kyle decided to ignore Darius' statement and said bitterly, "And when you retire, it'll put more money into our pockets. You're paid far more than you're worth." He shook his head with frustration and a look of disgust at his companion. "Let's get this loaded, and I'll ride back with you. I'm done for the weekend too. The hell with it. I'll go to Branson for the weekend to enjoy myself for a change. Everyone else has fun around here, so why shouldn't I?"

Darius frowned with disappointment and a trace of anger at the irony of being criticized by the younger man for not being worth his wages. This was said by one whose consistently shallow work ethic depended on his particular mood on any given day. Still, he held his tongue, shoved his hayfork into the stack of hay, and tossed it into the wagon. Kyle wasn't his concern anyway. He was Annie's husband, and was therefore a problem for her to deal with—and knowing her, she would.

"Yep," Kyle said as he tossed hay into the wagon's bed with vigor born of anger rather than enthusiasm. "Screw it, I need some time off. The ranch won't go under if I'm not here to help. There's no sign of rain either, so there's no hurry."

His companion ignored him and began to whistle a hymn as he worked. Kyle could drain him with his complaining and whining, especially when the days were long and exhaustion was shared by all. He could get along with anyone just fine, but the young man had a way of making it that much harder to tolerate him when he began to complain like a spoiled child. If the truth was told, he complained constantly.

"Let's get this damn thing loaded and go home," Kyle said bitterly. It irritated him to be ignored by an overpaid hired hand.

DARIUS DROVE the wagon across the Big Z to the large hay barn near the homestead and stopped beneath a double door under the overhanging eve near the top of the structure. The doors were open, and a large grappler fork dangled lifelessly, waiting to be lowered from a block pulley connected to a metal track attached to the ceiling inside the barn. Standing in the shade of the building were Charlie Ziegler, Steven Bannister, Steven's friend Johnny Barso, and Annie Lenning. They drank sweetened water from a glass pitcher, and all were covered in hay dust and stalks.

Annie watched the two men draw up in the wagon. She immediately noticed by his frown that Kyle looked irritated, and offered him her glass of sweetened water, "You act like you're hot or something," she said cheerfully. "You should try stacking the hay up there!. It has to be close to a hundred and fifteen degrees."

Kyle drank the water quickly and stepped out of the wagon. He handed the empty glass to her. "It doesn't matter.

I'm done for the day. You guys finish up." He walked quickly toward his house next to Charlie's and Mary's and about a hundred yards away from the barn.

Annie watched him walk away, perplexed for a moment. "Where do you think you're going?" she called.

He waved her question away without looking back. "I'm done," was all he said. He kept walking.

"Done?" she asked quietly and turned to look at Darius. "What's wrong with him?"

He shrugged. "I don't know. When he heard Charlie sent the boys home, he got upset. He wants time off too, I guess."

Charlie sighed and shook his head. He turned to Steven and Johnny. "Well, let's get this hay unloaded."

Steven frowned. "Maybe I should go tell him we're hot and tired too, but we're still working. You might want to remind him of that," Steven said to his little sister.

Annie shrugged in disgust. "Oh, he's been grumpy for days. Let's finish with this load, and I'll go back with Darius for the next one."

Charlie peered at Kyle, who had neared his front porch. "What's eating at him? Work?"

She drew a deep breath as she pulled her cowhide gloves on. "I guess."

Her uncle studied her but didn't need to say anything more. His disappointment showed in his aging green eyes. He turned to his nephew and Johnny. "Let's get back up there and get some work done."

"You bet," Steven said, and headed into the barn to go upstairs, followed by his friend.

Darius locked the brakes on the wagon and stood on the bench seat to climb onto the hay, which was stacked eight feet high. The wagon had a modified flatbed that was eight feet wide and ten feet long. The stack of hay was a little over eight feet high from the wagon's bed. He looked at Annie, who carried two wooden buckets of water from the creek for the horses to drink.

She set the water down for the animals and frowned at him. "You irritated my husband again, huh?"

He smiled. "I suppose so. But what I *do* know that is you get to do his job now."

"Yeah, I'll help you get the next load. But you know this is the last year we're doing it like this, don't you? I don't care what Uncle Charlie says, we will buy a loader this winter. It will load the hay for us and cut our labor down to nothing," Annie said with real determination.

Darius shook his head. "Yeah, it figures you all would wait until I'm about to retire to make the job easier."

Charlie had bought a horse-drawn mower to cut the hay and a horse-drawn rake to line it into windrows for drying. However, he had never invested in a hay loader that connected to the back of the wagon to gather the hay and drop it on the wagon bed. It would have been a useful and time-saving piece of equipment, but he had decided to use the money elsewhere for the ranch and put off buying another piece of equipment he would use for only a week or two a year.

He had used the rake to lay out the long line of windrows to dry the hay and then used it again to pull the windrows into piles of dry hay for the boys to throw onto the wagon by hand. He had also invested in a modern iron hay carrier and rail system for his barn, an impressive upgrade from the wood rail system he had used in the past. His hay crop had cost him a small fortune, but he figured that with all the machinery and time saved, hand-loading the wagons was still far too small a matter to justify spending so much

money on something with such a short season of useful-
ness. His niece disagreed.

Annie walked to a young horse tethered to a post a short
distance away, which had a long rope tied to its harness. The
rope fed to the large block pulley mounted under the overhanging gable above the large double doors of the loft. A
large hayfork with four three-foot-long tangs hung above
the wagon, suspended by the pulley. She untied the halter
and walked the horse backward to lower the grapple fork
down toward Darius. He watched carefully and grabbed it
as soon as he could.

It took him only a moment to shove the fork into the pile of
hay he was perched on, and he stood back as Annie walked the
horse forward. As she did so, a large pile of loose hay was hauled
into the air and toward the loft. Steven Bannister stood in the
door and waited for the load to arrive. The grapple fork halted
once it reached the hay carrier, and Annie stopped the horse.
Steven tugged a short rope, and the carrier—a square frame
with built-in rollers on top—trundled easily to the other end of
the barn over a series of iron flat rails mounted on the ceiling.

Once they reached the stack of hay, he pulled another
rope and the grapple hook tilted upward and dropped its
load onto the growing pile. From there, Charlie and Johnny
would move it to wherever they wanted it on the stack.

Steven dragged the heavy iron carriage back to the door
and the end of the rail and Annie backed the horse up to
lower the grapple fork again. The work in the loft was dusty,
dry, and terribly hot, but it needed to be done. They'd had
two wagon crews bringing hay in throughout the past week,
and for three days, Adam Bannister and his two young sons
helped with a third wagon.

The hayloft was more than a two-thirds full of tightly-packed hay that reached almost to the roof. They had brought in a substantial supply, but there was still much more to bring in before it rained. It had been a strange summer, with more rain thus far than usual, but as of now, the cut hay was dry, and there was no indication of rain in the near future.

It was a Friday afternoon, and Charlie had decided he would give the four teenage boys the afternoon off to go swimming or something while there was plenty of daylight left for them to go be boys. The only days off they'd had were Sundays, and they'd worked hard and long enough hours without complaining that he felt they deserved to have the afternoon off to enjoy their pay and rest up over the weekend. Come Monday morning, he knew they'd be rejuvenated enough to do whatever work he had for them. Little did he know that by doing so, it would lose him another pair of hands in Kyle. It frustrated him.

When the last of the hay had been raised and dropped in front of him, the old man wiped the heavy sweat from his face. He called to Steven, who looked damp and uncomfortably hot as he did. "Leave the grapple on the floor and close the doors. Tell Darius to put the horses away, and you and Johnny go home to your families. The rest of the hay can wait until tomorrow."

Steven hesitated. "We could get another load or two, Uncle Charlie. Johnny and I could load the other wagon."

"No, let's stop for the day."

"It's still fairly early," Johnny Barso protested. He was the new Willow Falls deputy, after the unexpected death of long-time deputy Clyde Waltz the previous winter. Sheriff Tom Smith was good enough to let Johnny help Charlie bring his hay in.

The old man leaned on his hayfork. "I appreciate the

offer, but we can't get it all in today anyway. We might as well quit early and rest up. Go spend some time with your families. If you want to help tomorrow, we'll be at it again."

"I'll be here," Johnny said.

ANNIE HELPED DARIUS put the horses away before she returned to her house. She walked inside and asked her oldest son Ira, who'd watched his younger siblings all day, "Where's your pa?"

"Upstairs in your room," the boy answered. He usually spent the day on the multiple chores that needed to be done while everyone else hauled hay, but he had been needed to watch his younger siblings today. Rory Jackson, Darius' twenty-six-year-old daughter and Annie's best friend, had not been feeling well and was unable to do so.

She climbed the stairs wearily and opened the bedroom door. Kyle leaned shirtless over a wash basin and sponged his body off with a wash rag.

"What are you doing?" she asked pointedly. "Couldn't you stick around and help us unload?"

He looked at her and noted the blue denim jeans held up by suspenders over a striped blue-and-white long-sleeved man's shirt. Her boots were covered in dust, and she clutched her leather gloves in her left hand. She'd pulled her long black hair into a ponytail beneath her straw hat, which was covered in a thin layer of dust and sweat. He shook his head as he completed his scrutiny. "No, I am done with hay. I need a break."

"Great," Annie said sarcastically. "We're done for the day, so take a break. But tomorrow morning, we must get back to work. So rest up, because we want to get this hay finished."

Kyle sighed. "I'm not helping—"

"What do you mean, you're not helping? We have hay to bring in, so you'll help bring it in."

"I'm not a rancher, Annie. I'm a merchant. I'd be better at managing the ranch than working it, and you know that," he retorted as he washed his underarms.

She frowned irritably. "The ranch doesn't need a manager. We need the hay brought in. We manage fine."

He tossed the wash rag down into the basin. "I've worked my hands to the bone fixing fences, herding cattle, branding calves, doctoring sores, and getting kicked in the shin, and all for the sake of saving calves. Now, it's hay. Cut hay, rake hay, pile hay, and now, *harvesting* hay. *Damn it, Annie, I need a break.* I don't want my whole life to be about the damn Big Z Ranch and working all the time. I don't love it the way you do. I don't. So, I am taking a break and going to Branson for the weekend to see my friends. I'll have some fun and enjoy myself for a change."

"You're *not* going to Branson," Annie exclaimed immediately, angered by his remarks. "We have work to do, and you can help us do it. This ranch you apparently can't stand is what puts the money you gamble away in your pocket. I don't hear you complaining about that, though, only the work. Let me tell you something else. I'll never leave this ranch, and as long as you're married to me, neither will you. If you don't want to do the work, open a petty little store in Willow Falls and peddle your goods, but don't ask me to share my bank account with you. If you don't want to work this ranch, you won't benefit from it."

Kyle glared at his wife in anger. "Fine."

"Fine?" she questioned. "Is that where Catherine gets it? Fine? She's *six years old*, Kyle! You sound like your little girl. Fine?"

He turned away from her and yanked a dresser drawer

open to pull out a clean shirt and pants. "I'm going to Branson whether you like it or not. I intend to have some fun before I die of boredom. If I had known that our marriage would be about the Big Z and not us, I would never have married you. I need some excitement in my life, not more work than a man can stand."

Annie paused. Tears threatened at the cutting words her husband had spoken to her. Her twenty-ninth birthday was the following day, but if that wasn't important enough for him to remember, she wouldn't remind him. She refused to use her birthday to persuade him to stay. She spoke calmly. "You can leave anytime you want to."

"I am, in about twenty minutes. Let me dress and pack an extra shirt or two, and I'll be going. I'll be back Sunday evening and ready for work on Monday. No big deal, but at least I will have had some fun in the meantime," he said as he sat on the bed to button his suspenders to a pair of clean tan pants.

"I meant for good," Annie said, and the tears in her eyes reflected the fading sunlight.

Kyle looked up at her in surprise, and, a moment later, concern. "I'm not leaving you. You're my wife, and this is my family. I simply need to take a break to see my parents and a few old friends, perhaps."

"Yeah, I know. You do it all the time," she said dryly. "I think maybe it's time we really consider if this is how we want to live our lives . You don't like the ranch, and I don't like your going to town to carouse with your friends. This is my life too, Kyle. While you're out there getting drunk, gambling, and whoring around, this is what matters to me right here—our home. You and our children, Aunt Mary and Uncle Charlie, my brothers, and this ranch."

She paused and continued softly, "Maybe this weekend,

you really need to consider what it is you want in life—your family or Branson. We had this same conversation barely a month ago. Remember, we rented a room at the Monarch Hotel and were supposed to spend time together, just the two of us, and you..." She shook her head, disappointed. "You preferred to drink with your friends all weekend. I told you then that the weekends in Branson had to end. It has hardly been a month and here you are, desperate to get back there like a drunk dying for a beer. I need you to be my husband and help me get things organized and completed around here, not run away to whore around with your old school buddies and act like you're seventeen again. I need you here to help me raise our children and keep this place running."

Kyle shook his head slightly, giving her a soft, reassuring smile. "First of all, I don't whore around. I may drink and gamble, but I've never whored around. I promise you that, and my friends can verify it. You're my wife, Annie. I have always loved you too much to cheat on you." He stood from the bed and moved to hug her, but she stepped away.

"Then why are you going? Why not stay here and be a husband and a father to your children, rather than run off to relive your childhood with your drunken friends?"

He sighed heavily as he sat on the edge of the bed once more. "Do you ever feel like a calf stuck in a stall? I mean, this is my life—this ranch, this house, and the same people day after day. And all I do is work. Like I already said, I need to get away and have some fun occasionally too."

Annie gasped. "I just told you this is my life, and you have the audacity to say, 'I don't like the ranch, and I'm tired of being stuck around the same people day after day?' Well, I don't appreciate that. Everything you don't like, I love, and everything I can't stand, you seem to enjoy. Actually, you said it was the only fun you have." She exhaled and shook her head in frustration. "Enjoy your time away from us, because your weekends in Branson have come to an end. Unlike other women out there, I don't need you to support me.

"I own this ranch, and if it was anyone else doing what you did out there today, they'd be fired. Part of being an owner is being an example to the employees. If you don't care about getting the work done, why should they? I won't have it! I have every intention of moving away from cattle and starting a horse company. If you want to talk about work, it's only beginning. I won't have my dreams derailed by laziness and irresponsibility, which you displayed today, and have continuously shown over the years. It's time for you to decide what you want, Kyle—me and your family, or your old school chums and their bachelor life. You can no longer have both," she said sternly.

A flicker of anger passed through his eyes. "You don't own the ranch yet, and I doubt Charlie will let his ranch be turned into a horse farm. When we do inherit this place, though, trust me... I'll manage it from my desk and make this place three times more successful than it is now."

She laughed slightly despite her anger. "Let me tell you a little secret. *You* won't inherit the ranch. *I* will, and I will manage it as I see fit. But one thing I do know is that you will *not* sit on your butt while there's work to be done."

"Do you think I will be out there doing manual labor like I am now when we own the ranch? We can hire people for that."

Annie glared at Kyle for a moment before answering. "Um, yes, I *do* think you'll do manual labor. I will not run this ranch and work harder than everyone else, only to have my husband pout like an eight-year-old boy and quit for the day because he's not *having fun!* That is unacceptable and downright embarrassing." She finished with a raised voice, and her hard eyes glared into Kyle's.

He waved his hand and shook his head in frustration. "I'm not talking to you anymore—"

"Of course not!" she said heatedly, interrupting him. "Well, I have to go downstairs and make dinner for our children after working in the barn all day, but you don't hear me complaining about not having fun, do you? No, you don't. A rancher's life is work, Kyle. Nothing comes for free unless you're you. You don't want to work, but you'll gladly waste the money drinking and gambling while your family stays home working to make the money."

She leaned toward Kyle with heat in her eyes and a sneer on her lips and spoke purposefully. "My father owned a ranch, too. Oddly enough, he didn't like to work either after he got a taste for drinking and gambling. He lost the entire estate that my grandfather had built. I won't let that happen to me. Hear me, and hear me well. I warned you back in June that your drinking and gambling days were over. You're supposed to be a Christian, Kyle. I don't know what has come over you in the past few months, but you better get right with God, because after this weekend, if you ever leave like this again, you won't have a home to come back to. I love you, but I don't need you. And I will never let you destroy this ranch. Not ever. Go have your damn fun, but you better come home a changed man or you won't be here for long." She left the room and slammed the door behind her.

Kyle dressed hastily in tan-colored pants and a light-gray pullover. He pulled his suspenders over his shoulders and looked in the mirror above the dresser as he put his brown hat on. It wasn't his worn, flat-rimmed, dust-covered work hat, but a clean and sharp-looking derby. He grabbed two other shirts from his drawer and a pair of pants to roll up and put in a clean cloth bag, then added his leather pocketbook. He took hold of his bag and walked downstairs.

Annie had traded her leather gloves for an apron, and she laid a zucchini from the garden on a cutting board to slice. A fire had already been made in the cook stove, and she held a knife in her hand as she glared at him when he came into view from the stairs.

"I'll be back on Sunday," he said.

Her heart plummeted into her stomach as deep sadness overwhelmed her. He had either forgotten it was her birthday or he simply didn't care. She had already decided that she would not remind him. He could come home on Sunday and feel like the heel he was.

"I'm frying up some zucchini and boiled beets and spinach for dinner if you want to wait," she answered. "Ira, go to the cellar and get a jar of applesauce," she instructed her oldest son.

"Okay, Ma. Where are you going, Pa?" he asked, although he already knew since he had overheard them earlier.

On hearing Ira's question, six-year-old Catherine also took an interest in her father's departure. She ran across the room and grabbed his legs. "Where are you going, Daddy? Can I go too?"

Kyle frowned. "No, not this time."

"Why not?" she whined sadly as she sat on his foot and held his leg, looking up at him with a pouting bottom lip.

Annie spoke from the kitchen, "Yeah, Kyle, why can't she go?"

He looked at his wife with growing frustration but didn't say anything.

The child continued, encouraged by her mother's words, "Yeah, why not, Daddy? Mommy said I could go."

"Can I go too?" asked eight-year-old Ira.

"No, you two cannot go," Kyle answered quickly. "Neither of you are coming with me. For crying out loud, do you see what you started?" he asked Annie irritably. Catherine removed herself from his leg to sit on the floor and cry.

Annie shrugged her shoulders carelessly. "I'm not the one wanting to leave my family to go get drunk and lose money. You should take them with you so I can have some fun for a change. Are you going to eat dinner here or not?" she asked over her daughter's wails.

He answered bitterly, "No. I'd rather have steak than another night of vegetables."

The disgust in her eyes left him in no doubt about her disappointment. "You better go then, because we're having garden vegetables again. And applesauce. Ira, get to the cellar and bring in some applesauce. I won't tell you again."

"Okay, Ma, but I was saying goodbye to Pa."

"Your father will be back in a couple of days, so tell him goodbye and go get it. It's dinnertime," she said irritably and flashed a hard look at Kyle. "You better go. I know you're in a hurry to get there, but remember what I said. This is the last time. I won't be married to a man who'd rather play with his old friends than do the work that needs to be done or spend the evening with his family, especially—" She almost mentioned it being her birthday weekend.

"It's *one weekend!*" he yelled. "I'm going to see my parents. I didn't realize it was against the prison's rules to do so."

"*Prison?*" Annie asked, astonished. "I wasn't aware that this was a prison. If that's how you feel, consider yourself liberated and *get out!*" she shouted as she pointed the knife toward the door.

He took a deep breath and looked at his children. Ira stood nearby and seemed afraid of his parents' unusual raised voices, and Catherine grabbed his leg. "Don't go, Daddy. Don't leave me," she cried.

Kyle looked at his angry wife, and the foolishness of his words penetrated the deepest part of his soul. Remorse at what he'd spoken in the heat of an argument had a way of bringing the sincerest guilt. "I'm sorry, that was the wrong choice of words. I shouldn't have said that, Annie. You know I love you and our children." He bent and picked Catherine up to break her hold on his leg. Gently, he set her on the davenport, continued toward Annie, and put his hands on her shoulders to look into her eyes. "I love you," he said and stooped to kiss her, but she turned her head away from him.

"It won't work."

"What?" he asked, taken back by the coldness of her response.

She looked into his eyes. "You're sweet-talking yourself out of trouble. Kyle, I have five brothers, and have been married to you for nine years. Do you really think I don't know what you're trying to do? You're still going, aren't you? So this little sweet-talk is only a line of crap. But I mean it. You can't run off to Branson when you're tired of us. It won't happen anymore."

Kyle stood back defensively. "I'm not tired of you. I'm merely going to visit my parents and see some old friends while I'm there, that's all."

"Bull! I know what you're going there to do. Keep in mind that your friends aren't married and don't have a family, but you do. I've put up with this for long enough. You need to either grow up or move on. You embarrassed me today, and it's not the first time you've done that either. I love you, but I won't have my children growing up watching their father refuse to work or cry about it when he has to."

His lips twisted into a sneer as he grew more angered by her words. He suddenly yelled, "A man needs a break occasionally, okay? Damn it, Annie, everything is about this damn ranch. I am so sick and tired of it." He grabbed a beet off the counter and threw it across the kitchen in anger. It struck a cupboard door and cracked it. He continued, "What difference does it make if I go to Branson occasionally to let loose and have some damn fun? That's what makes this house feel like a prison. Kyle, do this, Kyle, do that. I don't care if I embarrassed you today, I really don't. I have had enough, and you know, I won't apologize for that. The hell with it. I am going to Branson. You deal with it however you want. I will see you on Sunday. Goodbye," he said, and strode out of the kitchen.

"I've said my piece," Annie told him as a warning.

Kyle stopped and turned back to look at her. "So have I."

She simply shrugged. "Goodbye."

He grabbed his bag, in a hurry to be gone. He paused as he opened the door and looked back at her. "Let me ask you: if I said we were moving to Branson, would you come with me?"

Annie shook her head. "No. I told you a long time ago that I would never leave the Big Z Ranch. This is my home."

"You love this damn ranch more than you ever loved me." Kyle shook his head in frustration. "Well, let me tell you something, Annie: the Big Z is not my home. Branson is. Goodbye." He closed the door hard behind him.

Catherine began to cry as she ran to her mother and hugged her legs. "Daddy didn't give me a kiss goodbye."

"Mom, you didn't have to be so mean. He's only going to

Branson," Ira said. He had never seen his father this angry with his mother before.

Annie brushed Catherine quickly from her legs and stepped toward Ira. She slapped his cheek hard with her right hand. "You don't speak to me like that, young man. Do you understand me?" she yelled.

"Yes, Mom," he whimpered.

"A man with a family has no business drinking and gambling his family's money away, do you understand that?"

"Yes."

"Then you do as you were told and go get that applesauce from the cellar before I grab a switch and beat your butt to the cellar and back for having to ask you three times to do it."

"Okay," Ira said meekly, with tears in his eyes. He immediately went outside and toward the cellar.

Annie looked out the window and watched Kyle stride toward the barn to saddle his horse. In the deepest part of her soul, she recognized that her marriage was over and her life as she knew it would change. She closed her eyes as a single tear trickled down her cheek. "Catherine, set the table for dinner. We only need four plates. Daddy's not eating with us tonight."

2

Kyle Lenning had grown up in Branson. His parents owned the W.R. Lenning Hardware Store on 1st Street and a nice home in the center of town. He was welcome to stay there anytime, but he seldom came to Branson to see his parents. His trips to Branson were to meet with his old friends, drink, and gamble at his favorite saloon, the Green Toad. Most of the time, he stayed in a hotel on Rose Street next to the Green Toad, but as he discovered, it was full on this weekend. He tried two other hotels on the street before he arrived unexpectedly at Paul Johnson and Sam Troyer's small rented house. He knocked on the door.

It was opened by a blue-eyed, medium-built man in his mid-to-late twenties with an oval-shaped face. He had short blond hair and a blond goatee, and sported a mustache above his smile.

"Kyle! What are you doing here? Come on in. Hey, Paul, Kyle's here!" Sam Troyer said loudly. "What's going on?" He gave his friend a quick hug and continued before he could answer. "I was just telling Paul that we don't get to see you enough anymore."

Kyle smiled broadly. "I know, it's been a while. So, is it okay if I stay here with you guys for a couple of days?"

"Yeah. Anytime, you know that," Sam replied, and closed the door behind them.

Paul stepped out of his bedroom wearing grey pants with suspenders, but he didn't have a shirt on. He was well over six feet tall and thin. His face was long and narrow, and his black hair had grown past his ears to mid-neck. He had also grown a black beard since Kyle had seen him last.

"Hey!" Paul laughed as he walked quickly to hug his old friend. "It's good to see you. Are you ready to get drunk? I can't think of any other reason you'd be in town."

Kyle nodded. "I am. So, are you trying to imitate my brother-in-law Matt with that long hair and beard?" he joked.

The other man smiled. "Hey, he has all the girls swooning over him around here. There's something about his hair and beard that they like. I've even had a couple of ladies swoon over me since I decided to let it grow out. Granted, that's after they drink a quart of beer or so. They swoon over me before puking," he finished dryly.

Kyle chuckled. "At least they swooned for ya, huh?"

"Yeah. So how are you and the family?"

"Oh, they're good," Kyle answered with a yawn. He sat on the wood-framed davenport.

Sam said, "Did you bring Annie to town with you again? You know, I've looked around, and she's still the best-looking wife in the county. Now, your sister-in-law Regina is a close second, but she's married to our landlord, so we might end up losing our house if I looked at her too long."

"What are you looking at married women for anyway? I thought you were excited about that Slater girl? You know, the pretty girl you saw on the street and followed into the

Slater Mining Office, not realizing she was the princess of the company. What was her name again?" Kyle chuckled at the memory of one his friend's more embarrassing moments.

Sam frowned. "Debra Slater."

"Yeah, Debra," Kyle repeated. "I thought you wanted to court Debra? Isn't that what you were hoping for the last time I was here?"

His friend nodded. "Things didn't pan out so well. She apparently has larger aspirations for a husband than a laborer at the sawmill."

Paul added with a hint of laughter, "Yeah, the princess of the Slater Silver kingdom has her eyes on your brother-in-law Matt. Everyone's talking about it around here. The rumor is her father bought his badge, and now he's likely to marry into the Slater family. This town is becoming like a twelfth-century Shakespearean play with all the drama, corruption, and power players pulling favors for one another, all to secure more control over every one of us peasants who live here.

"I mean, it's ridiculous. The wealthy stick to the wealthy. Matt's not wealthy yet, but he has the authority and power. By the way, did you know that Matt is the U.S. Marshal, but is also the county sheriff? He has total authority, federal, state, and county. Think of the power and political ties someone must have to arrange something like that! Trust me, there are some folks around here who are not pleased about it at all. Everyone knows it was William Slater and his son Josh who initiated it, but all those power players, including your other brothers-in-law, had a hand in setting that up.

"The Branson Elite have bought the sheriff in town, that's no secret, but now they have the federal, state, and county law bought as well. Not by vote, mind you, but appointed by the President of the United States and the Oregon Governor. Imagine the power it takes to do that. Well, that's Debra's father, William R. Slater. Now, do you really think she'd be interested in a scruffy man who works in a sawmill for three dollars and fifty cents a day? Come on, her lunches cost more than that."

"Thanks," Sam muttered with a frown.

Kyle laughed. "I knew they set had Matt up well enough to enforce the law without any restrictions. So, is that why you're growing your hair out? Because Debra might look at you twice if you look like Matt?"

Paul laughed. "That's right. If my three dollars and fifty cents a day won't impress her, perhaps my hair will."

"She's interested in Matt, huh? Annie thinks he'll end up marrying Rory Jackson someday, but he told me not too long ago that he would never get married. So maybe you still have a chance with Debra, Sam."

The other man grinned. "No, I think I lost my chance when I followed her into their office on Main Street and tried making small talk, thinking she was a secretary. How was I to know her family owned the whole corporation? She was very rude, though, and said I was in luck because they were hiring and it looked like I needed a job. I was taken back by the disgust in her arrogant eyes when I told her I came in to ask her name. She didn't say much, only asked if I wanted a job at the mine. I said the only thing I could think of. I said, 'Sorry, darling, but I prefer not to be buried alive for less than I'm making now.' She was rude. Very rude."

"They only make three dollars a day in that mine, and work a whole lot harder than we do," Paul added. "Not to say we don't work hard, but we're treated better, compara-tively. The Slaters are tyrants."

Sam turned his attention back to Kyle. "You never answered my question. How is Annie?"

Kyle sighed, "Oh, she's fine."

"That doesn't sound very convincing. What's up, bud? Is there trouble in paradise?"

"Paradise?" he asked skeptically.

"Yeah. Hell, Kyle, you're married to the prettiest girl in the county, you own a ranch, and have a nice family. It sounds like paradise to me," Sam said.

"Well, let me tell you guys, it isn't all it's supposed to be."

"What?" Paul was surprised by his tone. "You married into the Bannister family. You have it made. Hell, Sam and I should come over to your place for the weekend so we can get in good with the Bannisters. They could open doors for us we never dreamed of."

Kyle sighed. "That's half the problem. Annie doesn't like you guys, and whoever Annie doesn't like, none of the family will either."

Sam looked skeptical. "What do you mean, Annie doesn't like us? We were at your wedding, for crying out loud! She's always liked us. Lee likes us just fine."

He smirked. "You came to our wedding drunk and you have been ever since, according to her. Her family isn't particularly fond of drunk and rowdy people, especially after the first impressions you two made at our wedding."

"Rowdy?" Sam questioned, "We were only having fun."

Kyle raised his eyebrows for effect. "You harassed Billy Jo to the point of almost getting into a fight with her father, Uncle Luther. Then, after they left, you started to harass Annie's best friend Rory. You don't mess with Rory or Annie will cut your heart out. And if she doesn't, one her brothers or Uncle Charlie will. I'll remind you that you called Rory a whore, no one talks that way to her. Annie hasn't liked you guys since then. Haven't you ever noticed that you haven't been invited to the ranch once in all these years?" he asked loudly.

Sam shook his head. "No, I didn't call her a whore. I asked if she was one. There is a difference. I thought we weren't invited over because we don't own a horse and no one wants to walk that far," he said with a shrug, sounding slightly troubled. "She really doesn't like us?"

Paul asked, "So what does she think of you coming to town to see us?"

Kyle shook his head before answering. "We had a huge fight when I left. She gave me an ultimatum to quit coming here, or she'll divorce me."

"What?" Sam asked with concern. "Isn't that what she said the last time you were here when she came banging on the door?"

He continued, "Basically. She wants a rancher for a husband, and the fact is, I hate working on the ranch. I told her I'd be better at managing the business than I am at working it, but she made it clear that I will never run it. I'm a laborer, that's all."

Paul spoke sarcastically, "You could buy the Green Toad here in town if you want to manage a business. I know it's your favorite place to go. Herb's selling out."

"Seriously?" he asked, real interest in his voice.

"Yup. He wants to buy a place over in the Willamette Valley. You might wanna talk to him about it if you're serious."

"I will. I don't know if I could pull enough out of our savings to make an offer. I could pull some—maybe enough for a down payment if Herb will work with me on monthly installments. Annie would probably divorce me, but at least I'd have a business I'd enjoy working in. I wouldn't have to haul hay anymore, that's for sure. I swear there are better ways of making a living than hauling hay day after day. And I'd be around you guys more often. You know, like we were in the good old days."

Sam looked at him with a curious expression. "I thought you loved Annie? Every time you've come here, all we've ever heard was what a great and amazing lady she was. Today, you're singing a different song. Why?"

"I don't like being penned up like a pig. You know I could run that ranch far better than Charlie or Annie ever dreamed of. I could make it ten times more profitable, and have a bigger house, and a carriage like Lee and Albert have. We could afford to travel to Boston or Europe if we wanted to if I managed the ranch. But no, Annie likes it exactly the way it is—a business with big potential profit settling for only enough to get by. Listen to this. We could add a substantial amount to our personal earnings by paying Darius a ranch hand's wage, rather than splitting the total profits three ways. Darius makes almost as much as Charlie, Annie, and me. It isn't right, and it is a waste of money. He isn't an owner. He's an old cowboy who can't even do what he's hired to do anymore. It irritates the hell out of me. The first thing I'd do is cut his wages down to where they belong and pocket the savings," he said, his frustration evident.

"What does that have to do with Annie?" Paul asked. "Kyle, what's really going on with you two?"

Kyle took a deep breath. "She loves the ranch more than she does me. She's already made it clear that even when Darius dies, his daughter Rory will inherit his wages for the rest of her life, and she doesn't even work it," he said bitterly. "It's pointless, Paul. I can't compete against the Big Z. I hate cows, and I hate hay. I belong behind a counter selling goods, whether a pound of nails or whiskey by the shot. It doesn't matter right now. I simply don't want to work the ranch anymore."

"So, it's your job, and not Annie, then?"

"It's both. You can't separate the two, because they're the same thing."

"What about opening a store of some kind in Willow Falls? Then you could get away from the ranch work."

Kyle shook his head with a slight chuckle. "She doesn't want to be married to a merchant. She wants a husband who works with her and shares her passion. Unfortunately, I don't."

Sam chuckled. "She married a store clerk. What does she expect?"

"A cowboy," he said softly. "She expects me to be a cowboy, and to love being one. In most marriages, it's the woman who changes her name and her life for her husband, but with Annie, it's the other way around. I must sacrifice everything I want in life to satisfy her desires. And by the way, her desires are not pretty dresses or a big house, but more horses. She plans to buy twenty more horses to get her new business started—a horse company. And she bought three horses without asking me, with our money. I'm surprised she didn't ask me to change my name to Bannister."

Paul laughed. "Come on, it can't be that bad. This is the first time you've ever complained about her in what...almost ten years? I think you need a weekend away to relax and have some fun, and then you'll feel better."

"Maybe, but I don't know. I'm tired of it, Paul. Maybe I'm tired of being married. Every day, I wish I was here in Branson instead of being there. Don't get me wrong. I love

Annie and her family. They are great people, but I'm looking for something different. Maybe it would simply be nice to have a wife who wanted the same kinds of things in life that I do. It seems to me that Annie and I have come to a big letter Y in our lives. We started off walking together in a good direction, but now we want different things, and we may never be on the same path again," he said with a shrug. "So you see, it's not as simple as having a weekend with you guys to make it all better. According to her, this is my last weekend to see you guys, or she will divorce me. That is my life."

Sam scoffed with mock disgust to change the subject. "Well, that's enough of that talk for now, because we're taking you to Bella's tonight."

"Who's that?"

Sam answered with a smirk, "Not who, but what. A new dance hall opened in June, named Bella's Dance Hall. It's far more fun than the Green Toad or anywhere else, and it has girls. Lots of pretty girls!"

Kyle shook his head. "I'm still married, guys."

"I didn't say whores, I said girls. In fact, you should meet Helen and Edith. We have spent so much time talking about you that we haven't told you about them. They're a couple of girls we've gotten to know a little since they've come to town. I know you think I'm hooked on Debra Slater, but I'm courting Helen," Sam said with a smile and a gleeful shrug.

"You're courting a whore? What's new with that?" Kyle asked and laughed.

"Shut up," Sam said lightly. "She's not a whore, she's a dancer. You know, like a hurdy-gurdy, but it's just a dance hall."

"They're respectable girls," Paul added as he walked into his room to change his clothes.

46

Kyle looked at Sam. "You have a lady? Like a real courting commitment?"

Sam smiled at his friend. "Yes...but it all depends on you really."

"How's that?" Kyle asked.

"Well, if you get a divorce from Annie, do you think I could court her? Do you think she'd forgive me for calling her friend a whore if I asked?"

"You're kidding, right?" he said with a laugh.

"Honestly," Sam said, "I hope you and Annie can work through this, because I really do think she is the greatest girl in the world. Even if she doesn't like me."

Kyle's expression faded to somber sincerity. "I hope so, but I deserve some of the things that *I* want in life too. We don't have to get divorced if we can only find a compromise. Maybe then we can find that spark again. I hope so, anyway."

3

___

Kyle Lenning and his two friends had stopped by his favorite saloon for a few drinks to start their night, and he had approached the proprietor of the Green Toad, Herb Gannon, about buying the establishment. They had spoken at length, and he had left with high hopes of buying it. The three friends walked four more blocks down Rose Street to a newly constructed large, two-story building that appeared to be the busiest of all the saloons, gambling halls, and whorehouses on Rose Street. It was the new and thriving Bella's Dance Hall. The inviting sound of music and laughter could be heard from two blocks away.

Like many towns and cities, Branson allowed certain less civilized businesses to exist on the far west side of town on Rose Street. Originally, it was a small red-light district, but over the past few years, it had expanded to a full twelve-block long street leading to Branson's segregated China-town. With the influx of immigrants, prospectors, and Chinese in Branson, it not only filled Rose Street with new businesses but brought a demand to annex a sister street one block over named Flower Lane.

A common joke to the locals was that street was *blooming* with new business as well. The Chinese were permitted to have public businesses in Chinatown originally, but now Flower Lane was open to them as well. Kyle was amazed by how much new construction there was on the street since he had last been in town a month before. The street now contained Chinese merchants of every kind—multiple laundries, restaurants, dry goods stores, and even a doctor or two.

However, as they walked down Flower Lane, he had no interest in what the Chinese had to offer. His attention was on the dance hall his friends were taking him to. An atmosphere of excitement exuded from the open windows and doors like the scent of sweet incense from the Chinese market. Kyle had never been to a real dance hall with dancing girls. The establishment was a two-story clapboard building painted pink, with a covered front porch and white trim around the doors and windows. It had large capital letters painted across the wide false front that simply read Bella's. In smaller letters underneath were the words Dance Hall.

Kyle followed his friends through the front door, and his excitement grew. They walked into a well-lit alcove where customers could hang their coats and hats on one of many golden hooks that lined the walls. The new white-based paisley wallpaper in the alcove was bright and cheerful. Above the double door leading into the dance hall, a hanging plaque made of unfinished myrtle wood with carved letters inlaid with black paint elegantly captured a single thought: A lady is a lady and must be respected as such. Along the right wall and hung vertically, a longer but matching piece of myrtle wood with bold lettering at the top listed the house rules.

. . .

No guns or knives beyond this point.

No fighting or quarreling or harassing our musicians beyond this point.

Our ladies are to be danced with, not touched, man-handled, or harassed in any way.

Beyond this point, dancing, drinking, laughing, and fun are the only things tolerated.

Enjoy,

Love, Bella.

A man stood at the double doors and smiled as Sam and Paul approached. Middle-aged and dressed in a respectable brown suit, he seemed friendly enough, . He was shorter than most but broad-shouldered and barrel-chested. His curly brown hair was short, and a thick brown mustache bristled on his square face. He smiled in a friendly way. "Well, boys, it's good to see you again. I hope you brought money because the band's playing well tonight."

"Of course, we brought money, Dave. We even brought a friend," Sam said and gestured toward Kyle. "This is our friend Kyle Lenning. He's the owner of the Big Z Ranch over in Willow Falls. He's come to spend the weekend with us poor laborers. Kyle, this is Dave. He's the owner of this fine establishment."

Dave stuck out his hand to shake Kyle's with interest. "A rancher, huh? How many acres if I may ask?" He shook Kyle's hand firmly.

"Too many. I thought this place was called Bella's?" Kyle asked.

"It's my wife's business, really. I merely manage the

door." He laughed. "Well, Kyle, let me tell you how it works. It's a dollar per dance and fifty cents per drink. You'll get a token with every drink you buy. When you have five tokens, bring them to the bar and you'll get a free drink."

Beyond the double doors was a wide room with a long bar to the right and an area of tables and chairs immediately beyond the entry. A wide hardwood dance floor was filled with men dancing happily with beautifully-dressed ladies. Every lady he could see wore their hair in different styles, but all of them had taken the time to make their hair look extremely pretty. Some even pinned feathers or flowers in it. They all wore a touch of makeup to make their smiling faces glow even more, and sported dresses of various colors and designs. Most of the dresses he could see were low-cut at the shoulders to reveal enough of the lady's bosom to keep the men coming back for one more dance. Many skirts reached to just below the knees, and when they'd step back and spin, the dress came up to give a quick glance at knee-high stockings held up by colorful garters and a teasing glance of the soft white flesh above.

Across the dance floor was an area fenced off from the main area, where the band played various instruments. On each side of the band was a narrow space with smaller, more private tables and chairs. At the far end of the building was a stage with a large green curtain that could be opened or closed for the show. Kyle took in the entire environment— the music, the dancing ladies, the many men who stood around drinking and talking with each other or to other well-dressed ladies who were not currently dancing, and the cigarette and cigar smoke that hung in the air. All of it filled his senses.

He smiled. It was all he ever dreamed his saloon could be and more. Excitement rippled through his veins. He was more excited than before to buy the Green Toad and make a saloon like Bella's Dance Hall. It was no wonder the Green Toad was going out of business. It simply could not compete with Bella's.

"Here," Paul said and handed him a thick glass filled with cold beer. It was a rarity in Branson to get a cold beer. The only other place that served it was the Monarch Lounge. "What do you think? It's better than sitting at a poker table at the Green Toad, isn't it?" his friend asked loudly over the music.

Kyle's smile widened. "I'm buying the Green Toad, and this is what I'll do with it. This is awesome."

"Yeah," Paul agreed. "Wait until you meet Edith."

"Who?"

"My lady friend Edith. That's her right there." He pointed at a thin lady who danced with another man along the edge of the dance floor. Her face was almost angelic, and she had clear blue eyes that lit up at the sight of Paul. Her wavy blonde hair was curled nearly perfectly into a neat mane that flowed down her back. Her smile widened as she danced past him.

"Her?" Kyle asked sounding surprised.

"That's her. Beautiful, isn't she?" Paul asked proudly.

He nodded in agreement. "You met her here?"

"This is where she lives and works."

Kyle looked slightly confused. "Back at the house, you mentioned someone special. Is this her? Or was that someone else?"

"No, that's her. That's Edith. We've become good friends, and I suppose you could say I'm courting her."

He grimaced. "So you're okay with her working here?"

"Oh, yeah. She makes more money than I do. Plus, she enjoys it."

His grimace settled into a confused expression.

Paul pointed across the dance floor. "And that dark-haired girl across the room wearing the red and gold dress? That's Helen. She's Sam's lady."

"Hmm." He grunted, unimpressed, and took a drink of beer.

"What? You don't find her attractive? Granted, Helen's not as attractive as Edith, but Sam likes her a lot. We met them on opening night, and we became friends with them right away. They're new around here and didn't know anyone, of course."

Kyle nodded at Edith as she danced past again. "Doesn't it bother you that she's with another man?"

His friend shrugged. "No, it's her job. Why would it bother me? She makes good money, and if we ever get married, we could buy a nice house and start a brewery with the money she makes. The truth is, she has saved up quite a bit of money by dancing. Kyle, she can make twenty-five dollars a night on the weekends, if not more. It takes me nearly two weeks to make that much."

"And you're okay with that?" he asked skeptically.

Paul looked at him astonished. "Who wouldn't be? You're no different. Your wife owns your ranch, so what's the difference?"

"My wife's not a whore. That's the difference," he answered simply.

The other man gasped. "Edith's not a whore."

"She's not?"

"No! Wait, did you think she was a whore?"

He shrugged. "Yeah."

"No." Paul laughed. "No, they're dancers. You can't bed them. Even if you offered them a lot of money, you'd be slapped and escorted out of here. No, she doesn't have sex with these guys. They only dance."

"Oh." Kyle smiled slightly. "I had no idea."

Sam joined them with a drink in his hand. "No idea about what?" he asked.

Paul answered. "He thought they were whores," he said and nodded toward the dancers.

"Nope," Sam said simply. "That's Helen over there." He pointed at Helen as she danced expertly with a young man who apparently didn't know how to dance too well. "Here, I bought you a ticket to go dance with one of these ladies. We'll have Helen and Edith set you up with one of the prettier ones."

Kyle laughed lightly as he took the paper ticket. "I am married, remember."

Paul answered for Sam, "Not if you buy the Green Toad, you're not. Or you won't be, anyway."

His smile faded. "That's true enough."

The band finished their tune, and the dance came to an end. The men on the dance floor tried to start a conversation with their dance partner, and many even produced a ticket for the next dance, but the ladies declined the tickets gently and made their way toward the bar.

A band member stood and spoke loudly through a megaphone. "We'll take a short break and begin the next dance in five minutes. So, gentlemen, have a cold drink, and be sure to buy the ladies one too. It gets awfully thirsty out there dancing all night. Be sure to find your partner for the Polka Redowa. It's coming up in five minutes."

Kyle watched as Helen left her dance partner and scurried over to Edith, who was talking to her dance partner about buying her a drink. Helen grabbed Edith's arm and pulled her excitedly toward where Paul and Sam stood not far from the bar.

"Hi," Helen said excitedly to Sam. The two women stopped a few paces away from them to keep a professional appearance during their working hours. "I began to worry that you weren't coming tonight." She was taller and a little plumper than her friend. Helen's hair was black and fell in two pigtails on either side of her head. Her face was oval-shaped, with thick lips and a prominent nose. She had blue eyes that appeared slightly too small for her nose. While she was an attractive lady at first sight, to Kyle, she didn't compare to Edith's natural beauty.

Sam motioned toward Kyle. "Our friend wanted to stop by the Green Toad. This is Kyle Lenning. The three of us used to be the Three Musketeers in our youth. We all grew up together. Kyle, this is Helen and Edith," he said as an introduction.

Kyle nodded at Helen, "Nice to meet you, and you," he added to Edith.

"Likewise, Mister Lenning," Edith said simply and then directed her attention to Paul. "Do you have a ticket?"

"Not yet,"

"Oh, Paul..." she whined.

"So, Mister Lenning," Helen began, "Why haven't you come to see us before? Any friend of Paul's and Sam's should most certainly be a friend of ours."

Kyle smiled at her friendliness and the flirtation in her eyes.

Sam spoke before he could answer, "Kyle's the owner of the Big Z Ranch over in Willow Falls. He's only here for the weekend."

Paul added, "Actually, he's thinking about buying the

Green Toad, but he's here for some fun tonight, so can you girls help him find a special lady to have it with?"

"Do you mean for right now, or after work?" Helen asked and raised her eyebrows up and down suggestively.

"Both," Paul answered with a small smile. "Are you two coming over tonight?" he asked Edith.

She replied, "You know we can't tonight, but you three can stick around after we close and have a few more drinks and talk. The drinks won't be free, but the time is," Edith said softly. There was sincerity in her manner.

"I thought that was against the rules?" Sam asked.

The two girls looked at each other with childlike smirks. "It was," Helen said slowly, "but we talked to Bella and Dave, and they have given us permission to have a few personal friends stay later if we want. We can't give you free drinks or tokens for drinks, but we can sell you some. We have to stay downstairs, and we can't leave the building except on Saturday nights, because we have Sunday off."

"So you can come over tomorrow night?" Paul asked Edith.

She nodded. "Tomorrow night we can do whatever we want to, but tonight you can stay late. Three o'clock at the latest, though."

Sam looked at Helen with a slightly confused expression. "I thought you said there were strict rules about that?"

Helen smiled secretively. "Let's say Bella understands what it's like to be a young lady. There are rules, but she allows some things."

Edith added simply, "So, what will you do with your friend? I see you have a ticket?" She pointed at the ticket in Kyle's hand.

He nodded. "I do."

"Then..." Edith looked around for another dancer.

"Christine! Christine, come here," she called. Another dancer eagerly but politely left the two men who seemed to have her cornered in a conversation she had no real interest in. She gladly joined her friends and rolled her eyes in real gratitude. "Christine, this is Paul."

"Oh," she said with interest and held her hand out to shake his. "Nice to finally meet you. I heard you work at the Seven Timber Lumber Mill?"

Paul nodded. "I do. It's nice to meet you."

Edith continued, "And this over here is Sam."

"Sam! It is just as nice to meet you too. I've heard a lot about both of you. Sam, you work at the Seven Timber Lumber Mill too?" she asked while shaking his hand. Her eyes moved to Kyle, and then back to Sam as he answered.

"Yeah, I do."

Helen said quickly, "They're staying after tonight."

"Great," Christine said. "I think someone you both work for will join us. He's not here yet, but he will be."

"Work for? Don't you mean with?" Paul asked. He had seen many other mill and timber employees at the dance hall in the past month, but he'd never seen a supervisor there.

"No," Christine said simply. "You work for him. Travis McKnight. He's the manager, I believe."

Sam answered slowly, "Oh! He's the big boss. We don't know him, though. He stays in the office. Never comes out into the working man's mill unless he's walking through."

"You don't know him?" She seemed surprised.

Both men shook their heads. "Not personally," Paul stated.

"Then you'll get to know him tonight. Who knows, maybe he'll promote you guys," Christine said. Her eyes went to Kyle once again, and she gave him a smile.

Paul asked curiously, "Why's he coming here?"

Christine frowned playfully. "To be with me, of course. The same reason you'll be staying after to visit with Edith."

"Isn't he married?" Paul asked.

"No, his wife died over a year ago. You guys should really get to know your boss," she said. "It was nice to meet you, gentlemen," she added with one last glance at Kyle before she began to walk away.

Edith stopped her. "Christine, this is Paul's and Sam's friend, Mister Lenning. He owns a large ranch and is buying a saloon here in town. He has a ticket but no one to dance with," she emphasized.

Christine smiled almost shyly as she walked back and spoke while looking into his eyes. "How rude of me. Mister Lenning. Hello, my name is Christine. Is this your first time here?"

"Call me Kyle, and yes, it is." He could not help but stare into her dark-brown eyes. She was, in one word, indescribable. Kyle was married to a beautiful woman. His sister-in-law, Regina Bannister, was known as perhaps the most beautiful woman in the county, but neither compared to the lady who stood before him. Christine was without a doubt simply gorgeous. He could not take his eyes off her. She was literally breathtaking.

"Give her the ticket," Edith instructed him with a nudge.

Kyle handed the ticket to Christine, and she slid it in a hidden pocket in her dress. "Kyle, I do believe the band is starting up in a minute. Shall we dance?"

He smiled slowly. "Sure," he said, and she took his arm in hers and led him out onto the dance floor.

"Ticket," Helen said to Sam, and held her hand out expectantly.

He smiled and handed it over and they stepped onto the

dance floor, although she was much closer to him than she had been anyone else she had escorted during the evening.

Edith frowned at Paul. "No ticket?"

He shook his head. "Next dance. Hey, I'm confused. Why is Travis McKnight coming to see your friend?"

Edith looked awkwardly at him. "Why do you come to see me?"

"Because I like you," Paul said honestly.

She smiled slightly. "It's the same thing. He likes her, and she likes him."

Paul shook his head. "His wife didn't die. He's still married."

"How do you know? You said yourself that you didn't know him."

"I don't know him personally, but I know who he is. And I know he's married."

Edith frowned. "He told her he wasn't. How do you know?"

"Because I know. I don't have to know him to know about him. He's the mill manager, and the mill's not so big that we don't know anything about him. He's married and has a kid and lives across town on Jefferson Street, I believe, in a big house. Also, he's best friends with Josh Slater, whose family owns the Slater Mining Company. He doesn't know me, and wouldn't know I worked for him if we were introduced. But I do know he's married," he said decisively.

Edith frowned thoughtfully. "He's courted her since we opened. So he's lying to her?"

Paul nodded. "Yeah, but you didn't hear it from Sam or me. We don't want to lose our jobs."

"Sure," she said and was suddenly distracted by an older man who handed her a shot glass of pink champagne. "Here's a quick drink for ya, pretty lady. Now, how about a dance? I have a ticket," he said, producing the ticket as the band began to play.

She smiled pleasantly. "Why, thank you. I'd love to, Mister Gallop," she said and took both drink and the ticket. She quickly drank the pink lemonade that was sold strictly for the ladies as champagne for a dollar a shot. They were not allowed to drink anything except water or the pink champagne bought for them by the customers. Edith handed the empty shot glass to Paul and took the gentleman by the arm to allow him to escort her out onto the dance floor.

He watched Edith dancing with the man, then looked at his friend dancing with Christine Knapp. Kyle wouldn't know how lucky he was to dance with the most beautiful and coveted of all the dance hall girls. Christine was also an angelic singer who could silence the rowdiest of men with her beautiful voice when she stood on the stage.

It surprised Paul that the lumber mill's manager would be seen on Rose Street, let alone court a dance hall girl. He had never seen Travis McKnight there, nor had anyone ever mentioned seeing him, but somehow he was getting in good with the most popular of all the ladies. In Travis' defense, though, Christine was a very beautiful woman. Even Kyle was taking an interest in her as they danced to the music.

4

Annie Lenning sat tiredly on her davenport, utterly exhausted. She'd spent another long day hauling hay in the summer heat, made dinner for her family, and done the evening chores before heating water for baths for her three children. Finally, she had put all her children to bed, read a Bible story to them, and told a funny story to her youngest before taking some time for herself.

Once she'd bailed out the dirty water out of the tub, she took the time to heat enough water for her to have a long, warm bath herself. She had sat as comfortably as she could in her mid-sized steel tub, but wished she had Lee's full-size bathtub with brass claw feet so she could recline fully and be soothed by the hot water as it was poured into the tub. Instead, she sat upright in a mid-sized tub as her friend Rory Jackson topped it up with warm water. She bathed often, but after this week of hot, sweat-saturated, and dusty work, even a bath once a day didn't feel like enough.

She was physically exhausted, and emotionally as well after the fight with Kyle that afternoon. The bath gave her some time to relax before another busy day came in the morning, with very little help where she needed it the most. Working the ranch was hard, but raising three kids practically alone despite being married brought another kind of exhaustion that she had come to know in recent months.

Refreshed slightly by the bath, Annie put on a light night dress to stay cool in the hot July night and the warmth from the cook stove that had burned all evening to heat the bath water. Rory had closed the damper to put the fire out, but the heat lingered in the house even with the opened windows and doors. There was no evening breeze to cool the house, only simmering heat with no place to go.

Annie kicked her feet up on a table in front of the davenport and wiped the sweat from her forehead. She had a brown towel wrapped around her hair on top of her head and appeared worn and tired, even after the refreshing wash.

Rory poured two glasses of cool tea from a pitcher and handed her one. "I don't have any ice, but it's cool enough," she said and sat on the other end of the davenport with her own beverage.

"We need to dig a deeper cellar and pack it with sawdust this winter. I say that every summer, but remind me, so we can do it. We need to pack a lot more ice this winter than we did last year," Annie said tiredly.

"You could hire those boys to dig it deeper. They wouldn't mind the extra money." Rory spoke of Gabriel Smith and a couple other teenage boys who worked summers on the Big Z Ranch.

"No, Kyle can do it," she said bitterly. "There's absolutely no reason he can't."

"Are you still mad about him going to Branson?" Rory asked, even though she already knew the answer.

Annie sighed and nodded. "It angers me no end. I grew

up with five brothers, and every one of them can put in a day's worth of work without a single complaint. Uncle Charlie and your dad are old men, and they haven't complained once. For crying out loud, Gabriel and those other boys don't whine about the heat or how tired they are. The only person who throws a fit like a woman is my husband. It's disgusting. And that's only part of it. Then he wants to go to town to carouse with his friends.

"And I'm sick of it. I'm not like Regina, Mellissa, or my other sisters-in-law. I'm not afraid to be alone. I don't need him to work the ranch or provide for me. What I *do* need is my husband to act like a man rather than a spoiled child. I need him to stop embarrassing me and act like a man instead of a little girl."

Rory laughed.

She looked at her friend with a serious expression. "What are you laughing at?"

"I always find it funny how you refer to girls as a bad thing. Like it's the biggest insult in the world," she said with a smile and added, "But you are one."

Annie nodded with a frown. "Well, it is insulting, especially for a man to act like a woman. Besides, we're not normal girls, Rory. We're ranchers. It's in our blood. I don't mind one bit getting my hands dirty or callused, but I take a negative view of men who do. Especially when it's this ranch that pays for his carousing in town." She looked at the other woman irritably. "If he hates this place so much, I wish he'd pack his crap up and leave."

"You don't mean that," Rory said softly.

"Yes, I do," she said slowly and added, "Today was the last straw. If he doesn't want to do his part around here, then he doesn't need to be here. I won't stay married to a lazy man, especially one who whines like a little girl."

Her companion smiled and shook her head. "You sound so much like your brothers."

"Yeah? Well, I should've known not to marry a merchant's son. He was a city dweller even before Branson was a real city. Every one of my brothers could go through him like a hot knife through warm butter. I should've known then that he didn't have the gumption for this kind of life," she said sadly and stared straight ahead. A light mist shimmered in her brown eyes.

Rory took a drink of her tea and wished she had some ice to put in it. "Kyle's not a bad man, Annie. You're only mad at him."

"No, I'm not mad, I am hurt. You know it isn't merely that he acted like a child, or even his having to go to town to play around. Do you know what irritates me the most? Aside from him breaking my cabinet door, he forgot my birthday. He left and said not one word about it. He knows how important that is to me, and he still got mad and left like it didn't matter to him at all. A year ago, he would never have gone to town on my birthday without me, but now it doesn't matter, I guess.

She sighed and sipped her tea. "I don't know where the man I married went to in the past year. We haven't talked like a husband and wife in a long time now, as you know. He hasn't been much of a help around the house, either. He simply sits and ignores the kids most of the time, and I have no idea why. It's like he doesn't care anymore, and what am I supposed to do, work harder and act happy? No, he must either commit to this family and me fully or leave. There won't be any more of this half-assed nonsense, because I don't need a man that badly, and I won't pretend that I do. I'd like to have my husband back, but this poor-me depression or whatever he has

64

going on has to come to a stop. I can't put up with it anymore."

Rory shrugged. "Well, he isn't cheating on you when he goes to town, Annie. He loves you too much for that."

Annie grimaced. "Of course, he isn't. I'd shoot him, or one of my brothers would. No, I know he doesn't." She sighed again, then continued softly, "As much as I love Kyle, it's not fair to either of us to live like this. If this ranch is so hard on him, then maybe he should leave it and go where he can do what he wants to do."

"Maybe he'll take more of an interest in the family if we hired some experienced cowboys to work the ranch and not boys. It might free him up more to be a husband and father."

She smirked at her friend. "We can't hire cowboys, because then I'd find a real man."

"Annie!" Rory exclaimed with a laugh. "That's terrible. I know your feelings are hurt right now, but he's still your husband. Kyle's a nice man, and that is why you fell in love with him—not because he was a cowboy. We both knew he couldn't ride a horse or rope a post when you met him." She laughed as if remembering.

"He's come a long way from being a store clerk. I don't know what's going on with him right now either, but he's still a good man. Today was a bad day for him. He'll come back refreshed and ready to get back to work, and he'll be very sorry to have missed your birthday. In fact, it wouldn't surprise me if he came back tomorrow with candies and a new pair of boots or something for you. He loves you, Annie. I know he wouldn't miss your birthday intentionally."

Annie took a drink of her tea and looked at Rory with moisture in her eyes. "We had a big fight, Rory. I've never seen him get so mad. He threw a beet. He threw a darn beet at my cabinet. I don't think I've ever heard of anyone throwing a beet, but he did." She laughed lightly. "He threw a *beet*. That would be a hanging offense if it got back to the right person somewhere, I'm sure. Your pa will be mad because he'll have to make a new door for me."

Rory frowned with real empathy. She knew her friend too well to not know she was changing the subject to fight the tears she wanted to cry. "Pa will gladly replace the cabinet door. How were the children when that happened?"

She squeezed her lips tightly together so as not to let her tears fall and shook her head silently. "Here. They've never seen him act like that, and it scared them. I can't allow that to happen again either. My children should not be afraid of their father, and I won't take the blame. He made the choice to leave long before we argued." Her sadness was clearly visible on her attractive face. "I do not know what the future holds, but this I do know. I need someone who will help with the children at least, and he doesn't even do that."

"Annie, you can't get divorced. It's not biblical to do so. Once you're married, you're married for better or worse— for life."

Annie nodded sadly and sighed. "I don't want a divorce. I want my husband back the way he used to be. I miss his smile and the sound of his laughter. I haven't heard that in a while."

Rory spoke softly, "Have you ever asked him where his laughter went?"

She shook her head. "We were supposed to spend that weekend in Branson together in Lee's hotel. You know, have nice dinners and be served like we were important folks, but he ran off with his friends, and I stayed in the hotel room alone or with you. Kyle was nowhere to be found. I guess he'd rather be with his friends than me. That's a sad thing. I must be losing my feminine attributes, huh?"

The other woman laughed lightly. "I'm sorry, Annie, but you never had any feminine attributes."

She smiled. "I'm kidding. You do."

Annie looked at Rory with a serious expression. "I am probably the only woman in the West who had to teach her husband how to ride a horse and throw a rope. He certainly wasn't ranch material, but I thought it was adorable at the time," she said with a reflective smile. "It isn't anymore."

Rory drew a deep breath and spoke the first thoughts that came to mind. "I do wish I could find someone who'd love me the way I am. I think that is the ultimate kind of love. Like you and Kyle have. He's going through a tough time, Annie. You'll have your doting husband back in no time, I am sure."

She frowned and shook her head lightly. "You will find someone in good time. But right now, I need to get some sleep. The sun rises early, and it's my birthday. Another day of chores, kids to feed, hay to haul, cows to milk, and dinner to cook. And where is my doting husband? Getting drunk with his friends and wasting our money while the rest of us do all the work. And *that,* my dear friend, is the very point I have faced day in and day out for a while now. If he loved me that much, he'd be here to celebrate my birthday and help me around our house, but I am left to do it all. Truthfully, I could do it all without him with less frustration."

5

Kyle unbuttoned the bottom button of his shirt and rolled the sleeves up to try to cool down. It was already hot in the dance hall, and after a few polkas, he began to sweat profusely. The drinks were cold, and he bought another round for himself and his two friends. As an expected gesture of appreciation, he bought a shot glass of pink champagne for the girl he had danced with. Her name was Mary, but his eyes looked past her to Christine Knapp.

He had danced twice with the woman, but as he soon discovered, she was in high demand, and he understood why. She was very beautiful. Christine had thick dark-auburn hair that was long and straight and was arranged in a woven bun. Her dark-brown eyes could've been a work of art, they were so hypnotic. They glowed with something deep, passionate, and kind, and had an immense depth of goodness, but beyond the goodness were smiles and beauty. Despite that, there was a hint of sadness that could not be hidden in her eyes.

People often said the eyes were the gateway to the soul, but Kyle had always thought it was a mere old wives' tale until now. He could not look away from her, and when he did, her oval face and gentle smile drew his attention right back to her. Despite the ring on his finger, he was attracted to her in a way he had not experienced since he'd first seen Annie ten years before. Christine was a flame that tempted him like a moth seeking the light.

He watched her walk toward the bar with a young man who looked excited to be in her company. The fellow would undoubtedly buy himself a drink and her a glass of pink champagne. It occurred to Kyle that many of the men in the dance hall more than likely didn't have a whole lot of money to spend on a dollar per glass of pink champagne for a girl, but if it bought Christine's attention even for a moment, it might be worth every cent.

Kyle approached her before any other man had the opportunity to ask her for the last dance of the night. "Miss Christine?"

She paused to look at him with a coy smile. "Yes, Mister Lenning?"

"You remember my name. That's a good sign."

"Of course. It's not every day I get to meet a ranch owner."

He smiled. "Say, the last dance is coming up, and I would like to dance with you again."

Christine smiled politely. "Mister Lenning, I can't promise you that. The last dance is an auction. If you want it badly enough, you'll have to pay the price for it. Now, if you'll excuse me, I'm terribly thirsty, and Mister Connors here is buying me a drink," she said with a friendly smile. She turned her attention back to the man whose arm she held.

"Well, what's the price, usually?" he asked.

She turned to look at him again. "Last night it was ten tickets, but on the weekend, twenty is about average."

"Then I'll buy twenty-one," he said with finality.

A man who approached from behind her spoke quickly to Kyle, "Don't waste your time buying tickets, son. I already have a pocket full, and a thousand dollars isn't too much to spend on my Christina."

Her eyes lit up at the sound of the man's voice, and she turned quickly to face him. He was about six feet tall, with broad shoulders and a powerful build. His short, curly brown hair matched the neatly-trimmed thick mustache on his otherwise clean-shaven face. He was in his late thirties or early forties, and well-dressed in a checkered tan suit with an ironed white shirt and a starched collar beneath his matching checkered vest. A gold pocket watch's chain trailed from a vest button to the pocket. He had obviously hung his suit coat in the front entryway, although he held a new derby hat in his hand. He was a man of means and exuberant confidence.

"Hi!" Christine said with real excitement in her voice. Her pleasure at seeing this gentleman was significantly more than she had shown for anyone else in the dance hall. A strange and unexpected twinge of jealousy ran from the pit of Kyle's stomach and erupted like twin flames of fury behind his eyes. He knew right then that he wanted her to look at him with the same expression she looked at the well-dressed man with. "I'll see you in a while," she said, then tapped his chest and continued to the bar with the young man whose arm she held onto. She paid no attention to Kyle.

"I'll wait right here," the man answered with a satisfied smirk as he watched her walk away. Kyle looked at him and extended his hand. "I'm Kyle Lenning."

The man scrutinized him with slight annoyance and ignored the hand. "Save your pennies. You couldn't afford her anyway," he said with a condescending smirk, then turned his back and walked toward the bar.

Kyle was indignant. He watched the arrogant stranger stride to the bar and order a drink like he was ten feet tall and walked on water. He was tempted to go over and put his fist into the man's nose to see if he bled. The man obviously had no idea who he was. He had money. He simply wasn't wearing a suit. It wasn't because he didn't have the means, but his wife didn't believe in spending it on anything that couldn't be worn on the ranch. Perhaps his tan wool pants with suspenders holding them up and his V-neck shirt weren't his Sunday best, but he wasn't dressed in rags, either.

His resentment at being belittled by a pompous ass grew quickly. He watched the man take his drink and make his way rudely through the crowd of men to stand beside another man in a suit near the entry door. Kyle recognized the other man as Branson's sheriff, Tim Wright. He had met the sheriff several times, and they had spoken at length this past December in Willow Falls. Tim had brought his deputies to Willow Falls to control the crowd and be there when Kyle's brother-in-law Matt Bannister brought the bodies of the Moskin Gang back to town after saving the woman they had kidnapped. It was the most exciting thing to happen in Willow Falls' history as far as Kyle was concerned. Seeing the sheriff standing beside the arrogant stranger who had belittled him brought a small smirk to his lips. He walked to the bar to refill his drink, then sauntered over and stood beside the arrogant, well-dressed man, intentionally close enough to listen to his conversation with the sheriff.

"I commend you," Sheriff Wright was saying. "She is a gem."

The man nodded with a smirk. "Indeed."

"For now, anyway," the sheriff added with a large grin.

"For now, yeah, but maybe longer than most."

Kyle turned to face the two men. "Hello, Tim. You'll remember we did some talking in Willow Falls last Christmas. I'm Kyle Lenning, owner of the Big Z Ranch." He had emphasized his professional title for the pompous stranger.

Sheriff Wright frowned in quick thought and then his face lit up with recognition. "Yes, Mister Lenning," he said with enthusiasm, and shook Kyle's hand. "You're Matt's and Lee's brother-in-law, right?"

"I am," he said proudly. He watched with satisfaction as the other man's eyes looked at him with some interest.

Tim tapped his friend's chest with the back of his hand and pointed at Kyle with a partly extended finger. "This is Matt and Lee Bannister's brother-in-law, Kyle Lenning. He and his beautiful wife own the Big Z cattle ranch over in Willow Falls. Kyle, this is my friend Travis McKnight. He's the general manager of the Seven Timber Lumber Mill."

Travis now shook Kyle's hand with more interest. "I didn't know the Bannisters had a sister."

"Yeah, she's the youngest of the six children. She has five elder brothers."

"Five? I thought there were three, Lee, Albert, and Matt."

Kyle smirked. "No, there are five brothers," he clarified. He added for good measure, "You'll have to excuse me if I'm not dressed in a suit, but I don't have much use for one when working with a thousand head of cattle, give or take a few. Why would I?" he asked with a smirk of his own. True, he had embellished the number of beeves a little, but he did say "give or take a few," so he wasn't necessarily lying. He'd simply misled the man.

"I suppose not," Travis said agreeably.

Kyle nodded toward Christine, who was now voluntarily teaching an old man—who looked to be a poor placer miner—how to dance a schottische on the empty dance floor. Her smile and joy were authentic as she laughed with the old man and looked toward the three men who stood by the door. "Just to let you know, I can afford more than you think I can. Perhaps even her."

Travis looked at Kyle strangely for a second and laughed good-naturedly. "Oh! I forgot about that. No hard feelings, I hope."

"No, none," he said with an internal sense of victory. He had been acknowledged and given his due respect by two of Branson's more prominent men. That satisfied him.

Tim spoke of a more serious topic at hand. "So, while your brother-in-law is over in Idaho looking for a lady-killer, we seem to have our own lady-killer here. He'll have a late start tracking this one down when he gets back."

Kyle immediately forgot his personal slights. "I don't know anything about it. What woman was killed here?"

Tim shrugged uncaringly. "I don't know who she was. Probably some vagrant miners, most likely, who cheated the wrong person. A man and woman were burned in a cabin up near Fairmont Creek. It may have been a murder-suicide, I don't know, but they were both shot and burned beyond recognition. It's out of my jurisdiction, so it's Matt's mess to clean up."

"No one knows who they were?"

"Not that I'm aware of. We have so many people coming and going that nobody knows anyone anymore. I assume they're placer miners, but they didn't have a claim as far as I can tell. But then again, I don't know who they are." He laughed.

"When he gets back, he'll figure it out, I'm sure," Kyle said simply.

"Perhaps not. Rumor has it the Sperry Helms Gang was involved. I don't know if that's true, but that's what I heard from the Rose Street gossip."

"Well, gentlemen," Travis said, "I'm going to go dance with my lady." He stepped forward to meet Christine as she laughed with the old man over his clumsiness.

Kyle watched as the band leader announced the last dance and began to auction off each of the dancers to the highest bidders, with a ten-ticket minimum for each of them. The last to be auctioned was Christine, and the minimum bid was raised to twenty tickets to have the last dance with her. Most of the girls ended with less than three bids, except Edith, who was won with a fifteen-ticket bid by a burly, heavy-set logger. Travis, of course, bid twenty-five tickets to dance with Christine. The last dance was the slowest of the night, and lasted longer than any other to make it worth the auction price. When the band began playing and the couples took to the floor, Tim Wright stepped closer to Kyle and said, "He's sure lucky to find her, ain't he? She is pure gold."

"Do you know her?" he asked as his low-gauge jealousy began to curl again.

"No, I've never met her, but when he's done with her, I plan to introduce myself. That there is the biggest scam in America or absolute brilliance, wouldn't you say?" he said and gestured toward the dance floor.

"What?"

"Auctioning the last dance. I've never heard of anyplace else doing that before, but it brings the money in. I didn't think they could compete with the saloons, but barely a month in, they've run the Green Toad out of business. All the others are losing money too. I guess you can't compete with beautiful dancing girls, even though the prices are inflated on the drinks. Nobody is supposed to know this, but that pink champagne everyone buys the ladies is nothing more than pink lemonade. Of course, if you want some, they'll sell you real champagne. It's all a hoax.

"It cost them a ton of money to build this place, but they're making a fortune. They pay a licensing fee of four hundred dollars a month plus taxes. I thought they'd fold in the first month of business, but I was very wrong. The only real problem they'll have internally is the girls getting pregnant or married. It's kind of the nature of the beast. Externally, there's already some folks who want to run them out of town to save their own business—and marriages too, I reckon." He finished with a smile.

"I was told they weren't whores," Kyle stated more than asked.

"They're not, but you don't think these girls are proper, do you? Not one of them is pure, I promise you. And when they fall for a man, marriage is what's on their mind. Unless, of course, they get pregnant first, but I am sure Bella has a solution to get rid of that. She ran a large brothel in Colorado before moving her dance hall here. It's likely that most of these girls were her whores, and probably still are for the right price. All except Travis' lady there."

"Christine?"

"Yeah. It's my understanding that she's a widow. She and her husband were coming West, and a fever of some sort took him and the kid, I think. At that point, she hooked up with Bella. Travis says she wasn't a whore. Her morals are too high to be a whore, so she only sings and dances. I heard her sing two weeks ago, and it's like listening to an angel. Travis has had his eye on her since their opening night and has courted her ever since. Of course, he told your brother-in-law Matt that she was a prostitute to chase him away, and you know Matt. He never came back."

"Matt was interested in her?" he asked, genuinely surprised.

"I don't know, but Travis wasn't taking any chances." He laughed. "Apparently, Matt was taken by her like everyone else around here, but he left after Travis told him she had given four or five of his employees gonorrhea or something." He laughed and shook his head. "Travis is a funny guy. Anyway, she is hooked on *him* now, so it worked."

"What a snake! Matt's a good man. Do you think they'll get married?" Kyle asked. He watched Christine's face glow with pleasure while she and Travis held each other's hands and turned slowly in a continuous large circle around the floor. Their eyes never left one another's.

Tim chuckled good-naturedly. "Now that would be scandalous, wouldn't it?"

Kyle looked at Tim in silent inquiry. "I wouldn't know."

"It would cause quite a stir around here."

He remembered what his friends had said earlier about their boss Travis McKnight being married. While he didn't question Tim about it, a hollow jealous rage began to build in his stomach as he watched the man stare into her eyes and dance confidently while living a lie. He sipped his drink and remained quiet. There really was no humor at all in the horrible lies Travis had told his brother in law about Christine, yet part of him rejoiced in knowing that Matt was out of the picture and Christine could be free of Travis as soon as she found out he was married and lying to other would-be suitors about her in despicable ways.

When the dance was over, the gentleman and the dancers all applauded the band, as did many of the men standing around the bar and tables. Travis took Christine by the hand and led her off the dance floor with childlike excitement on his face. He guided her to where Tim and Kyle stood along the wall by the entry door. "Christina, I want to introduce you to my friend Tim Wright. He's the sheriff here. Tim, this is Christina."

"Miss." Tim greeted her with a slight bow and kissed the top of her hand politely.

Travis continued, "And I think you met Kyle. He owns a large and successful ranch. Even though he doesn't know how to dress for success, he is related to some of the most influential men in our county, the Bannisters."

Christine looked at Kyle with more sincere interest than she had all night. "Like Matt Bannister?" she asked.

He nodded. "Yeah, do you know him?"

She grinned flirtatiously and rolled her eyes. "No, but I have read a book about him, and I saw him outside his office one day. He is very handsome." She looked at Travis as she explained further. "He's never come back in here after that first time, but if he does, I'll dance with him, so I can tell my grandkids that I did." She exhaled heavily. "It's too bad he's the way he is. I thought he was a Christian."

Travis spoke quickly to change the subject. "So, will you serenade me like you promised one of these days?"

"Maybe someday," she said with a smile.

Tim spoke seriously, rather embittered by her comment about dancing with Matt. "Matt won't come in here. It's not his jurisdiction, it's mine. Plus, he is too refined in his own way to come into a place like this. The more I get to know him, the more I realize he hates crowds and prefers to be alone. He's rather peculiar that way."

Christine responded, "I suppose that's what makes him mysterious at first."

"You're not missing much," Tim said with a hint of bitterness to his tone. "Is she?" he asked Travis.

The other man shrugged. "I don't really know him. I know his brothers, and I work with Albert here and there, but I don't know Matt very well. I met him a few times, but he doesn't say much to me."

Kyle could feel the effects of the beer he'd drunk and interjected sarcastically, "But you've said quite a bit to him, from what I've heard. Christine, he is a Christian and a very honorable man. I've gotten to know him some, and he's not as hardened as you'd think he is. He's a very caring man. I think he'd help anyone in need, but he doesn't scream it out loud to get recognition for it. If you ever hear anything different about him, don't believe it. It'll probably be from someone lying to you to make themselves look better than they are. Perhaps they're not who you think they are," he hinted boldly, glancing toward Travis.

Tim scowled irritably at him and then looked away as innocently as he could in the growing discomfort that had infiltrated the conversation.

Travis ignored him and turned to Christine. "I have arranged for us to have a late dinner at the Monarch Lounge, so if you'd like to change, we can go. My carriage is outside."

Kyle grimaced. "I thought women weren't allowed in there?" His brother-in-law Lee Bannister owned the Monarch Hotel. It was the largest and only high-class hotel in Branson, and it housed the Monarch restaurant, which was the only fine dining in the county. It also housed the Monarch Lounge, which was a private gentlemen's club reserved strictly for hotel guests and paid memberships by

Branson's elite. Kyle knew the restaurant was closed at this hour, and women were not allowed in the lounge.

The man looked at him with irritation. "I made special arrangements for a side room."

"Side room?" he asked skeptically. "Oh, you mean a hotel room."

Travis laughed uncomfortably, but it didn't hide his irritation. He explained to Christine, who looked from one to the other in confusion, "The Monarch restaurant has the finest food anywhere. It has the finest wines as well. It closes early, or I'd take you there. I have arranged for a private meal to be served to us tonight. But Kyle's right, even though I have a membership to the lounge, women are not allowed, so I had to get a formal room for the evening. It was expensive to set this up, but you deserve the very best."

Christine frowned. She had not missed Travis' irritation and hesitation when Kyle questioned him about the room, nor the change in the atmosphere between the two men. It waved a red flag she couldn't ignore, and she paused to consider his motives. "Thank you for thinking so, but you could take me to dinner when they're open. Why do our buggy rides and picnics always have to be far from town? And you never come here until almost closing time on any given night. You've never even shown me where you live, despite my asking you to—"

"Trust me, my house is most unimpressive, and—"

"No, one more question," she said calmly. "You have never wanted to take me anywhere in town until now, and that's to a hotel after midnight for fine dining. Are you afraid to be seen with me?"

Travis smiled reassuringly. "Absolutely not. Listen, I work late quite often, and when I'm done, you're working. It's simply the way things have been lately. It's summer, and it's always busy at the mill at this time of year. As far as my house goes, I'm afraid it leaves a lot to be desired, and I'm waiting for it to be painted before I show you where I live. The paint's all peeling off, and I need to hire a maid. If you think I'm rich, you'll be disappointed. I'm afraid the mansion on the hill belongs to my friends the Slater family, not me." He laughed. "Christine, I really don't have anything to hide. But there is one concern I guess I should explain. My wife died only last year, and you know how people talk. I simply don't want to ruin your reputation if you are seen with me in public too soon. So, if you would change your dress, we can go."

Christine smiled carefully. "Okay, but I'll come back here after dinner, so don't think I'll stay there. Agreed?"

"Of course. We'll have dinner, and I'll bring you back here."

"Very well," she said, nodding agreeably. "Gentlemen, it was nice to meet you, and I hope to see you both again," she said and excused herself politely to walk toward the alcove in the dance hall's entrance to go up the stairs to her room. Bella's hired security guard Phil stood at the bottom of the stairs, guarding access to the upper floor.

The three men watched her disappear around the corner. Sheriff Tim Wright wasted no time and quickly said goodnight to his friend. "You have a great night. She is a gold-star gem. Mister Lenning, it was good to see you again."

After Tim left, Kyle looked at Travis and said, "I get to stay after here while everyone else goes home. Perhaps I'll see you when you bring Christine back, huh? I might even get to talk to her about Matt for an hour or two, if that's what it takes to get in good with her." He'd had a few drinks and felt bolder than usual.

The other man looked at him with no friendliness in his

expression. He was clearly still irritated about Kyle questioning him about his plans at the Monarch Hotel. "Enjoy your time of...staying after, as you put it. Unfortunately for you, Christine will be with me," he said with an arrogant smirk. He put his derby hat on and walked toward the entrance to talk to Phil at the bottom of the stairs while he waited for Christine to return.

Kyle was approached by his two friends, who were with their lady friends Edith and Helen. Sam looked curious. "That was Travis McKnight. How do you know him?"

He shook his head. "I don't know the snake."

"It looked like you knew both him and the sheriff fairly well. Did you put a good word in for Paul and me? You should've introduced us so we could get on his good side."

"Next time," he said quietly, "but I don't think a good word from me would benefit you any." A surge of jealousy strained through his chest as he watched Travis laugh with Phil and Bella's husband Dave. Kyle knew exactly what Travis had in mind. He knew the Monarch Restaurant closed after dinner, so to hire the cook to make a special meal this late at night would cost extra money. Added to that would be the cost of a room for the night with all its luxuries, a soft bed with satin sheets, and undoubtedly he would have a bottle of imported wine to go with the meal. It was a first-class seduction of a beautiful woman by a married man. While it was none of his business, Christine was far too valuable a person to be misled, mistreated, and misused by a lying, arrogant piece of trash like Travis McKnight. Kyle liked Christine. In fact, he felt a kinship with her that surpassed any first introductions he had ever known before. It was almost crazy. He had just met the lady and danced with her a couple of times, but he was smitten. Simply put, he could not take his eyes off her and would jump at any opportunity to be near her.

"Is something wrong?" Sam asked curiously.

Kyle looked at Helen and Edith. "You girls need to go tell Christine that piece of bull dung over there"—he nodded at Travis—"is married. His wife's waiting for him at home, and he has a room lined up at the Monarch Hotel for Christine. He was telling the sheriff about it while I talked to them. Don't let her go, that's all I can say. She deserves better."

Edith spoke plainly. "We intended to. We need to go now before she comes back down, Helen. We'll be back." They walked quickly toward the stairs. Both ignored Travis when he tipped his hat and tried to start a conversation with them, and quickly disappeared upstairs.

Sam reached into his pocket and pulled out five drink tokens. "I have a free drink that says it doesn't matter to her and she goes with him."

Paul shook his head slowly. "You're on. I've heard enough about the ladies here from Edith to know Christine is strictly marriage-first material. No, I say we find a good seat and watch the show."

Kyle stated, "I don't know what she sees in a guy like that anyway."

"Money!" Sam laughed. "Lots of money."

6

Christine Knapp went to her room to change her low-cut dress for a more appropriate evening gown to ride in Travis' buggy to the Monarch Hotel for dinner. She emptied the hidden pocket of her dress and counted the dance tickets she had collected. There were twenty-five tickets, which was her usual number since she danced to every song the band played. With the twenty-five tickets acquired for the last dance auction, she had earned the dance hall fifty dance tickets. Combined with the dollar champagnes that the bartender kept careful tabs on, she had probably earned another thirty-five dollars, bringing in an estimated eighty-five dollars for the dance hall on her own, not including the drinks the men bought for themselves.

With a quick division by splitting it with the dance hall, who took sixty percent, she had made thirty-five dollars or so for the night's work. The word *work* was misleading, though. She had actually made thirty-some dollars for a night of fun, dancing, and being nice to people. It wasn't a bad living, and the money added up quickly on a weekly basis if it was saved.

She saved her money, except for an occasional new dress and the monthly fifty-dollar fee she paid for her room and board to Bella. All of the girls had their own rooms above the dance hall. They were a decent size, with one girl per room to give her privacy and comfort. If Bella hired a new girl, she would share a room with the dancer of the lowest seniority. Everything was based upon seniority since the proprietor herself had started at the bottom with nothing of her own and worked her way up to the wealth and status she now had. She knew girls, and she knew how to treat them fairly. Bella wasn't a cruel or demanding woman, but a smart businesswoman who could be tough. She was genuinely caring and did all she could to help her girls succeed in life if they wanted to. For Christine, Bella had been a lifesaver and a friend. If it had not been for her and her dance hall, she doubted she would have a life at all.

Christine was an only child who had been raised by her grandparents in rural Indiana. Her mother had been a beautiful sixteen-year-old young lady named Evelyn Harper. It wasn't uncommon for her to be approached by would-be suitors wanting to court her. She was nearing marrying age, and there was no shortage of single men of all ages hoping to court Evelyn and win her heart. One of the more persistent suitors was twenty-seven-year-old Roger Yount. The Younts were a powerful family of local politicians, including U.S. Senator John Yount.

Evelyn had no interest in Roger Yount, but he refused to leave her alone and sought her attention all the more when she rejected his advances. One afternoon, while walking home from town, Evelyn was surprised to see Roger and three of his friends step out of the bushes as she approached them. This time, Roger and his friends had no intention of asking. They dragged her off the road and raped her. None of the men were prosecuted, due to Roger's last name and the weight it carried in their small community. Evelyn was shattered, but her nightmare was just beginning when she discovered she was pregnant with what might well be Roger's baby.

Christine was born nine months later and was adored by her mother. However, Evelyn's reputation in town had gone from a wonderful sweet girl to a vile whore of the worst kind. She was unable to go to town without running into at least one of Roger's many friends, who would mock her with cutting remarks and obscene offers. The townsfolk, who had once given her the small-town warmth of a communal family, now treated her like she had the plague. No one would believe she had been raped by four men in such good standing within the town's social circle. The story spread around town that the unwed mother was lying about the four men for the purpose of trying to blackmail them for money.

One rainy afternoon she went to the store for her mother, and Roger Yount, his new young wife, and a group of their friends circled her in the middle of the muddy street and forced her to admit to everyone within hearing distance that she had lied about being raped. Roger's young wife, who had been Evelyn's best friend, and her older sister physically attacked Evelyn in front of the crowd and beat her until she bled. They forced her to painfully cry out for all to hear that she had lied about being raped and to admit that she planned it all to blackmail money from the Yount family and their friends.

Satisfied with her public admission, the group of former friends and townspeople walked away laughing while Evelyn lay on the wet ground and wept harder than she ever had before. Not one person cared enough to help her up out of the mud or ask if she was okay. They all simply closed their doors and let her wail. She lost all hope of ever being able to live a decent life again, and that night she drank a bottle of laudanum before going to sleep. In the morning, Evelyn's mother found her dead in bed with two-year-old Christine, who lay beside her singing softly while waiting for her mother to wake up like she usually did.

Her grandparents had no choice but to raise the child as their own daughter in a good Christian home. Although they were poor, they cherished each other and spent many evenings sitting around the piano teaching Christine how to play the notes and sing hymns like an angel. The finest memories of her youth were singing with her grandparents around their piano. As she grew older, she transformed into a beautiful young lady like her mother, and soon caught the attention of several suitors, including grown men in their thirties.

This time, Christine's grandfather had sworn not to permit anything to happen to her like it had his darling only daughter. It did not matter who showed interest in winning her affections, her devotion had already been won by the neighbor boy who had always been her best friend. She had grown up with Richard Knapp and could tell him anything with the greatest confidence. He not only cared, but loved her in such a way that he always considered what was best for her.

When she was nineteen years old, she and Richard married. They lived with his parents until they could invest in a modest place of their own to farm. Richard worked at a small flour mill while he waited for his crops to come in. It was hard times and they had no money to spare, but for four years, they struggled to make a living. Christine, in the meantime, did the household chores and kept the small farm going. She conceived three times, but each pregnancy ended in a miscarriage. Finally, after four years, Christine gave birth to a daughter, who they named Carmen.

Six months later, Christine's grandfather was kicked in the abdomen by a new horse he had bought, and he passed away two days later from internal bleeding. It was a devastating loss, but it was made sadder when her Grandmother decided to sell their family farm and refused to sell it to Richard and Christine. She gave no reason as to why, but simply rejected their offer to buy it. When the farm sold, her grandmother decided to move in with her only living sister over a hundred miles away. On her last day with Christine, she gave her granddaughter a long hug, told her she loved her, and handed her an envelope filled with money.

"There's enough there to buy farmland in Oregon, where you can do well. Sell your place and get out of this dark town. Take Carmen and Richard, and make a good life for yourselves. This is your chance to leave here, Christine. Don't waste it." It was the last time she had ever seen her dear grandmother. Although it had always been a dream, they were now able to go West and start a new life. There was a certain sadness in leaving Indiana, but it was also very exciting to adventure out into the unknown wilds to make a home.

The possibilities were endless, and so were the nights they lay awake dreaming of the kind of house they'd build, how many acres they'd plant, and even buying a new piano to play and sing hymns with. They had grand dreams, and every reason to expect to achieve those dreams with hard work. As best friends do, they would work together to earn what they wanted. While crossing the Kansas plains, influenza virus struck the wagon train. Christine and her small family contracted the disease and became extremely ill. Christine and Richard recovered, but little Carmen wasn't so strong and succumbed to the disease. They buried their beloved child on the Kansas plains with only a cross made from a broken board with no name on it as her grave marker. Broken-hearted, they continued west with only their dreams to hold onto. They weren't the only ones, though. Several children and some of the elderly from their wagon train were buried on the Kansas plains as well.

In Denver, Colorado, they hoped to stock up on supplies and prepare to cross the Rocky Mountains. Richard, on the second night of their short time of rest from the trail, went to a saloon with some of the other men to have a drink or two. Later that night, one of his companions raced to the wagon train to tell Christine that her husband had been stabbed. He had accidentally knocked a drink out of a man's hand. In a normal situation, it wouldn't have been blown out of proportion, but this other man had held a glass that had been given to him by someone special apparently, and it broke when it hit the floor. The man screamed in horror while he stared at the shards, and quickly drew his knife. Richard tried to apologize, but the crazed man attacked before anyone realized his intention.

Christine found his body in the doctor's office. He had been stabbed seventeen times and died almost immediately. She was devastated. Her family had been entirely snuffed out, and she was inconsolable. Although the ladies in their wagon train tried to comfort her, they could not delay for too long because they had families and a long, arduous journey across the Rocky Mountains awaiting them. A few men who had lost their wives on the trail west assumed Richard's death to be a sign from God that the young, beautiful, new widow should marry them. She, of course, had no interest in or even entertained the notion, not when she had lost her best friend and the love of her life. Her future and her joy in life were gone. Despite seeing his body, she simply could not believe Richard was dead.

Despite her shock and mourning, she had decisions to make, and she had to make them quickly. The wagon train would leave with or without her, and she had no idea what she should do or how she could do it. She had nowhere to go unless she went back to Indiana and stayed with Richard's family or perhaps tracked her grandmother down. Christine felt scared and hopeless for the first time in her life. The wagon train was leaving for Oregon in the morning, and the wagon master pressed her for an answer. She was simply too devastated to care about anything besides mourning her husband.

Across town, Bella had heard the news that a young woman had lost her husband the night before. By all accounts, the young lady was beautiful, and was now alone with nowhere to go. She was stirred by compassion, and went to the wagon train to seek Christine out. Bella offered her a place to stay for a few days so she could mourn and collect her thoughts in peace. She didn't ask for money, simply offered Christine a safe place until she was ready to go home, if that was what she wanted to do. Christine accepted Bella's offer and sold her supplies and wagon to others among the wagon train before they left.

Although the woman owned a brothel and a dance hall in Denver, the only thing she found in her benefactor was a kind mother-figure who seemed to genuinely care about her. After a few days, she questioned the young woman about any future plans she might have had now that her husband was gone. Christine shrugged and told Bella that she had no plans. She had no idea what she would do.

Bella offered her a job and then explained, "There are

two kinds of ladies. There are those who sell themselves, and those who don't. Those who do have already done so when they come to work for me. Those who don't, dance. I prefer the ladies who dance. If you work for me, there are rules—a lot of rules—but the main one is that for the first year you work for me, there will be no men in your life. You will dance with different men, and not see any man alone for that first year. Once the year is over, you will have the freedom to be courted and find yourself an honorable husband. Dancing is a fine profession, but your youth, beauty, and spirit will fade in time. You'll be in the poor-house if you don't save your money and find a decent husband while you still have the beauty to do so."

Christine began her dancing career, and within six months, she was the highest-earning of all of the dancers. When Bella heard her sing accompanied by a piano, she immediately asked her to sing a song or two for their gentlemen guests nightly. Her popularity grew, and men came to dance specifically with her and to hear her sing. Many men tried to court her, but not only was she not allowed to, she genuinely had no interest in any man she laid eyes on or danced with. No one could take the place of the dirty farm boy who had been the great love of her life.

It wasn't easy to dance with other men, and she felt guilty, as if she were unfaithful to her husband—or to his memory, at the very least. A certain sense of shame that plagued her night after night, knowing that Richard was buried a mile away with only a wooden cross to represent his life. Richard Knapp had been an amazing and loving man, but not one person in Denver would ever care about him or his grave. She danced night after night and wore a fake smile for the men who lined up and spent good money to dance with her.

Every night, she clung to the fact that she was not selling herself. She knew Richard would understand if she could speak to him one last time. She knew he would sell all he had to share one last dance with her if he could. The fact was, he was gone, and he wasn't coming back. The most she could do was buy a large granite tombstone and have the words My beloved forever etched under his name and the dates of his tragically short lifespan.

Over time, she reconciled her emotions and danced and manipulated men into buying her glasses of pink champagne. It was business, and that mindset, once she accepted it, kept her smiling on the dancefloor and flirting enough to keep the men coming back. Some days it was harder to smile on than others, like hers and Richard's anniversary or his birthday, but business was business, separate from her emotions. She was the star attraction, and was expected to dance and sing. No matter how she felt, she still had a job to do. It was the farmer's work ethic in another type of profession—a profession she had never imagined she'd be involved in. Despite the circumstances that she endured, Bella's Dance Hall was a good place for her to be.

It was true that Bella hoped her ladies would find decent husbands and start a good family life for themselves. Of course, she made money from her ladies, but she took a personal interest in and cared for each of the girls. She wanted them to do well, and when one moved on in marriage, Bella hired someone new to take their place. There was no shortage of girls who wanted to be a part of Bella's Dance Hall. The ladies were well-dressed, well-fed, looked after, kept safe, and enjoyed their lives for the most part.

The proprietor looked after them like a mother and advised them to not rush into marriage too fast, but to get to know the gentleman before giving their lives to them. Bella often emphasized certain realities, and would point out that it took work to communicate, effort to get along, and real heart to endure the tough times that came along to make a marriage a joyful one. One thing she knew too well was that marriage could be a beautiful thing, but there wasn't a sorrier life than marrying a man of the wrong kind.

As for Christine, she had danced with hundreds of men in her three years in Colorado, and now in Branson. Not one of those men had ever swept her off her feet or even captured her interest for a moment. Hundreds of men had bought her drinks, talked to her, flirted with her, and tried to attract her interest in a thousand different ways. Still, not one man had ever won her interest until she saw Matt Bannister up close outside his office. She had suddenly felt butterflies swirl in her stomach as their eyes met on the boardwalk as if they were the only persons present.

It was the first time since her wedding day that those butterflies took flight within her. She'd thought it was fate later that night when she saw Matt step into the dance hall and begin speaking to a man she had met named Travis McKnight. She was saddened to see Matt leave as quickly as he had, and later, talking to Travis, she was disappointed to learn that the intriguing marshal had thought she was a prostitute. That was the only reason he had entered the dance hall. For some unknown reason—mostly from what she had read about him—she'd expected much more. It was rumored he was a Christian man, but apparently, he wasn't after all.

Travis McKnight was handsome, powerfully built, well-dressed, and smelled of sweet cologne. His confidence was the kind that came from leading others and commanding other men's respect. He was obviously a person of importance, intelligence, and success. Travis made her feel like a curious child when he looked at her, and she wasn't sure why. He simply had that confidence that made him seem like a king and her a mere peasant. For the first time in almost three years since Richard's death, Christine had a desire to get to know another man in a personal way.

The dance hall had opened in June, and Travis had been her constant customer and suitor since then. She learned that he was a widower like herself, and that gave them common ground on which to begin building a foundation. He was well-spoken, sincere, and easy to talk to, but most uncommonly, he listened to her the way Richard used to. Despite her innate wariness at first, she felt he was self-sufficient, kind, loving, and genuine with her. He shared his dreams and his weaknesses and would be a very suitable husband and father someday.

Christine wasn't one to fall quickly into a relationship. She knew well that relationships, especially intimate ones, were built with time, communication, and openness, among other things. It was a process of building a foundation of friendship that could withstand the mutual attraction when it grew into the flames of love. Truly, a love based upon the secure foundation of friendship could hold true when the storms and tragedies of life tore at the seams of a marriage. However, a marriage based upon a dream, hope, desire, or whim had no chance of surviving when the fires of love were doused by life's storms and the realities that often follow the wedding day's bliss. The most miserable people in the world could very well be those who were committed to their marriage but lacked the foundation of friendship.

Having both lost the love they had committed their lives to, their hearts were fragile and still on the mend. Even though she was cautious, excitement began to flow through her veins at the possibility that maybe Travis was another chance for her to fall in love. She could never replace the beautiful family she had lost, but she could begin again. Perhaps she could have a real home, a real future to look forward to, and a real chance to achieve happiness in her empty life. Travis McKnight was the kind of man she thought she could love for the rest of her life, when and if they were ever ready to take the next step in their relationship. For the first time in almost three years, Christine was ready to leave the past behind and move forward. It had come out of nowhere, and it scared her somewhat, but she was ready.

Or so it seemed, until the words of her friends resounded like a slap across her face. She sank heavily onto a cushioned chair in her room and stared at Edith and Helen with a stunned expression—not immediate acceptance, but strong bewilderment. "Wh-what are you saying?"

"He's lied to you. Travis is married," Edith repeated gently but firmly to her friend. "His wife and kids live across town. That's probably why he only comes here late at night and never takes you any place where you can be seen."

"His wife died. Her name was Rhonda. We've talked about her and Richard many times. He wouldn't lie about that!" Christine stared at her friends and began to grow angry at their accusation. "He wouldn't lie about that. There's no reason to."

Helen scoffed bitterly. "Have you done him yet?"

"What kind of a question is that, Helen? Seriously, you two. I am about sick of your—"

"Have you been bedded by him yet? It's a yes or no question, Christine," Helen interrupted hastily. She glared a challenge at her and waited for the answer.

"No!" she said in a raised voice, and stood to continue

getting dressed. "What does that have to do with anything? You're telling me he's married, and he's not. Now you're asking if we made love, and the answer is no. What do you two want? Because he's waiting for me and I don't want to keep him waiting too long. He planned a dinner at the Monarch Hotel for us, so if you'll excuse me..." She paused to look at her friends. "I don't appreciate hearing your gossip, by the way."

"It's not gossip, Christine, it's the truth," Edith said softly.

Helen added sarcastically, "At the Monarch Hotel, imagine that! Hmm..."

Christine glared at Helen, angered by her tone. "What is with you tonight, Helen? Why can't you be happy for me? I finally meet a gentleman I'm interested in, and when he sets up a nice romantic evening, you belittle me? I know him, and I know his wife died, so please stop it, okay? I won't let you two ruin my chance to find happiness because of some stupid rumor you heard. A rumor probably started by some jealous man who was irritated because Travis danced with me. You know how those things go. Some of those men are worse than women when it comes to manipulating others to get what they want."

Helen raised her arms as if handing Christine a platter. "There you are. Exactly."

Christine merely grimaced and shook her head in frustration.

Edith continued, "We heard it from the guys, and they work for him. They've known him a lot longer than you have."

She sighed as she leaned back against her vanity. "If you're talking about your sweethearts, they said they didn't know him, so how in the world could they know if he was married? I won't have a good thing ruined by rumors. I won't even listen to them. Now, will you please leave so I can finish getting ready to go?"

Helen sighed and turned to leave, but spun back and added with real irritation, "Here's an idea. Tell him if he takes you to his house you'll sleep with him, and see what he does. If there's nothing to hide, he'll take you there, trust me. If he doesn't, he's either a homosexual or hiding his wife. Try it and see," she finished with a sarcastic shrug.

"He's already made plans for tonight, thank you!" Christine snapped at her.

Edith shook her head at the other woman's remark and spoke softly. "Christine, I know you like him a lot, and he seems very genuine, but deep down, you know something's not right. He's courted you all this time, and still hasn't taken you to his house or mentioned where he lives. He hasn't taken you anywhere near town in daylight, nor the Monarch Restaurant until tonight—which again, is too late for anyone to see you with him. Do you ever have the feeling he's hiding something, and maybe that something is you? Maybe he's hiding you from the people in town who know his wife? Listen, you know as well as I do that if he were serious about you, he would be proud to show you off. No other man in this whole dance hall would keep you hidden away like Travis does—"

"He doesn't keep me hidden away like some kind of mistress!" she interrupted with disgust.

"Listen to me," Edith said pointedly. "You don't have to believe us, but hear me for a minute. I know Paul, and I know he is telling the truth. He may not know Travis personally, but he does know *about* him. Paul has no reason to lie, but Travis does if he's married. Obviously, Travis rented a room at the hotel—which I find very presumptuous, by the way. I don't like it, and I don't think a man in his position is used to hearing the word 'no.' So before you leave with him and put yourself in a position where you could potentially be forced, know that we love you and care about you. We are trying to be true friends, and we don't want to see you get hurt. Paul and Sam both say he's married without any doubt, and I believe them." Her eyes were bright with sympathy.

Christine sat in her chair again, now deep in thought as Edith's words sank in and doubt began to fill her mind. "He's not married. He can't be. I can't imagine he'd lie to me, especially about his wife dying. I mean, why would he lie about that?"

"To get to you through the most vulnerable door you have," Helen said simply.

"But why? I mean, how could anyone lie about something like that? It's inconceivable. No, she has to be dead. There's no other reason he'd say that if she wasn't," she debated quietly.

"Christine, Paul knows where he lives. He has seen Travis' wife and son in the yard. Branson's not a big city," Edith said softly.

Christine looked at her. "Do you think his wife is alive and he lied about that?"

Edith nodded. "I do, and you need to ask him about that before you go anywhere tonight."

Helen spoke with a heavy dose of venom in her voice, "And then you need to let everyone know what a piece of crap he is."

She looked at Helen. "How do you know Sam is not married?"

The woman grimaced. "Because I've been to his house. Sam ain't rich, but at least he's honest. I'll take that over money any day."

Christine nodded in agreement and looked down to collect the thoughts that now whirled in a hundred different directions. The most troubling thought was whether Travis was lying about his wife dying. How could a man be so callous as to lie about such a thing? The *why* plagued her thoughts as well, but the *how* was simply inconceivable to her.

Helen's voice drew her out of her contemplation. "You should take another look at Sam's friend Kyle. He seems like a nice man, and he owns a ranch."

"He's married," she said, and added with a mischievous smile, "And he is related to Matt Bannister, and Matt is not married...although Matt likes prostitutes, Travis said."

Edith spoke questionably, "Well, I would question that too if Travis said it. I know men fairly well, and I didn't get that impression when we walked past Matt that day. He couldn't keep his eyes off you. You'll remember how disgusted he looked when that old man offered a dollar or two for us to bed his son in the wagon?" She shook her head and grimaced in disgust at the thought, then continued in an accusatory tone, "And if you'll remember correctly, Travis was the one who talked to Matt that night before he walked out. If he lied about his wife and has played you all this time, who knows what he told the marshal? Ask Paul's friend Kyle. He would know. The answers are downstairs."

"He did say Matt was an honorable man this evening. In fact, maybe he tried to..." Christine paused to consider the words Kyle had spoken earlier.

Helen smiled slightly. "So there you go—a link to your dream man. Now, let's get rid of this leech and get you set up with the marshal."

She looked awkwardly at her two friends. "Travis told me that night when Matt came in that he left because we weren't prostitutes. He said he had some disease and favored prostitutes."

Edith shook her head. "If the only person you have ever heard that from is Travis, don't believe him. None of us have ever heard that kind of stuff about him, not even from the prostitutes who live around the corner."

"That's an excellent idea," Helen said to Edith. "The least we can do is ask that Kyle guy if Travis was lying about Matt. Then you'll know," Edith said, her smile bright and encouraging.

Christine's frown deepened as she changed into a comfortable yet attractive gown for the remainder of the evening. She was nervous about confronting Travis, but she knew she had to. She hoped he was telling her the truth and her friends were wrong, of course. It would break her heart to learn that he had lied to her about his wife being dead. It made no sense, and it was simply beyond imagination to lie about such a horrible thing.

Ten minutes later, she stepped out of her room and walked down the hallway toward the stairs. Near the top, she paused to look nervously at her friends. They were right behind her, and Edith's comforting smile encouraged her to descend the stairs. Her heart pounded with each step. Travis waited near the bottom with his suit jacket and derby hat on.

"You look absolutely gorgeous!" he said with a smile. He paused when he saw her expression. "What's the matter, Christina? Are you not feeling well?"

She paused four steps from the bottom and took a deep breath before asking, "Are you married?"

His eyes widened quickly in surprise and then narrowed as he grimaced. "What? No, I'm not married. I told you, my wife died. I don't know why you'd even ask such a thing. But we'd better hurry. We don't want dinner getting cold before we get there," he said, and recovered his smile as he held his hand out to guide her down the remaining stairs.

She brought her hands up nervously to her chest and interlocked her fingers. "I was told you were married."

"I was until she died," he said. His hand remained out to grasp hers.

"I want to see your house."

Travis lowered his arm and frowned. Despite his growing impatience, he managed to hold onto his smile. "Why? I told you it would be a disappointment. It's nothing to brag about, trust me."

Christine shook her head. "I still want to see it, and I won't go anywhere until you promise to take me there."

"Fine. We'll drive past it on the way to dinner, but let's leave now. I'd like to eat while the food's warmer than the wine," he said with a hint of agitation. He flushed a little, possibly with embarrassment since a few people had gathered nearby and watched him curiously. They seemed to grow more uncomfortable by the minute.

She shook her head firmly. "No, I want to go inside, not merely drive past it. I want to go inside and see your home, and my friends will come with me."

"What?" Travis asked. He raised his voice "No! Look, I won't take you to my house so you and your friends can look around. I've already paid a small fortune for a room, a specially arranged dinner, and the best wine in the city for us to enjoy at the Monarch Hotel. I will not take you to my house tonight, okay?" He lowered his voice and continued, "Christina, it's already planned and paid for, so how about we enjoy the evening? I will take you there tomorrow if you want. This really isn't the place for a conversation, so let's discuss it over dinner." He flashed his charming smile.

"A conversation about what, Travis?" Her tone took him by surprise. She stood on the stairs and glared at him as her beautiful brown eyes glazed over with tears that she held back.

He began to look uncomfortable once more. "About *what*?" he asked. "About this ludicrous accusation. And why I would want to take you and your friends to my home to look around? Do I snoop around *your* home? It's ridiculous. Listen, we have dinner waiting for us right now, I'm sure, so can we drop the nonsense and leave?"

Christine shook her head. "Not until you prove to my friends and me that your wife is not at your house."

A sneer came over his face, and he looked down at the floor and exhaled slowly as his face reddened in anger. He shook his head, knowing that everyone around him now watched him intently.

"Well?" she snapped unexpectedly. "Are you married or not, Travis? Have you been lying to me this whole time?"

"No, I haven't been lying," he shouted at her. There was a moment of silence before he added in a lower voice as he stepped up the first two steps to be near her, "At least not about how I feel. Christina—listen, my lady, I *am* married, yes, but I hate her with a passion. I know I was wrong in saying what I did, but—"

Christine's upper lip curled into a snarl, and she slashed her right hand across his cheek. The impact sounded like a firework and sent his derby hat tumbling to the bottom of the stairs. "Get out of my sight," she yelled. "I never once lied to you, you lying bastard! My husband was murdered and I poured my heart out to you, and you had the gall to lie to me? Get out of here, and don't ever speak to me again. Not ever," she shrieked emotionally, then turned and bolted upstairs. The dam of tears broke as she ran.

"Christina!" Travis called after her.

"Time to go, Mister McKnight," Bella's husband Dave said as he and their security man guided him gently off the stairs. "She doesn't want to talk to you."

"I have to talk to her. Christina!" he bellowed up the stairs. "You don't understand! I didn't lie about my feeling for you, only about my wife. She doesn't matter, can't you see? I'm in love with you."

"Mister McKnight, I must ask you to leave for tonight," Dave said in an authoritative tone.

Travis nodded and shouted up the stairs, "I'll see you later, Christina." He turned to pick his hat up off the floor but froze. Kyle Lenning stood behind him and held his hat out to him with a broad grin. Travis snatched it from his hands. "Thank you."

The man shook his head, his smile amused. "You may not want to tell your wife about this," he said with a chuckle. Others laughed as well.

Travis looked at him, humiliated and angry. "I know who you are, Mister Lenning. We'll see how funny you really are later."

Kyle continued to laugh as if accepting the challenge. He raised his left hand to show his wedding ring. "I don't have to lie about being widowed for girls to talk to me. In fact, I think I'll talk to Christine tonight after all. Your name will come up, I imagine. I wouldn't want her to think I'm a liar too, so I'll keep my ring on." He laughed.

Travis pointed at him with an angry glare as he was led out the door by Dave and their hired security guard.

7

She had laid awake for most of the night and woke up late. Her hopes for finding romance and love had been torn apart, and she felt like a fool. How she could have been deceived so easily weighed heavily upon her mind. Travis McKnight had treated her with genuine respect and honor, unlike most men, who assumed they could get an hour in the privacy of her room for ten dollars. She was a dancer and she also sang, but she wasn't a prostitute, nor did she pretend to be. Christine had once been a very upright young lady, with an honorable husband and a beautiful family. She had been treated with respect then, and she longed to be treated the same way now, even though she sang for the men or danced for a dollar ticket and peddled drinks.

Being associated with Bella's Dance Hall already tarnished her reputation with the more righteous people in the city of Branson. Even the most common women in town looked at her with disdain, while the more affluent women looked at her with disgust—as if she were a diseased threat to their husbands. However, men of all classes looked at her with lust and desire, except for Travis McKnight. He'd courted her like a gentleman and gained her trust and affection. Foolishly, she'd allowed herself to feel affection she had not known since her husband was alive. It was all a lie, and now her heart was broken.

A knock on the door drew her from her thoughts. "Yes?" she called softly.

The door opened, and a young lady stepped inside with a smile. "Good morning, Christine. Bella wants to see you. She's in her office going over the schedule."

"Oh. Okay..." She yawned. "I'll be down in a few minutes."

Christine looked in the mirror, pulled her long hair up into a neat bun, and wiped her face with a wet towel to wash the sleep from her eyes. She added tooth powder to her toothbrush and brushed her teeth before rinsing her mouth and spitting the water out her opened window into the alley below. With a long cotton robe around her, she went down to Bella's office and knocked on the office door.

"Come in, Christine," Bella said loudly in her rough voice.

The dancer opened the door slowly. Her boss sat behind her desk, and in front of it, in two padded chairs, sat Helen Monroe and Edith Williams. They both smiled at Christine.

"Good morning," she said awkwardly as she stepped into the office.

Bella spoke quickly. "How are you feeling, young lady?"

"I'm okay."

"Yeah? Are you ready to work tonight? We can't have you teary-eyed and frowning on the busiest night of the week. You're my number one girl, and everyone expects a smile. Are you up to it?"

Christine frowned. "Of course."

"Really? Even though your heart was broken?"

"Yes," she said unconvincingly, and her eyes teared up.

Bella's eyes softened. "When we first came here to Branson, before you met that Travis bastard, you wanted to meet that handsome marshal. Matt Bannister, am I right?"

She smiled shyly while her two friends giggled. "Well, yeah. But Travis said he was only interested in prostitutes, and you know I'm not interested in men like that—if he was telling the truth."

The proprietor sighed, her expression gentle. "Christine, the girls here asked Kyle about that last night, and it's about as far from the truth as any lie that Kyle Lenning had ever heard. That's his brother-in-law, you know, so I think we can believe him over that lying McKnight bastard."

"Well, I'm not surprised," she replied, and her aggravation showed in her voice. She really shouldn't be shocked to find out about another verified lie.

"Anyway, the girls here asked me if they could have tonight off to spend an evening out with their two suitors, and they tell me Kyle's a friend who's in town only for tonight. He seems to have taken an interest in you, so I want you to take the night off and go out with these two ladies and have some fun. Find that beautiful smile again, and use this man to introduce you to that elusive Matt Bannister. I want you to meet him, Christine, and win his heart like only you can. He is a good man from all I understand and will treat you right."

Christine laughed nervously. "You act like he'd be interested in me. He won't set foot in here since Travis said something to him, so I don't think he'd be interested in someone who lives and works here."

"Don't sell yourself short. You have all the virtue of any other woman in town. And if he's half the man people say he is, he'll recognize that right away. Do you think it's a coincidence that you are both new to this town? He's only been here a few months longer than us. Take tonight off and have fun. Put your thoughts on someone other than that rat Travis."

"I don't know. It's the busiest night, and we're all here to make money," she stated uncertainly.

Helen responded quickly, "Oh, come on, Christine. We never have a Saturday night off, not ever! Come out with us, and let's do something different for a change. Kyle's coming, and it'll be fun."

Christine rolled her eyes slowly. "I don't even know him, and besides, he's married. I've had enough of married men being interested in me."

"He's not courting you. He'll introduce you to the marshal," Helen said. "Besides, he's happily married, so he won't try anything."

She smiled sadly. "Really, I would rather work."

Bella spoke firmly. "You'll take the night off and go out with these ladies. I don't want to hear any more about it. Get to know this Kyle, and impress the hell out of the marshal. The girls will do the rest."

"The rest of what?" she asked skeptically.

Bella smiled. "You don't worry about that. As you know, I am very protective of my girls, and I hate to see any girl leave our dance hall family unless they meet a solid man who's asked her to be his wife. I want all you ladies to get married and have a family when the right man comes along. I have watched those two men look at these girls, and I'm telling you, I think Edith and Helen are close to leaving us. I am giving them the night off to invest in their future. And you, too. Go meet the marshal, and when you do meet the right man, I will do my best to work with you to make that happen, just the way I am with them. We can afford a night without you three. Go have some fun with the ladies."

Christine frowned slightly. "Fine, but I don't want to. And just so you know, I don't have anything to wear that's casual enough to out with a rancher in this town."

Bella laughed loudly. "I sure love you! Now, all three of you go get bathed and freshened up, and steal some hearts tonight!"

8

Kyle had left his friends' house around three in the morning, after Sam and Paul had fallen asleep. He walked down to Rose Street with his thoughts swimming in wonder about Christine. What she had done to stimulate such emotions, he didn't know, but he couldn't get her off his mind. He had wandered past Bella's Dance Hall hoping she'd be looking out of an opened window or sitting outside to breathe in some fresh, cool air as he walked by. He yearned for a chance to speak with her in private without a crowd of men interrupting to dance with her. However, there no such luck when he walked by or for that matter, during the time he stood on the corner hoping for a chance to see her. Giving up, he wandered back to Sam's and Paul's house and slept on their davenport.

Kyle was just now waking up, and he sat on the davenport. He was not feeling too well, like always after a night of drinking. He held a cup of coffee in his hand and didn't feel like talking, but someone knocked on the door.

Sam stood up and opened the door. "Hey!" he said

enthusiastically. He was immediately wrapped in a hug by Helen.

"Good morning!" she said, and kissed him quickly.

"Morning," Sam replied, and kissed her again.

"Where's Edith? Didn't she come with you?" Paul asked. He was standing by the bedroom's door with no shirt on, just his baggy long johns with a button-up front.

"Nope. She went with Bella to get some supplies. I can't stay long either. I have to help clean until four, it turns out, but we have tonight off!" she said excitedly. "So, you better be ready for some fun!"

"Edith has tonight off too?" Paul asked.

"She does. We talked to Bella this morning, and she gave us the night off. And Christine, too," she continued, looking at Kyle, who remained on the davenport. "So, you better get cleaned up and try to look handsome, because she isn't impressed by hungover slobs."

Sam frowned. "Christine's coming with us?"

Helen scoffed. "Don't sound so stunned! She is just a woman, you know. But yes, she's coming with us. Well, him." She nodded at Kyle. She looked at Sam and spoke quietly. "We can't have your friend being a third wheel, now, can we? Perhaps Christine will keep him entertained so we can do our own thing."

Sam smiled. "That sounds good to me."

"Good, because since none of us work tomorrow, Edith and I plan on getting drunk! We have already decided that we're going to get Christine drunk tonight too. I'm afraid she's a little heartbroken today. I don't know why though, since her biggest crush is on your brother-in-law, the marshal, Kyle. I don't know why she liked Travis so much. I thought he was pompous and arrogant, but I suppose most guys with soft-skinned hands are."

Kyle spoke from the davenport, "Christina's coming?"

Helen nodded. "Yep. And she's prepping herself up very pretty, too. But don't you worry, Mister Lenning, she knows you're a happily married man. She's not dressing up for you. She wants to meet the marshal tonight."

For a moment, Kyle's chest had filled with excitement, but just as quickly as it had filled, his chest was deflated by her acknowledging he was married. Not just married, but *happily* married. Even her interest in making herself more beautiful than she already was had nothing to do with him. It was for a man she had never even met. It put a sour taste in Kyle's mouth as he said, "Matt's not in town. He's over in Sweethome, Idaho looking for a man that killed a woman."

Helen frowned. "Well, don't tell her that until after we're out and about, dummy! We do expect a nice dinner somewhere before you take us to that traveling Shakespearean troupe's play tonight. Bella said she will get the tickets for us. She also says a little class wouldn't hurt you guys any. So, meet us at five in the lobby of the dance hall and dress nice, because we're going to watch Shakespeare and mingle like classy folks!" She giggled.

Paul asked with a frown on his face, "I thought you said you wanted to get drunk?" He wasn't interested in going to a play at all.

"We will after the play. But don't think you can skip the play, because Edith is excited to see it. None of us have seen one before, and Christine wants to see it too."

"I'll take Christina to it," Kyle said, perfectly willing.

Helen spoke seriously to Kyle, "You might impress her more if you said her name right. Her name is Christine, not Christina."

"Oh. Well, that guy called her Christina," he replied.

"It was his pet name for her. I wouldn't call her that if I was you."

"I won't," he said with a slight smile.

"You know," Sam offered, "we're not really Shakespeare and theater kind of guys. A saloon, gambling hall, or perhaps or somewhere to dance. Maybe even getting together here sounds more fun than watching someone act out an old play where we can't understand what they're saying anyway."

"Have you ever read any Shakespeare?" she asked with a flirtatious smirk on her lips.

"No, I don't read much."

"*Can* you read?" she asked, and listened to the chuckles of Paul and Kyle.

"Yeah...but I don't like to. Now, if you want to raise some hell, I can help with that, but not at no opera or theater house."

"Sam, who knows how long it will be until we have another Saturday night off? We can go to a saloon anytime, but the traveling Shakespeare troupe will only be here this weekend. We all want to go, and we will go with you three gentlemen—or we'll go alone. You get to choose if we are worth it or not. I should go. See you at five?" She didn't wait for an answer, but gave him a quick kiss on his lips and stepped back out the door to leave.

"All right, see you then," Sam said as he watched her walk away. He left the door open to let some air into their house. It was going to be another hot July day.

"Well, it looks like we're going to a play," Paul said without any enthusiasm in his voice.

Sam smiled as he looked at his friend. "You do realize they're off tomorrow night too, so we might have a great weekend after we get through the play. We need to clean this place up and make it somewhat homey for the ladies. Just think, Kyle, if you weren't married, Christine might be all over you this weekend," he teased with a laugh.

Kyle groaned with frustration. "Whoever said I was *happily* married? I never said that! I was just telling you guys yesterday that we were fighting and going our different ways in life. I want to buy the Green Toad. I have always wanted to buy that place, and it just so happens it's for sale! And the night I come to terms with knowing what I want, I meet the most beautiful girl in the world! Seriously, guys, what are the odds of all this happening? Think about it: on the night I come to town and am thinking about ending my marriage, she finds out her suitor is married! Is that not a coincidence?"

"It is," Paul agreed, "but she's interested in your brother-in-law!" He laughed at his friend.

Sam laughed loudly too. "You just can't win for losing, can you?"

Kyle spoke seriously, "You just wait and see. I'll buy the Green Toad, and someday end up marrying Christina—I mean, Christine. She'll draw in customers from all over, and we'll have the best saloon in town."

Paul shook his head with a sarcastic smile. "That's quite a dream, especially for just meeting her last night. You don't even know what she looks like in the daylight, or what she's like when she's not dancing."

"It doesn't matter. We made a connection. It was almost like love at first sight. Do you know what I mean?" he asked curiously, trying to define the consuming emotions that overwhelmed his mind like a heavy fog of desire, affection, and surrender to the lady he had just met. It had hit him like a solid wall of bricks that he was magically transported through, and now he was on the other side, where nothing else mattered.

"What?" Paul asked astonished by his friend's words.

Sam spoke with no humor in his voice, "I think you're just desperate for some excitement in your life, so let's have some fun tonight and send you back home tomorrow before you make an ass of yourself. I don't know Christine very well, but from what I do know, I don't think she'd pair up with a man who left his family for her."

Kyle was agitated by Sam's tone. "I'm not leaving my family because of her! But I don't think it's all coincidence how my family's falling apart either. I mean, I have never felt this way before. It's like she's the one I'm destined to be with or something. I don't know how to explain it, but there's a connection from deep within, and I can't get her off my mind."

Paul answered quickly, "Every guy feels like that about her. That's why she's Christine! Every guy wants to be with her. Do you have any idea how much money she earns a night dancing? She makes more from the last dance auction in a single night than we do in a week. And do you know why that is? Because she pours on the charm to make every man feel special. Trust me, Kyle, you're not the only one infatuated with her. You're just another man paying for a dance to be near her. That's why they keep coming back."

Kyle glared at Paul sternly. "Wait and see."

"Are you serious?" Sam asked, raising his voice. His concern was evident in his expression. "What about Annie? You *are* married, you know."

"Yeah, I am. But, uh, I'm not going to be for long. I'm buying the Green Toad, and that will pretty much end my marriage. Yeah?"

Sam answered seriously, "Well, we'll just wait and see, I guess. But I'll remind you that it takes money to buy the Green Toad, and the Big Z isn't yours. I'm pretty sure your brothers-in-law won't loan you the money if you divorce their sister, and if you try to pull a fast one on them by running out on Annie, they'll call you to account and run you out of business faster than you can say goodbye. You married into the wrong family if you think you can just walk out. Annie will shoot you herself, and who's going to arrest her? Matt? He's the only real law around here, and you know he won't."

"There's no crime in getting a divorce."

"But why?" Paul asked loudly, becoming irritable with his friend. "Annie's awesome!"

Kyle looked at Paul sadly. "Yeah, she is...but not for me. I told you guys, I hate the ranch, and I hate my life. It's Annie's life, and I don't want any part of it—not anymore. I belong in the city. I belong here. I want to live my life and do what will make me happy, and not anyone else for a change. I'm tired of caring about what everyone else wants. I want to enjoy my life, and live it for me. And I'm going to do it! I know you're thinking I must be crazy, but I've been thinking about leaving Annie and the ranch for a while now. I don't believe in coincidences, so everything must be lining up like this for a reason. Like it's a God thing."

Sam frowned. "You're reading too much into a couple of coincidences. Or maybe you're seeing more than there is."

Paul added, "We're all friends, Kyle, and we will be no matter what, but I believe you're making a big mistake if you're thinking about leaving your family. Getting away sometimes is fine, but leaving your wife and kids to start a new life shouldn't be taken lightly."

"I'm not taking it lightly. I just told you that I've been thinking about it for a long time. It's just, now everything is lining up perfectly for me to do it. Call it what you will, but I don't believe in coincidences. Haven't you ever heard people say that for a Christian, there's no such thing as a coincidence?" Kyle asked.

Paul grimaced in thought and answered slowly, "Yeah, but you're not one."

Kyle paused and exhaled as a wave of conviction rolled through him. He nodded. "I am. I'm just...not living it like I'm supposed to be. I know that. But it doesn't stop the Lord from loving me and leading me. And all these coincidences are His way of showing me where to go. My dreams are right here at the doorstep, and all I have to do is grab them. Can't you see that?"

Sam chuckled softly and shook his head in disbelief at what he was hearing. "Sometimes people see what they want to, and not the rest of the picture."

"What's the rest of the picture, Sam? Since you know so much, what do you think it is, huh?" Kyle asked shortly. He was becoming angry with his friends.

Sam looked at Kyle evenly. "You're married to Annie, so nothing else needs to be said. Your responsibilities are to your family—period."

"You're not married, so you have no idea what it's like. Everything is about them. I don't get anything, except to work day after day on a ranch I hate! I want to do whatever the hell *I* want for a change. When is it *my* turn to have some fun in life? Everyone else is enjoying life except me!"

"You're right, I'm not married, Kyle, but when I do say my vows, they will mean something. I won't leave my children because I hate my job at the mill, either. I won't be so selfish as to leave them just so I can have fun and do what I want when I have a family at home depending on me to raise them!" Sam exclaimed.

"You don't know anything about having a family!" Kyle shouted. "How can you stand there and tell me what my responsibilities are when you haven't got a clue what I do for my family? I have been married for—"

"Oh, spare me the sad story!" Sam interrupted irritably, "You have it made with Annie. You just don't like working with your hands. If you could—"

"If I could *what*?" Kyle shouted.

"If Annie moved over here so you could tend bar, you would not leave her, and you know it!"

Kyle rolled his eyes and gasped, then spoke sincerely, "But that's the point, Sam. She won't. But now I've met Christina, and she will! Love at first sight is real, at least for me. I can't explain it beyond that, but yeah..." His voice trailed off as he watched Sam and Paul stare at him awkwardly.

Sam spoke through a restrained chuckle. "You don't even know her name. It's 'Christine.'"

Paul spoke slowly, "You mentioned something about being a Christian and coincidences being God things, right?"

"Yeah. God sets it all that up, so there are no coincidences. It's all part of His plan. It's called the providence of God , and that's how we know what His will is. Like right now, with the Green Toad up for sale and meeting *Christine*," he emphasized to Sam before continuing, "are coincidently the two areas in my life I need to change to make my life enjoyable. And with this..." he paused to find the right word, "love connection I have with Christine, it's plain to see! It's the Lord's will for me to leave Annie, marry Christine, and buy the Green Toad Saloon. It's so obvious. Can you guys not see that?"

"No," Paul said simply. "And I'll tell you why: because

from what I know, God hates divorce. I also have a very hard time understanding that the Lord above, who hates divorce, would encourage you to get divorced and buy a saloon where other men are going to be getting drunk and gambling. Both of which are, in my understanding, sins. Now, I'm not a Christian, and I don't claim to be, but you do. And you think God, in all his goodness, would want you to divorce your wife and leave your kids to go party at a saloon every night, marry a woman you don't know, and live your life having fun and encouraging others to sin? I don't think so."

"You're being stupid, in other words," Sam spat poisonously. "Honestly, all these years, you have never even one time mentioned leaving Annie or being unhappy in your marriage. Not one time have you ever, to my knowledge, been unfaithful to her. You have always been head over heels for her, so I am blown away by this stupidity you're talking about. Leaving Annie? Are you out of your damn mind? What is *wrong* with you?"

Kyle blew out a breath in frustration. "You don't understand—"

Sam interrupted sarcastically, "Oh, that's right: coincidences. So if I prayed, 'Lord, I need a new beautiful wife to be happy,' and I looked outside and saw Lee's wife Regina walk by, I should assume it's God's will that she become my wife, right? Because she is beautiful, and I asked for a beautiful wife, so it must be God's will that I marry Regina. Is that what you're saying?"

"No!" Kyle replied. "She's married."

Paul shrugged. "So are you."

Sam leaned toward Kyle and said, "Well, that's exactly what you're doing! Those coincidences don't mean a damn thing! And they're not even that. It's just life. God's not going to want you to do something that doesn't coincide with what the Bible says. I don't go to church, and *I* know that! I don't know what's wrong with you, Kyle, but you better go back to church or something to get your head on straight."

Kyle was suddenly irate. "I'm not going back to church! The last thing I need is Reverend Ash telling me how to live my life. I'll do what I want to do, and serve the Lord as I see fit. If I want to come see you guys, then I'll come see you guys. I don't need the Reverend dictating my life, or Annie, for that matter! No, I don't need to back to church. What I *do* need is a new life where I am first for once. I deserve to be happy too, and I'm going to be. Wait and see."

9

Charlie Ziegler drove the wagon back to the hayfield for another load with Annie sitting beside him on the bench seat. It had been a long and tiring day so far, since they had driven the wagon back and forth, loading it and unloading it themselves. The second wagon was being loaded, driven, and unloaded by Darius Jackson, his daughter Rory, and Annie's eight-year-old son Ira. Bringing in the hay was normally a well-organized and fluid rotation of continuous work with many hands to make the daunting task more manageable and timely, but on this day, they were short-handed and out of sync. Annie was feeling the aggravation of wasting so much of the day and getting so little work done. The hundred-plus-degree temperature wasn't making the work any more comfortable, and like the others, she was covered in sweat and hay dust. She wore denim jeans with suspenders to hold them up over a sweat-stained long-sleeve shirt covered with bits of hay. Her hair was in a pony-tail under a straw hat to keep the sun off her face, and she wore leather gloves on her hands.

She shook her head in frustration as her crusty mood

came to the surface. "I don't know why you gave those boys the day off. We could've gotten far more done today if they were here. If everyone was here helping today and we pressed hard, we could be finished with all of it by sundown. As it is, we're barely making a dent in what's left! And next week we're helping Adam with *his* fields. We have too much to do around here, and not enough manpower to do it, Uncle Charlie. That's not including cutting firewood, canning the garden, and taking the time to pick berries and apples before they're gone. There's just too much to do to be done, and time's running out on us!"

Charlie frowned and exhaled. "I wasn't really expecting your husband to leave the way he did yesterday, but it wouldn't be fair to call on those boys to work after I gave them the day off. They've worked hard without any complaints for a while now. We'll be okay. We just have to keep going one wagon load at a time."

"Oh, I know we'll be okay. That's not the point. The point is we won't get everything done that we had wanted to get done by summer's end. Furthermore, when my husband gets home, he and I are taking a ride to the northeast corner of the property so my children cannot hear what I have to say to him!"

"That loud, huh?" Charlie asked with a small smirk.

"I am done with this nonsense! We have work to do, and *we* can't run off and leave it whenever we want to, so why should he be able to? That's not how it works in a business, and surely not here on the ranch. If he was a hired hand, I'd fire him, just so you know!" She didn't want to mention being hurt by his forgetting her birthday, but it gnawed at her like a rat. She continued in the same irritated tone, "He's supposed to be an example to our hands, and more so to our children. Ira's out here working his butt off at eight years old to help his mama, and his father's in Branson drinking and gambling. It makes me sicker than...well, than I've ever been before."

Charlie looked at niece and said simply, "He'll be an example to them either way. Unfortunately, I don't think his heart's in ranching."

Annie sighed heavily. "I don't think so either. He wants to reap the rewards of somebody else doing the work while he sits in the shade. Or goes to town to gamble it away."

Charlie shook his head. "Having built this ranch from the ground up, I can tell you there's a lot more sowing than reaping, and the day the owner doesn't want to work is the day the ranch begins to fail. As you know, it takes a love for ranching to make it successful. Annie, you're going to be the sole owner of this ranch soon, and you'll run it as you see fit, I have no doubt. I'll still do my chores and piddle around here and there, but whether it flourishes or fails will be in your hands. Are you ready for that, or do we need to wait?"

Annie took a deep breath. "I am ready. I just need to straighten out some things with Kyle and see where he stands."

Charlie spoke honestly, "I have never wanted to talk bad about your father to you kids, but you know he had a ranch a lot bigger than this one, and he lost it all. The reason he lost it was because he didn't want to do the work. He had a great mind for business and the man knew cattle, but he didn't love the work part of it. He preferred to drink and gamble. I see that same work ethic in Kyle, and I'd be lying if I said I wasn't concerned about that."

Annie nodded quietly, with a deeply disheartened expression. "Concerned about him ruining the Big Z?" she asked softly.

"No. I'm more concerned about him ruining *you*. The

ranch has already served me well, and while I'm alive, it will continue to. But after I'm gone, it's all up to you to keep it going. He doesn't want it, and my concern is that he'll undermine you and your transactions to lose this place so he can go back to the city."

"I thought you liked Kyle, Uncle Charlie."

"I do. I just have more experience recognizing when someone's lost the desire to do a day's work."

Annie chuckled bitterly. "That doesn't take much experience. Well, we're going to have a serious conversation, because honestly, I don't need a man. I won't lose this ranch for anyone, so if he wants to go, he can. But if he wants to stay, he will have to make some changes, because I'm not putting up with the nonsense anymore."

"Good. Now you need to start thinking about renegotiating some beef contracts before spring," Charlie said with a wry smile.

"Funny you should mention that," she said, glancing at Charlie with a slight smile.

"Oh? What's so funny about it?"

"Well, we lost our biggest contracts, as you know." Annie hesitated and twisted on the bench seat to face him as she spoke. "So, how would you feel about a change in the direction of the Big Z?"

"What do you mean by 'direction?'"

Annie took a deep breath before answering. "Well, Uncle Charlie, as you already know, I've always dreamed of having a horse company. The beeves are our bread and butter, but the horse trade can become our steak and potatoes. You know how I love horses! Uncle Charlie," she said nervously, "I'm going to be spending all of my time building a horse company, and I don't want to split my responsibilities between my family, the horse company, and the cattle and everything that comes up, like the beef contracts you mentioned and rounding up strays. So, Adam and I were talking, and we plan on combining properties and herds. If it's okay with you, Adam will be taking over the cattle business of the ranch while I focus on the horse company. Of course, you and Aunt Mary will receive a percentage of both sides of the Big Z Ranch's two businesses. What do you think about that?" She waited anxiously for his response. He had already approved of her starting a horse company, but the agreement with her older brother Adam to take the lead on the cattle side had not yet been discussed with him.

Charlie stared straight ahead without any expression and then turned to look at Annie with a smirk on his lips. "I think the idea sounds better coming from you than it did from your aunt."

Annie sighed loudly in relief. "I *knew* she told you about that!"

Charlie smiled gently as a bead of sweat ran down his face. "She thinks it's a great idea, and so do I. I've already talked to Adam about it, but I wanted to hear it from you. I don't know why it took you so long to mention it. I have no doubt you'll both do well. Now's the time we need to start looking for some good horses and experienced riders to get you started."

"That we should!" Annie said with an excited smile.

"I'm curious though...how does Kyle like that idea?"

Annie shook her head. "He doesn't. It's more hands-on work than the cattle, and he's not gifted or fond of that." She took a deep breath. "We're going to have to hire some experienced cowboys, aren't we?" she asked, already knowing the answer.

Charlie nodded. "Yep. But there's a lot of them out there to find. First, we're going to need a bunkhouse to house your bronc busters and Adam's cowboys, though. You two better start planning where you want it and a cookhouse built. Just don't build it near my place. I don't want my peaceful evenings ruined by a bunch of single men. I had enough of that raising your brothers," he joked. "I suppose all that's left to say is when the hay's done, let's get this thing started."

Annie smiled at her uncle. "I love you, Uncle Charlie. I just want you to know that."

He smiled and looked at her fondly. "I know. I love you too."

10

"I don't particularly feel like going to a dirty saloon or a play where Travis and his wife might be, nor do I want to sit at your gentlemen friends' house acting like I'm enjoying myself while their married friend slobbers all over me. I'm sorry, but I have no desire to do anything except my job tonight," Christine Knapp said as she sat the small vanity in her room. She was speaking to her two friends, Helen and Edith.

Edith spoke sincerely, "Christine, Bella says you need to get away from this place and have fun for a night. No one's expecting you to sleep with Kyle. He's just here for tonight, is all. Helen and I have been trying to get a weekend off since we opened here, and Bella never let us before. The only reason we're getting tonight off, and it's the *only* reason, is because you're her favorite, and she wants you to go have fun with us. We have the night off to entertain you, and if you don't go, we'll have to work too. I don't know about you, but I want to start a family someday, and tonight is an opportunity for me to be with Paul. Helen feels the same way about Sam. Please, Christine, don't ruin it for us."

Helen added, "Sam and the guys are really excited about going to the play with us tonight. And Kyle is a nice man and happily married, so he won't try anything with you. And like Bella said, he's related to the marshal. And..." she paused, smiling hesitantly, "of all the girls here, Bella thinks he'd have the most interest in you."

Christine sighed. "She wants us all to find good husbands, including you two. Trust me, she's giving you both the night off with or without me. I don't feel like going anywhere except to work."

Helen looked at her seriously. "Christine, she called us into her office this morning and ordered us to get you out of here for the night. True, we are excited to be off and able to spend time with the guys, but it wasn't our idea, it was Bella's. It's her orders that we make Kyle introduce you to the marshal. You can refuse to go, but Bella's gonna make you. You might as well get ready to go and enjoy yourself, or I'll go down and tell Bella right now that you're not going."

Christine sighed, showing her lack of enthusiasm with a roll of her eyes. "She's not going to fire me because I don't want to take a night off. You two go enjoy yourselves. Honestly, I have no desire to go."

Edith said, "Bella has already bought the tickets for the play. She bought six, and if we don't use them, she'll be very upset. This whole evening was her idea. Besides, you're not like us. We need tonight to spend time with Paul and Sam..."

"What do you mean, I'm not like you and Helen?"

"In short, we were whores," Edith answered. "You're a proper Christian lady who, if you were still married, probably wouldn't associate with us if you saw us on the street, just like all those proper ladies in town."

"That's not true!"

"Yes, it is. Christine, you've been with us for three years now, and you're still innocent and pure. There's not one high-society lady in this town or any other out there who has more integrity, values, class, or honor than you. *That* is what makes you different than us. We've been around the block in a few towns and are lucky to have found two decent men who like us for who we are without having to take our clothes off. But you? You can have any man you want. Bella knows that, and that's why we're supposed to take you out and use Kyle to introduce you to the marshal. That way you can forget all about Travis."

Christine looked at Edith fondly. "You can have any man you want, too. What's in the past is in the past, and a good man will love you for who you are now. Those socialite women who put their noses up in the air when they see you don't matter. Don't waste a single minute worrying about them. Anyone who gets to know you two will love you like I do. You are my best friends, and I'm thankful to know you. I wouldn't want to know any of those socialites who stroll around here like they're the queen of England. Trust me, they're an empty show."

"Were you a socialite before you came to be with us?" Helen asked.

Christine smiled. "No. You already know I grew up poor, and my husband Richard and I were just simple small farmers. Well, we hoped to have a bigger farm when we got to Oregon…" Her voice trailed off sadly.

"Did you marry him to have a family or because you loved him?" Helen asked.

Christine smiled gently and had a faraway expression on her face. "I loved him. He was the love of my life. Richard courted me for a long time before he asked for my hand in marriage. I loved him very much, Helen. And to offer unsolicited advice, never marry any man you're not absolutely head over heels in love with."

"I was in love once," Edith said, crossing her arms. "I was fifteen, and living on the Nebraska prairie with my folks. We went to a town social one night where a tall, lean, handsome stranger asked me to dance. Oh, I had danced with some of the boys my age, but this man was in his thirties. I was hooked on him right then and there, and I knew it. His name was Johnny, Johnny 'Denmark' Gottwells, and he was a gambler. I didn't know that at the time since he told me he was an entrepreneur. I didn't even know what that was. Anyway, we danced all night, and my parents were fit to be tied. A young Christian girl like me wasn't supposed to be dancing with a man twice my age, let alone more than once...or as close.

"Anyway, a few weeks later I snuck out and we ran off to get married, I thought, but he wasn't interested in marriage after all. He was interested in taking my innocence and pleasing himself when he wanted to. He took me from Nebraska down to Cheyenne to gamble. He hit a losing streak and needed money to gamble, so he sweet-talked me into laying down with a couple of men to help us get back on our feet and into a home for the winter. He said he was going to work in a saloon as a bartender so we could marry properly, but we needed that starter money to get by with until he got paid. So...I reluctantly did it," she said with a shame-filled shrug. "It started with one man, and then another. Of course, Johnny would take the money and bring in new men. Before I knew it, I was a whore. That's how I got started in the business."

"He didn't love you," Christine stated.

Edith shook her head. "In his own way, he did. He never hit me, I can't say that about the next man I was with. I left

Johnny when I had enough money saved up to go back home. When I finally went home, my Pa said I was ruined and would ruin my younger sisters, so he sent me away. I had nowhere to go, so I ended up in Lincoln doing the only thing I knew how to do. That's where I met Amos Albright, one of the meanest men I've ever known. He seemed nice, though, and offered me a chance to escape the life of a whore. Amos didn't want to marry me, he just wanted a woman.

"He had a farm twelve miles outside of Lincoln, and like I said, a meaner man I've never come across. I couldn't escape him until I climbed up into the rafters of the wood-shed and hid on two boards above the door. If he had looked up, he would have seen me, but he didn't. I waited there for hours while him and his brothers went looking for me. I was able to avoid them long enough to work my way to Kansas, then eventually to Colorado, which is where I met Bella. She thought I was too pretty to be a whore."

She paused to speak sincerely to Christine. "The reason I'm sharing that is that if I don't find a husband, I'll have to go back to whoring when I get too old to dance. So, you can see why it's important for Helen and me to have tonight off to spend with Paul and Sam. Unlike you, our options beyond this place are quite limited. If I don't get married, I don't have a future."

"Edith, honestly," Christine replied softly, "you're too wonderful of a person to not have a good man fall in love with you. I don't mean a compromise of living arrange-ments, but someone who really loves you. It may be Paul, or it may be someone else down the road, but whatever you do, don't compromise your future with the first man who asks for your hand if you're not absolutely in love with him. You're too beautiful inside and out for that. Trust me, the right man will come along and love you just the way you are."

"I don't know about that," Edith stated doubtfully.

"Trust me, he will."

Helen spoke from beside the door, "There's lots of men that don't mind us being ex-whores. They're just glad to have a woman to cook, clean, and bed with. Sam and Paul overlook all that past-life stuff." She added pointedly to Christine, "However, Edith doesn't think anyone will actually love her because she sold herself to so many men. It goes back to being raised in a religious family, I think."

"Helen—" Edith said quickly but was interrupted immediately.

"No, it does, Edith. Your parents rejected you after you ran off with Johnny, and that rejection still hurts. You think since your parents don't love you anymore, no one will. Certainly not a good man." She turned to Christine and continued, "So what she does is find these wretched men like that Amos guy she told you about, or Orlando, a real creep back in Denver. Men who beat on her and treat her like rubbish. She knows what a good man is because her father was one. But since he rejected her, she doesn't think a good man will ever love her because her father doesn't. Deep down she doesn't think she deserves a good man, just another abusive man who will treat her like trash. That's the way she sees herself."

"That's not true. What about Paul, huh?" Edith asked defensively.

"You wouldn't even know him if it wasn't for me. You would've hooked up with that creep Joe Thorn or that other guy, Jesse Helms. A criminal is what he is! Yeah, they would've treated you really well."

"He was nice."

"I know men like him. Yeah, he would've been sweet as honey until he showed you his real colors. There's nothing except blackness inside Jesse Helms, I'm telling you that right now. Now, Paul will treat you right if you to let him love you."

Edith scoffed defensively. "What do you mean, 'if I let him love me?'" she questioned. "How would I know if he loves me or not? He's not as affectionate as Sam. I can't force him to love me any more than I can force the wind to stop blowing or the sun to cool down. I could clean his house and make him dinner, listen to him and tell him how great he is. I could even sleep with him every night, but I've done all of that before, and no one's ever loved me. I want Paul to be as dopey over me as Sam is over you, but he isn't. I want someone to love me like Christine's husband loved her, but no one has. Not even Paul."

Christine smiled sadly.

Helen smiled. "Sam *is* dopey over me, isn't he? I sure love that man."

Edith shook her head with mock disgust. "It's sickening."

"Well," Helen added seriously, "what I meant by *if* you let him love you is, you have been hurt by every man in your life. Even your own father. You have these invisible walls up around you, and no matter how hard Paul tries to get to know you, you pull back and shut him out. You won't let him get close to you, Edith. He could hire a maid to cook and clean, and a whore too, but what he wants is to know you."

"We're getting to know each other," Edith answered quickly.

"You are, but every time he wants to talk to you, you change the conversation back to him or come find me. You never do anything with him by yourself, it's always a couples' thing with Sam and me. If you want him to love you, you have to trust him enough to open up and let your walls down so he can get to know you."

Edith shifted her eyes from the floor to Helen's. "I like Paul a lot, but I don't want to get hurt again. Every guy I have ever known was nice to me at first, so how do I know Paul won't treat me like everyone else has? You're right, my own father can't love me, so why would Paul?" she asked sadly.

"Edith, you are my best friend, and I promise that if you give him a chance, he will love you. But he can't love someone he doesn't know, and he won't wait forever to get to know you. You have to open yourself up and take a chance."

"Edith," Christine offered, "I was married to a great man who loved me like no other ever could, probably. I never thought I'd be interested in another man, but then I met Travis. Granted, he may be a lying creep, but for a moment, I felt the excitement of falling in love again. I know it was all a lie, it was real on my part. You see, it isn't so much about whether he was honest with me, but that I was honest with him. I was willing to risk my heart and expose who I am to him. Now, he may not have cared about that, but I do. If I ever want to find love again, I should open myself up to being loved. Helen's right. There's no other way to have a relationship than to take a chance and open yourself up. It can be scary to share your thoughts, emotions, and fears, but love is a friendship that grows closer as those things are shared. A love without sharing isn't much of a love at all. You have to let him into your private world."

Helen spoke excitedly. "Come on, Edith! He already knows you were a whore, and he still likes you. How much worse could getting to know you be?"

Edith laughed uncertainly. "So how do I open up?"

Christine answered pointedly, "You quit worrying about getting hurt and share your hopes and dreams with him, and then you strive to make him the best he can be by being his best friend. That is a good place to start."

Edith looked at Christine. "Come with us, Christine. Please? If I want a marriage like you had, maybe you can see it happening better than I can. Maybe you can see if Paul is for real."

Christine smiled despite her broken heart. "Have you forgotten that I was just deceived by a smooth-talking liar? I don't know if I'm the person you should seek advice from. What do I know, since I was falling for a liar myself?"

"Yeah, but you were what my mom used to call being love-blind. We can't always see things too clearly when we're close to it, and maybe that's what's wrong with me, except instead of being love-blind, I'm seeing it too clearly. Maybe even looking for reasons why it's not for real."

Helen jumped in. "I'd believe that! Paul's the best man you've ever met, and you're slowly chasing him away because you're scared to let yourself fall in love with him."

Edith shrugged. "Maybe. Christine, I know you have good sense. You may not have seen Travis was a fake, but none of us did. Some men are just camouflaged like a copperhead in the fallen leaves, and you can't tell the truth from the lies until it's too late. But your integrity held fast, and he got nothing from you. That speaks highly for you, and I really want you to pay attention and tell me if I should continue and take a chance with Paul or close that door and look elsewhere for a better man. I trust you and your judgment. Please come with us tonight. I need your input."

"Come on, Christine! We will have fun!" Helen urged.

Christine smiled. "Fine, I'll go, but do not leave me alone with Mister Lenning, or Travis if we happen to see him. I don't want to be alone with anyone."

"What about the marshal?" Helen asked with a smile as

she wiggled her eyebrows up and down. She was perfectly aware that Matt Bannister was not in town, but she wouldn't mention that to anyone right away. She had her own plans, and she needed Christine to go out with her and Edith to guarantee she'd get the night off to spend with Sam.

"Him either," Christine said of the marshal, then added, "But if I meet him, I don't want you embarrassing me like you did last time we saw him. Just be quiet, is all I ask."

Helen laughed. "Come on, Edith, let's go get ready to go."

11

Kyle Lenning walked into Sam's and Paul's little house dressed in a new pair of tan pants and a new long-sleeved red shirt. He had stopped by the barbershop and had his blonde hair trimmed and his face shaven clean. He looked quite impressive, except for the aggravation on his face as he tossed down a bundle of his old clothes wrapped in a gunny sack.

"Wow, you look like it's your wedding day," Sam acknowledged. "Did you talk to Herb?" Herb Gannon was the owner of the Green Toad.

"Yeah!" Kyle exclaimed with frustration as he sat down on the davenport heavily. "He's selling it for four thousand dollars. I haven't got that kind of money. I think he's asking too much, but I also think he's hoping to sell it to my brother-in-law Lee. I went to Lee's office and asked him for a loan to buy it. He owns enough property that I thought he'd help his family out. But do you know what he said?"

Paul shrugged. "I'm guessing...no?"

Sam chuckled at Paul's response. Kyle glared at Sam for laughing at him. He answered, "No, he said he'd have to talk to Annie about it! I'm her damn husband, so why would he have to talk to Annie about it? It's not her business, it's mine! Or it would be. So now I'm out of options unless I can sweet-talk Annie into borrowing the money from her brother. I can't believe he won't help me. I told him my plans, and now he'll probably go down there and hand over four thousand dollars in cash and buy it out from under me! Have I ever told you guys, I hate being married? It doesn't matter how long I've been in that family, I'll never be considered a part of it because I'm just Annie's husband—basically the hired help, and Lee's got to go talk to my Massa before he can help me. It makes me sick!" He paused to look at Sam irritably. "What are you laughing at?"

Sam shook his head with a wide grin. "You."

"What's so funny about me?"

Sam shrugged sarcastically. "Nothing."

Kyle shook his head. "Albert won't loan me the money without Annie's approval either. He won't want to cause any marital strife. I already know that about Albert. And my parents? You know they wouldn't help me buy a saloon on Rose Street. They already want everything on Rose Street to burn down. Besides, they don't have that kind of money."

Paul asked bluntly, "Since you think you want to leave your wife anyway, why don't you just move back in with your parents and work at the hardware store? They always wanted you to take it over, didn't they?"

"Because I'd rather count drinks than nails!"

Sam laughed at disgust evident in his tone.

"What?" Kyle yelled at Sam. "What are you laughing about?"

"You!"

"What about me?"

Sam spoke through a smirk as he shook his head. "I'm

just dumbfounded. I mean, you found out yesterday that the Green Toad's for sale and now you're desperately trying to throw your life away to buy it."

"Throw my life away? I don't *have* a life! For crying out loud, Sam, I don't have a life except for feeding hogs, cutting hay, hauling hay, and putting it away so I can feed the cows later! I hate my life, so I really don't think I'm throwing anything away!" he hollered.

Sam raised his eyebrows and said pointedly, "Your family."

Kyle hesitated before answering. "I wasn't meant to get married, and my marriage is over. I love Annie, but I'm not in love with Annie anymore. She's a plow strapped to my back slowing me down, and I want out. As far as my children go, it'll be hard to leave them, but it's best for me."

"What's best for them, though?" Sam asked curtly. "All I've heard since you've been here is about you. *You're* not happy, *you're* not having fun, *you're* not wealthy enough, *you* don't like the ranch, but *you* do like Christine, and *you're* going to marry her, right? Even though *you're* not meant for marriage now, supposedly. Come on, Kyle! Are you kidding me? You don't want to work at the lumber mill like we do, or the Big Z Ranch, or your parents' hardware store. Did you really expect your brother-in-law to hand you thousands of dollars when the truth is that you just don't like to work? I hate to be the one to tell you, but running a saloon takes work to keep it going."

"I work my butt off!" Kyle exclaimed angrily.

Sam raised his eyebrows questionably. "No, you probably do just enough to get by, and I'm guessing it isn't enough, or Annie wouldn't be hounding you. I know you, Kyle. You're a great guy, but you get bored, and when you do, you throw everything away to make a change. To be honest, I'm impressed that you've stuck with Annie this long."

"Shut up, Sam! I work as hard as anyone else on that ranch! Who do you think does it all, Charlie? Darius? They're getting so old they can barely make a dent in the work we do."

"And you work as hard as they do?"

"Yeah, I do!"

Sam laughed.

"What's so funny, Sam? Seriously, what are you laughing at?" Kyle demanded.

"Nothing."

"Something is apparently funny! I'll tell you this much: I know how hard I labor for nothing, and I'm sick of it!"

"That's exactly my point!" Sam said quickly. "Of all the people who would complain about inheriting the Big Z Ranch, it would be you. Do you know how many men would love to *be* you? You have a beautiful wife, a beautiful family in a nice house, and an established ranch just waiting to be yours. That's a dream come true for almost every man alive, and you'll throw it away for what...a saloon you can't afford and a girl you met once?"

Kyle glared at Sam and spoke heatedly. "Well, I'm not them, now, am I? I don't want to be a rancher for the rest of my life. Can't you understand that? And Annie's no prize either. For crying out loud, my wife's the only woman in the county, probably in the state, who breaks her own horses and plans on starting a business doing just that! She's more of a man than a lady! I want a wife who's a lady through and through. Maybe I'm asking for too much from her, but I'd like a wife who cared more about cleaning our house than the pigs' pen! Or cleaning my daughter up instead of a calf with scours! It would just be nice to have a wife like..." He paused and shook his head in frustration.

"Like Christine?" Sam asked.

Kyle looked at Sam seriously. "Yeah, like Christine. She's a lady, and she'd at least teach my daughters to be ladies instead of sitting in a mud puddle making mud cakes! Do you know that for two months this past spring, we had a baby pig living in our house? Chickens, bull snakes, a calf, and her damn goat have all lived in our house at one time or another. I want a nice place that's decorated neatly and has clean floors, instead of muddy boot prints everywhere. I want to come home to a beautiful lady, not work beside my mannish wife."

Sam and Paul both chuckled at their friend. Paul said through his smile, "Sam's right, you don't know anything about Christine. Absolutely nothing."

"Well, I'll get to know her tonight, won't I?" he spat rudely.

Sam spoke sarcastically. "Yeah, why don't you tell her you're leaving your family for her tonight and see what happens?"

"Oh, right, Sam, why don't I just tell her I love her too? Why are you being such an ass today? What happened to my old friends who loved to drink and carouse the weekend away? The independent guys who only cared about having fun? You guys are acting like whipped pups that have been married for ten years already. I thought you guys would be excited for me to finally break loose and rejoin you as single, free men like we used to be!"

Sam stared at his friend awkwardly. "First of all, I'm not being an ass, but you're being ridiculous. Are you even listening to yourself? In one day, you have decided to divorce your wife, leave your children, buy a saloon, and marry a woman you met one time. And you expect us to be excited for you? Hell, no! You're out of your damn mind!"

Kyle stood up from the davenport and pointed his finger at Sam. "This is not an overnight decision, you ass! I have agonized over this for a long time now. Annie wants more than I can give, and I want something she is not! We don't bring out the best in each other, and isn't that what love is supposed to do? All we bring out nowadays is hostility. I have nothing left to offer, and I am done with the ranch. I don't want to brand another calf or mend another fence. I'm done, and that's all there is to say about it." He sat back down on the davenport, seemingly exhausted. "I'm a merchant. That's what I know."

Sam laughed. "You were never a merchant. You hated the hardware store as much as you do the ranch, apparently. If I remember right, you were as excited about becoming a rancher as you are about the Green Toad."

"I was wrong, okay?" he asked Sam with a harsh glare.

Paul asked sincerely, "You've been head over heels in love with Annie for all these years, so what happened?"

Kyle exhaled heavily. "The ranch. We spend so much time working on it, and even when we're not, Annie's still consumed by it. She looks for work to do, and keeps piling on a wheelbarrow-load of future plans every day. It never ends. I guess, to answer your question, we quit talking, and somewhere along the way, that became okay," he said softly.

"So talk to her," Sam suggested simply.

Kyle frowned sadly. "It's not that easy to do now. I think we've crossed the line where we've lost everything that made us friends. We're just married now. That's all, guys, just married, with nothing left except the piece of paper in a drawer somewhere that used to hang on the wall that says we were married."

Paul replied, "So hang it on the wall again and court your wife like we do our ladies. Begin again, but don't throw your family away."

Sam added, "You better think about what you're doing, because once you leave your family, someone else will swoop in and steal Annie's heart and take your place. You're going to be a sad dog sitting on a barstool crying the 'poor me' song every night for the rest of your life. We see it all the time; just go talk to some of those sad old dogs drinking themselves to death in the saloons. It's awful, Kyle, and you're better than that. Make it work out somehow with Annie, even if you have to shovel crap day and night for the rest of your life. We've grown up, man. I don't know about Paul, but I'm thinking about asking Helen to marry me. Those old days are gone. We're not eighteen anymore, and I'm sure not going to act like it once I get married. It's time to move on. Go home tomorrow and make it work with your wife. You committed yourself to her, so go home and be the father and husband you promised to be."

12

Annie Lenning washed the sweat and dust from her face in a bucket of water set out by the well in front of Charlie's and Mary's house. Dinner was already prepared and set out on the table in the yard under a large tree.

Charlie handed her a towel to dry her face and said, "I think we got quite a bit done, considering our work crew today."

Annie dried her face and looked at Charlie with a frustrated expression. "There's still plenty of daylight left. We averaged one load in the time it usually takes for us to get three, so I wouldn't say we got much done. We can still haul in another load or two, and it would be that much less to do tomorrow."

Charlie took the towel from Annie to dry his own hands and face. "No, Annie, I think we'll call it a day. We've worked hard all week. I think we deserve to rest up and enjoy life a bit before Monday, don't you? I mean, it's your birthday after all," he said with a loving smirk on his face.

"Monday?" she asked sounding irritated. "We could finish up that field tomorrow if we pressed hard enough. My birthday doesn't mean much, apparently. Not much to my husband, anyway."

Charlie frowned. "That's to his own shame. We are celebrating because it matters to us. We worked today, but tomorrow's Sunday, and we're going to church and then taking the day off. Your Aunt Mary says we're having a picnic down on Pearl Creek. How's that sound, Darius?" he asked Darius Jackson as the other man washed his hands and face.

"Like a plan. I'm afraid I'm about half-exhausted, and could use a day of rest and some good food. Are you going to invite some of the church folks, or will it just be us for Annie's birthday picnic?"

"We'll invite Steven and his family, of course, but anyone else you'd better talk to Mary about since she's doing the cooking."

Darius chuckled. "If I want a piece of apple pie, I'd best not invite anyone at all. Huh, Annie? And birthday cake too!"

Annie frowned despite Darius's comment, and replied seriously, "Uncle Charlie, I'd like to get that field done before Kyle gets home tomorrow. That way I can tell him what an ass I think he is for not helping us get it finished. I don't want him thinking we couldn't get it done without him. He doesn't deserve that satisfaction."

Darius grew serious and answered for Charlie. "Annie, it's not my place to say, but do you really think he cares one way or the other about that field? By the way, he told me I wasn't worth my wages yesterday, and threatened to dock them when he takes over the ranch. Not that your uncle has kept me in the poor house after all these years." He laughed.

Charlie's eyes hardened with irritation as he glanced at Darius. "He's walking on thin ice there! I'll be taking him to the North Forty myself to discuss his talking to you like that!" He narrowed his eyes at Annie. "I'll discuss his comment about Darius with him personally when he gets home tomorrow. In the meantime, Darius is right. Do you think us working our asses off to finish that field would affect him either way? Don't you think it would bother him more to know that we celebrated your birthday without him?"

Darius's statement had angered Annie as well. Her eyes clouded with moisture because of the anger and embarrassment that welled up inside her from what Kyle'd had the nerve to say to Darius. "He'll be hungover tomorrow, so it won't make any difference if we were having fun or hauling hay. He'd just be glad no one is in the house so he can sleep all afternoon! I apologize for what he said, Darius. I am...so finished with him!"

Charlie put his arm around her comfortingly. "Well, while we were all out there getting dusty, your aunt made you a good birthday dinner, so let's go enjoy the evening with her."

They all sat down at the table under an old elm tree, enjoying the cool of the shade on a very warm evening. By the time, Annie had finished eating, she could honestly admit she no longer desired to go back to the fields. Like everyone else, she was physically exhausted. She would help her Aunt Mary clear the table and wash the dishes, and then and only then would she be able to soak in a warm bath and feel clean when she climbed into her bed for a rare but needed good night of sleep. Her exhaustion was evident now that she had eaten, and her Aunt Mary took notice of it.

"Annie, you look plum beaten down to nothing," Mary told her caringly.

"I am. I was telling Uncle Charlie that I wanted to finish

that the field tonight, but I am done." She yawned. "I just want to take a bath and go to bed."

"Well," Charlie said to no one in particular, "I feel better. Let's go haul in some more hay. Maybe we can get that field done tonight after all, Annie."

Annie looked at Charlie with a scowl. "You better be kidding."

Charlie laughed. "Rest up tonight, and tomorrow we'll go have some fun. Ira?" he said to Annie's oldest boy, "We already put the teams away, but would you feed them for me and make sure they have plenty of water? They worked hard today."

Ira sighed. "I'm too tired to move."

Annie turned her head and glared at her son ferociously, "Don't you dare sass your uncle! Now, get down there and do what you're told!" she ordered.

Ira looked at his mother, surprised by her angry tone. "I didn't say I wasn't going!"

"Then get!" Annie snapped.

Ira sent an embarrassed glance at his aunt and uncle, then got up and walked toward the barn.

"He's a good boy, Annie," Mary said softly. "He worked out there in the sun today too."

Annie sighed dramatically. "I know. I'm just not in the mood to listen to his whining. I get enough of that from his father. I know I'm not supposed to bad-talk my husband, but I am so tired of listening to him complain about how bad he has it," she yawned. "I'm about ready to make him cook and clean so I can get more work done around here."

Darius and the others chuckled, and he said, "Annie, I swear, you sound more like your uncle every day! We just finished for the day, and you're already talking about doing more work."

She nodded seriously. "Have you seen the grass in my yard?"

"It's as dry as any of it around here," Darius answered.

"Yeah. It's also getting tall, and it needs some fertilizer for the rainy season. That's the only time my grass is green. When my grass is green, it matches the yellow paint of my house really well, but it needs fertilizer! I need to fence my yard off and put those spring calves in there for a week or two. I've decided Kyle can do that while he does the house-work. Someone has to do it, and it isn't going to be me."

"Oh, Annie," Mary chided with a smile. She continued enthusiastically, "Speaking of yards, I wish Charlie would get me one of those push-mower thingies like Lee has for his grass. I took off my moccasins and walked barefoot through his yard because his grass is always so short, green, and soft. I've never seen a finer yard. I asked him how he got his yard so beautiful, and he said the secret was lots of water and that grass-cutter thing he pushes around. I made him show it to me, and it's just these blades that roll with the wheels and cut the grass, leaving it about one inch high!"

Annie frowned. "Lee doesn't push it, Aunt Mary. He has his butler, gardener, baby sitter, or whatever else he is—the carriage driver, James, and his wife—do it all."

"Well, it's Lee's yard, regardless of who does the work. All I know is, I want my yard as soft and green as his, not fenced off like a corral with heifers peeking in my windows and making my porch smell like a barn."

"Oh, it isn't that bad," Charlie commented.

"Charles," Mary said with a tone of authority, "the next time I walk out to the privy or to hang clothes to dry and step in a pile of manure, it will be the last time you use those animals to keep the grass down. I have been putting up with that all these years, but now I want a lawn like Lee's. All it takes is water and that grass-cutter thing."

"I'm sure it takes more than water and a new cutter. That James and his wife spend a whole lot of time working on that lawn to make it as nice as it is. Time is the one thing I *don't* have a lot of to spend on making the grass pretty."

"But if we had a yard like Lee's instead of this dry, clumpy, hard grass, I wouldn't have to wear shoes at all, not even moccasins."

Annie offered, "I think your yard's mostly weeds anyway, Aunt Mary. Lee must have a special kind of grass because it's not like ours at all."

"Well, I like his, and I could certainly have one of those boys work in the yard for me to make it more like his. I really liked walking barefoot through his grass. It felt so nice and cool on my feet," Mary said to Charlie.

"When the hay's done, I can spare a boy or two to make you a nicer yard, hon. Until then..." He yawned. "Let us finish with the hay."

"Tired?" she asked.

He nodded.

Annie commented, "Rory must be exhausted. She hasn't said a word."

"Rory, you do look tired, young lady," Mary said, glancing at Rory Jackson. She had worked in the fields loading hay with her father.

Rory smiled slightly. "I am. I must've gotten too much sun or something."

Darius stood from the table. "I best get her home and let her sleep. The poor girl worked hard today. Thank you for the great meal, Mary. I will help clear the table before I leave, though."

"No," Mary said, "You all worked hard, so go home and get some rest. Annie's here if I need help."

"Are you sure? I don't mind helping."

"Darius, take Rory home. The poor girl looks like she needs to get out of the heat and rest for a while."

"Yeah, go home. We'll see you at church tomorrow," Charlie chimed in.

As Darius and Rory walked toward the barn to hitch up their wagon, Mary looked at Annie and said, "Why don't you go heat up a bath and rest for the night?"

"No, I will help clean up."

"Hogwash. I can clean up just fine. You go on home. I'll need your help tomorrow, but not today."

Annie hesitated before answering, "I will, but before I go, can I ask you both something while none of the kids are around?"

"Of course," Mary said. Charlie gave her his attention as well.

Annie looked at them anxiously and then asked, "What do you think about divorce?"

Mary's expression grew serious. "Are you considering that?"

Annie nodded slowly as moisture filled her eyes. She forced the tears away. "Is it ever okay to do so, Aunt Mary?"

"Well, yeah, there *are* reasons to divorce, but why are you considering it?"

"You already know why. I know the Bible condemns it, except for adultery, and I don't know if Kyle has committed adultery. He always swears not, and I've believed him up until now. But we don't get along so well anymore. I guess, if our love was a fire, it's burned down to nothing, and there's no more wood. Not even a dry cow chip. I don't know what he wants anymore, but I know he *doesn't* want...to be here or with me. I guess my question is, what's the right thing to do? Do you think I am justified in divorcing him?"

"Annie, honey," Mary said taking Annie's hand in hers. "I don't know if divorce is ever really justified, just because of the damage it does to the family. I would suggest maybe you two should go away from here for a week or two and find some fresh kindling before you make a decision like that. Go to the ocean for a week or two and see if that flame doesn't spark back to life. I've heard the sunsets over the Pacific Ocean are some of the most beautiful sights south of Heaven."

Annie smiled slightly. "I guess we haven't done anything together except work in a very long time. Even our weekend together in Branson last June was for buying horses. Maybe we could take some time away from the kids and this place and get to know each other again without thinking about the ranch. Maybe if we weren't so busy and tired all the time, we might be able to talk like we used to. I don't know. Maybe we can find ourselves again and save our marriage. I would like to."

"Are you are still in love with him?" Mary asked.

"I am," Annie answered slowly. "Perhaps we just need to take your advice and get away by ourselves for a while. Talk about things like we used to do. We haven't taken a trip anywhere since we got married. We can afford to take a real trip to somewhere across the state and try to get our fire back, especially if we don't have any distractions like his friends, or on my part, a horse auction. You know, I thought that would be a romantic weekend for us to get away and spend time together, but I never considered it was a business trip. But it was, and my mind was on horses."

"I am glad to hear you realized that. A romantic weekend with no thinking about the ranch might just make all the difference in the world. You don't want to give up on your marriage, because not only does divorce tear apart families, and especially the children, the other thing about getting a divorce is, it would tarnish your reputation as a lady," Mary said gently.

Annie chuckled. "Aunt Mary, in case you didn't know, my reputation isn't all that lady-ish anyway."

Charlie spoke for the first time. "I hope that works out for the better, Annie. Sometimes you have to leave work at work and focus on each other. I'm still going to lay into him about speaking to Darius the way he did, though. I won't have Darius threatened or insulted by a man who couldn't wear Darius's boots if he had to. I'm a bit upset about that. I mentioned earlier today that I was afraid Kyle would try to undercut your business dealings to lose this ranch like your father did. It's my gut feeling that he wants to live in the city and run his parents' store, or something else easier than we do here. If you two can get yourselves set right and he comes back willing to do the work, great. There will be no problem. But if he doesn't change his attitude about working here, then he'll never change. He will be siphoning off your earnings until you have none left and fold. You need to think about that too while you're trying to relight that flame. Sometimes it turns out the kindling's too damp."

Mary spoke to Charlie with a touch of frustration to her voice, "She was just talking about going away to find that missing link in their marriage with a sense of hope, and you go and run it down with a statement like that? What about hoping they can fix their marriage, Charlie?"

"I do hope so, but the fact is, starting a horse company is tough work, and I want her to do well. A leaky bucket doesn't hold water for long, and neither does a drunk gambler."

Annie sighed, discouraged. "I can't put a bit in his mouth and control the reins, Uncle Charlie. I suppose it's up to him. I'm not afraid of being alone, but I hope he'll want to invest in our marriage before we let it end. I know I talk about the ranch too much and get preoccupied with what I want to do and need to get done. I suppose I push it too hard sometimes."

"I wonder where you get that from?" Mary asked sarcastically, giving Charlie a disapproving glare.

Charlie just laughed at her.

13

<hr/>

"I don't understand how a city can have a top-notch hotel with a private men's lounge, expensive rooms, and fine dining, but it doesn't have an opera house," Bella said, perplexed by the notion that Branson didn't have that kind of establishment. The J.R. Worley Shakespearean Troupe was in town to put on three showings of *Romeo and Juliet* over the weekend, and the only suitable place they could perform their play was in the city's dance hall, which in Bella's opinion was embarrassing for the city of Branson. A city by any definition should have an opera house or another facility to hold such a special event.

Helen Monroe answered, "It's not like they're from Europe and one of the great Shakespearean performing companies. It's my understanding that the J.R. Worley Troupe is a family that travels together. They're from Tennessee if I understood right."

"Like the Booth family, huh? I understand they did Othello and other plays very well before John Booth murdered the President. That seemed to ruin their family's career," Bella stated sarcastically.

"I'm sure it did," Helen agreed. "But I doubt this group of actors has any plans of assassinating...I don't even know who the mayor of this town is."

Christine Knapp answered, "Mister William R. Slater is the mayor. He owns the mining company, and Travis is best friends with his son Josh. I've met Josh Slater, and he's quite pompous. I didn't like him from the beginning."

"Is he rich?" Helen asked with a mischievous smile.

Christine nodded. "Very. He's also married."

Helen shrugged. "Well, I've never heard of them."

Edith offered as she laced up her boots, "You've never heard of them because people like that don't associate with places like this. We're on Rose Street, and people like them wouldn't dare stain their reputations by being seen on this side of town."

Bella stated, "You might see those pukes at the play tonight."

Christine looked at Bella anxiously. "I hope not. I don't ever want to see Travis again."

Bella continued, "Even if that puke is there, he won't be looking at you with his wife on his arm. If they *are* there, you should confront him. She deserves to know what a wretched snake he is. She might be one of those snooty women who walk around here looking at us like we're street trash, but I know all those uppity men they're married to are all members of the Monarch Lounge. That respectable and established club of honor has its own dirty little secrets, namely a stable of whores hidden behind closed doors." She paused to gaze at her three employees. "If any of those snooty wives look down upon you girls, just tell them you work in the Monarch Lounge and you know their husbands well."

"Bella!" Edith exclaimed with a wide smile. "That's terrible. A good idea, but still terrible."

"Don't let them get away with it. That's all I'm saying."

Christine added quietly, "Travis is a member of that club. He goes there all the time. We were supposed to have a late dinner there last night, supposedly. It was Kyle who said women weren't allowed in there, and then it came out that Travis had rented a room."

"He was expecting far more than a dinner, Christine," Bella said pointedly, her eyes burning into the girl.

Christine shook her head slowly. "He would've been very disappointed. I wonder if he goes to those women there? If what you're saying is true?"

"Oh, I guarantee it! If he's sniffing around here lying about his wife, rest assured he's one of the Monarch Lounge's best customers! It wouldn't surprise me if he didn't have one of those women tied around his finger like he almost had you. You should thank Helen's and Edith's two men tonight, and Mister Lenning. They saved you a world of heartache."

Helen added suddenly, "That's how I know Sam's going to be faithful. He's an honest man."

Edith asked her, "By the way, Helen, did you happen to ask them where they're taking us to dinner? I am famished."

"I told Sam that they're taking us somewhere to eat, but I didn't say where. All I do know is that Kyle friend of theirs was excited to hear that Christine was coming. I think he's smitten with you," she said to Christine.

Christine frowned, uninterested. "That would be to his own shame, if so."

Bella spoke seriously. "You girls, don't encourage that man. Christine's already been swindled by one married man. If word spreads about her being seen with two married men, it will harm her reputation more than being employed here does. The only reason I want her going out tonight is to meet the marshal, so find a way to get Mister Lenning to introduce you to his brother-in-law. Now, you ladies better make sure you're ready, because those boys will be here shortly. And you two," she said sternly to Edith and Helen. "Do not leave Christine alone with that man, understood?"

"We won't," Helen said, "because she's going to babysit *us*." She laughed.

"No laying down for those boys, girls! The last thing we need is for either of you getting pregnant and not be married. Make those boys marry you before taking that risk, understood, ladies?" Bella asked firmly.

"Of course," Helen answered. "I'll try to keep Edith off Paul," she teased her friend.

"It's not me you have to worry about," Edith said plainly.

Bella said, "I won't worry about either of you because I know you'll do what I say. When your dancing career comes to an end, there's only one place left for you if you're not married, and both of you are too wonderful to be whores again. Make those men want to marry you."

14

Kyle Lenning had dressed in his new clothes, paid for a shave and a haircut, and had his hair oiled and combed over to the side to make him look as respectable and handsome as could be. He had made a decent first impression on Christine the night before, he thought, but tonight he wanted to sweep her off her feet if he could. He was nervous when his two friends knocked on the door of Bella's Dance Hall and were escorted by Bella herself into a nice sitting room off to the side where none of them had been before.

Bella was a flamboyantly dressed woman of some thickness, with a rough face and a deep, raspy, loud voice. She was quite pleased to see the three men, though. Her attention went primarily to Sam and Paul, but eventually, she looked at Kyle with an expression that differed from the one she gave his friends.

"Mister Lenning, I understand you own a ranch?" she asked with interest.

"No, I don't. My wife and her family own the Big Z Ranch over in Willow Falls."

"Oh," she said, sounding disappointed. "How long have

you been married? I understand you married into the Bannister family, is that right?"

He nodded. "I did. But I'm thinking about getting a divorce and moving over here. I'm working on a business deal to get myself set up to make a solid living, just as soon as I can secure a loan."

Bella frowned. "I'm sorry to hear you're thinking about getting a divorce. May I ask why?"

Kyle hesitated before answering.

Sam chided through a tight smirk, "Go ahead and tell her, Kyle."

"I'll just say that we have separate interests and goals," he said unconvincingly with an uncomfortable shrug.

"Do you have children?" she asked pointedly.

"Three. One boy and two girls," he said softly.

"Where are they going to live, with you or their mother?" she asked, narrowing her eyes.

Kyle laughed uncertainly. "With their mother, but I'll see them often. I love my children, but I can't stand living there anymore."

"How old are they?"

Kyle raised his eyebrows in thought. "Ira's eight, Catherine's six, and our youngest, Erica, is four."

Bella took a deep breath and rolled her eyes disappointedly. "You mentioned needing a loan for some type of investment. May I inquire what you want to get into?"

"Absolutely. I am thinking about buying the Green Toad Saloon up the road a few blocks. It is up for sale, and it's always been my dream to own it, so now I'm trying to secure a loan of around six thousand dollars to purchase it. Do some remodeling and upgrades, and stock it with better liquor. If you're interested in becoming a silent partner, we could discuss numbers, perhaps?"

Bella waved him off. "I'm afraid not, Mister Lenning. I have no interest in buying into a dying saloon. Now, if you'll excuse me, I'll go get the ladies," she said and left the parlor.

Kyle was offended. "It's not a dying saloon," he muttered to his friends.

Soon Bella led Edith, Helen, and Christine into the parlor and smiled as the men looked at the three beautiful women. They were all wearing elegant dresses of the most modest designs, and their hair was up in decorative buns. They sported floral hats and had ornamented fans in their hands.

"You look gorgeous," Sam said sincerely as he looked fondly at Helen.

She smiled. "Thank you,"

Paul also acknowledged how beautiful Edith looked, but Kyle stood awkwardly and stared at Christine wordlessly. In truth, she looked far more stunning than the others. She was even more beautiful than she had been the night before. Kyle couldn't say any of the words that came to mind other than, "Hi."

Bella shook her head disappointedly. "Well, go on. You men take those ladies to someplace nice to eat, and you make sure that... I mean, make sure to introduce Christine to the marshal," she said as they walked toward the door.

Kyle asked, "How? He's not—"

"We will!" Helen said loudly, cutting Kyle off and physically turning him toward the door to leave. "Come on, Kyle, you're slowing us down. We're hungry, so move it!" she said, pushing him out the door with a laugh.

They walked to Main Street and stopped at the Regory Italian Café for a meal. Since none of them had ever had Italian food before, they had no idea what the strange names on the menu were. After seeing a plate being delivered to an older couple across from them, they all agreed to have the same meal as the couple. They ordered six plates of Chicken Tetrazzini, and a loaf of warm bread came with it. The food was good and the men ate hungrily, while the ladies ate more sparingly. Their conversation flowed, although it was primarily Sam and Paul talking with their two ladies. Kyle had tried to speak to Christine, but her responses were short and to the point, leaving little room to continue a conversation.

After they had finished their meal, they walked to a local confectionary and bought a few pieces of hard candy for the walk to the Branson Community Hall. It was an old two-story clapboard building used for community meetings and dances that had once been named the Branson Dance Hall. The name had recently been changed. The bottom floor was normally used for the food and drinks and meetings, while upstairs there was a large dancefloor and a small stage for a band. There was nothing special about the hall. It was just a space used for multiple purposes by the community.

Although many folks loitered downstairs, talking by the food and drink tables, Kyle and the others immediately went upstairs to get good seats for the play. They had hoped to sit near the front to see clearly, but they were quite disappointed. The seating was arranged into two long sections of folding wooden chairs lined up in rows separated by a center aisle. Near the front, about a third of the way back, a red velvet rope separated the seats. A man stood in the aisle with his hand on the rope, using it as a gate. It had become apparent that the tickets had been segregated by First Class and General Audience. First Class had assigned seats, while for general audience tickets like theirs, it was a free-for-all to find empty seats. The six could only find enough empty seats in the second to the last row, so they went ahead and sat down and waited for the play to begin. Of course, Paul sat beside Edith, and Sam sat beside Helen. Christine sat between Helen and Kyle, but she was noticeably closer to Helen.

Before too long, the folks who had been loitering carelessly downstairs came up and walked down the center aisle, continuing their conversations with the ladies on their arms. None of them seemed to take notice of anyone in the general audience section, except for a few ladies who looked at the people sitting down with an arrogance that only wealth could provide. With a wave of surprise, Kyle watched two of his brothers-in-law walk past him, Lee and his beautiful wife Regina, and Albert and his sweet wife Mellissa. Both men were dressed in suits and held their wives' arms lovingly. Not far behind them, strolled Travis McKnight with a blonde lady on his arm. She was one of the ones casting looks of disgust at the general audience people. None of them noticed Kyle sitting near the back row with Christine, and they all took their seats.

Before too long, J.R. Worley stepped up onto a portable stage about two feet high. He introduced himself and welcomed everyone to the J.R. Worley Shakespearean Troupe's presentation of *Romeo and Juliet*. Applause followed, and a flowing curtain across above the front of the stage opened. Behind the stage was a large canvas backdrop of a city square painted on it. A series of rolled up canvas backdrops that would be used to create the setting for the many scenes could be seen to one side. The actors all wore period Elizabethan costumes. The men wore daggers on their belts, and they spoke in loud, dramatic voices as they delivered their lines. Juliet and the other women wore beautiful gowns, and spoke with great sincerity and emotion as they gazed out into the crowd, seemingly not noticing the audience. Kyle watched with interest as the actors of brought the ancient play of *Romeo and Juliet* to life. The play, well-acted as it was, brought the dusty book on Kyle's bookshelf to life. He watched the actors and listened to every word with great interest. There was more emotion than he had been expecting. The actress playing Juliet was in her twenties, and was quite attractive and dressed in a beautiful Elizabethan gown. She had long dark straight hair very much like Christine's, so he found watching the actress to be as intoxicating as watching Christine. As the scenes changed, the large black curtain was closed to hide the stage, and J.R. Worley would step on stage to introduce a juggler to entertain the audience while the players changed the stage settings and clothing if necessary. J.R. Worley would then entertain the audience with a fascinating card trick or a quick story with a humorous ending, which was met with hearty laughs from the audience.

Kyle wasn't amused by the funny stories, though. It was hot in the dance hall, with two hundred people crowded together in rows of seats to watch the play. The windows were open, but there was no evening breeze to cool the mid-90s temperature of the July evening. Needless to say, the top floor of the dance hall was far too stuffy to be comfortable. While many of the men who wore suits dabbed their faces with a clean handkerchief, Kyle and his friends wiped the sweat off their faces with their shirtsleeves. Kyle sweated for another reason besides the heat, though. He was sitting beside Christine Knapp and didn't know what to say. He was nervous, and it caused him to perspire profusely.

He wanted to have a worthy conversation, but so far, all his attempts to converse with Christine had ended with short courtesies. She was friendly enough and as polite as a lady should be, but she was very reserved, and careful to not make eye contact for very long. Christine was the most beautiful woman he had ever seen—even more beautiful than Annie or his sister-in-law Regina. Regina Bannister had the reputation of being the most beautiful lady in the county, and Kyle had agreed with that until he saw Christine. There was simply no one more beautiful than her, and that bit of truth had been confirmed multiple times by all the men who had looked at her as they walked from Rose Street toward the play. Now that he sat beside her, he felt the desperate need to impress her while he could.

How he wished he take her hand. He could see her soft hands on her lap, but she offered no invitation. He empathized with Romeo as he said in the fifth scene in front of a backdrop of the Capulets' hall, "Did my heart love till now? Foreswear it, sight! For I ne'er saw true beauty till this night."

He stared at Christine longingly as she watched the play with interest. Kyle's heart beat faster as Romeo spoke the very words he wanted to come out of his own mouth. Had he ever known love until this moment? Truly, could beauty be correctly defined without Christine as the example? Could love at first sight ever be more clearly recognized?

The feelings within him were as true as any he'd ever had for Annie. His friends thought him foolish, but he needed to rid himself of his mistaken marriage to Annie. It was becoming apparent to him that it was the Lord's will to clear the path to begin a new life with the woman God had always intended for him from the beginning—Christine. He had always heard that there was no such thing as a coincidence in a Christian life. Everything was by the Lord's hand, moved and directed by the Lord himself in the lives of his children.

Was it a coincidence that his marriage was for all practical purposes over at the same moment he realized that the Green Toad Saloon was for sale? It had been his lifelong dream to own the Green Toad. Was it a coincidence that he had met Christine the night her suitor was found to be a liar? And was it a coincidence that, despite all odds, he'd be sitting beside her at a play about strangers from different worlds falling in love at first sight? A story about Romeo realizing he loved the beautiful Juliet and leaving behind his oath of chastity and love for Rosaline?

It was not just a coincidence, but appeared to be a sign from God. The desires that burned within him were precisely what he was supposed to feel. Kyle had never believed in love at first sight, but he had experienced it when he had seen Christine the night before. Now, as he looked at her, the love he felt could only be explained by her being the woman God had created for him before time began. He didn't need any more confirmation than that, because every word Romeo said concerning his passionate love for Juliet echoed his own longing to share his life with Christine. That alone was more than a coincidence.

She turned her head to look at him. She smiled slightly, and then turned back to watch the play.

Kyle glowed as the warmth of her smile swept through him. Satisfied, he turned back to watch the rest of the play. Perhaps her turning to face him and the warmth of her smile was a sign that she was feeling about him the way Juliet felt about Romeo.

15

The Branson Community Hall had never been more silent than it was when Romeo found Juliet's body in the tomb. His emotions were genuine and sincere as he wept and spoke his lines with a brokenness that only the death of the girl he loved could bring. His heart was so broken that life itself seemed devoid of joy, purpose, or hope.

He opened the small blue bottle of poison and drank the poison, and a few moments later, Friar Laurence came into the tomb and saw the body of young Romeo lying on the ground.

Juliet awoke slowly and looked at the priest, and after a short time, he hurried away. She knelt beside the body of Romeo and reached for the small blue bottle in Romeo's hand as the watchman's voice echoed from outside the sepulcher. Juliet looked toward the door and then back down at Romeo's body.

She grabbed the dagger from Romeo's belt and drove it into her heart, then fell across Romeo's body and breathed her last. Of course, all of these actions had been accompanied by the immortal words of the Bard.

Kyle Lenning, like everyone else, was transfixed by the actors, but his attention went to Christine when he heard her sniffle. She had cupped her hands over her face to sob quietly. He was going to ask if she was okay, but Helen nudged Christine's shoulder and stated quietly, "Come on, Christine, it's not that sad." She snickered.

Christine sniffled again and replied through her tears, "It is for me."

Helen laughed quietly. "It's just a play."

"Not to me," Christine responded.

Kyle leaned toward her and whispered, "Are you all right?"

She nodded and wiped her eyes, intentionally staring straight ahead to finish watching the play undisturbed. She wished Helen and Kyle would just leave her alone to weep, be with her thoughts, and work through her own emotions without interruptions.

The actors playing the elder Capulets and the Montagues entered the tomb at the news of their children's suicides, learning from Friar Lawrence that Romeo and Juliet had been married and had to die to love each other because of their family feud.

They made amends with each other, and an actor playing the part of the Prince spoke the play's last words pointedly. "A glooming peace this morning with it brings. The sun, for sorrow, will not show his head. Go hence, to have more talk of these sad things. Some shall be pardoned, and some punished, for never was a story of more woe than this of Juliet and her beloved Romeo."

The curtain closed for the final time and a momentary silence filled the community hall as the powerful emotions of the play settled into the minds and hearts of all who were there. Many of the spectators had read the story, but seeing it portrayed by the actors was a whole new experience that brought the tragic love story to life. After a moment of silence, a few beginning claps of appreciation turned into a loud standing ovation, including some whistling and cheers. J.R. Worley stepped in front of the closed curtain and bowed. The curtain opened, and all the performers were standing in line and bowed or curtsied with large smiles on their faces while the applause continued.

J.R. Worley spoke loudly to quiet the applause and get the audience to sit back down. "Thank you. Thank you. That completes our show for tonight, thank you. We invite all of you to come downstairs for some refreshments and hors d'oeuvres, courtesy of the Branson Gazette, Slater Mining Company, and the Monarch Hotel, where we have been staying. Now, as a custom of our troupe, we would ask everyone to remain seated while the ushers excuse the rows from the front to back in order. Again, come downstairs and introduce yourselves, and meet our many fine actors and performers. Ushers, if you will begin once we have left the room?" He waited for his troupe to leave the stage and walk up the center aisle through the applauding crowd to go downstairs.

Kyle glanced at Christine and watched a series of quiet tears roll slowly down her cheeks. She wiped her eyes to hide them with her handkerchief when she noticed Kyle looking at her. Once again, Helen nudged her and said with a slight laugh, "Seriously, it's not that sad."

"I know," Christine replied without any conviction.

Kyle wanted to say something to her, but he didn't know what to say that would invite a conversation or lift her spirits. To make her smile would be ideal, but if she confided in him why her tears fell so heavily, it would be the beginning of a true relationship. However, he didn't know what to say, and saying the wrong thing could lose him the opportunity to get to know her. Kyle thought of a sensitive word or two to invite her to confide in him, but before he could say them, he froze and stared toward the front rows. In a line of first-class ticketholders escorting their ladies up the aisle, he saw Lee and Regina Bannister. He hoped not to make eye contact, but Lee looked at him and paused. He stepped forward slowly and waved at Kyle to get his attention, "Hi, Kyle. I'll see you downstairs," he said as resumed walking. Regina smiled at him awkwardly when she noticed who he was sitting with. Just behind Lee and Regina were Albert and Mellissa Bannister. They also waved at him and looked awkward about him sitting beside a beautiful lady who wasn't Annie.

A moment later, Christine turned her head downward and tensed as Travis McKnight walked by with a blonde-haired woman holding onto his arm. Kyle couldn't resist a condescending smirk toward him as he passed. Travis stared at Christine, surprised to see her in the audience.

Finally, as the ushers neared the back row, Christine wiped her eyes for a final time and stood up to go down-stairs to the reception area. As they moved toward the stair-case, Christine unexpectedly took hold of Kyle's arm and asked, "Don't leave my side, okay? I don't want to see Travis, let alone talk to him. Don't leave me alone down there, please."

"Sure," he said with a hint of reservation to his voice. He didn't know how he would explain her holding onto his arm the way she was to his brothers-in-law and their wives. "Maybe we could skip it and get out of here?"

"That sounds good to me," Christine said. "Helen and Edith, we don't want to stay here, so would you mind if we called it a night and left?"

Edith answered, "I wanted to meet the actors, but you two can meet us outside if you want."

"No," Christine said simply, "I think I will just go back home."

"Oh, no, you're not!" Helen exclaimed. "You're not going back home until we all do. You're just afraid of seeing Travis, so the answer is very simple: don't look at him. He'll be with his wife anyway, and he's not going to introduce you to her, so relax."

Edith added, "If you don't want to go downstairs, you can wait outside for us. I just want to meet the actors and maybe get a drink. We won't be that long, I promise. And then we can go to the Green Toad, or over to Paul's and Sam's house."

Christine frowned. "We're not supposed to go to their place. You know the rules."

Helen waved a hand at Christine with a scoff. "Well, Bella knows we do, and she hasn't said anything, so I suppose it's fine."

"I don't think it's a good idea to go to their place, and I don't have any desire to go to a saloon. If there's nothing else to do, I'd just like to go back to my room."

"What else do you want to do, Christine?" Helen asked sharply. "You can't go back without us, and we're supposed to get you drunk so you'll loosen up and laugh a little! Now, if you don't mind, I'm going to take my Romeo downstairs and have a few drinks." She began walking quickly down the stairs with Sam, but they paused when Paul stopped them.

"Listen, I don't think we should go back to our place either. It's way too hot to be inside anyway, so why don't we buy a few quarts of beer and a bottle of wine for the ladies and go out to Premro Island? Make a fire and enjoy the waterfall?"

Sam nodded. "That's a great idea! How's that sound to you?" he asked Helen.

"Great, but let's go downstairs right now," she said, pulling him down the stairs.

Paul looked at Christine. "How does that sound to you, Christine?"

"I don't know where that is," she said. She had no interest in going.

Paul smiled. "It's not far. Kyle, Sam, and I all grew up swimming there. If you like waterfalls, you'll enjoy it."

"You will enjoy it," Kyle repeated. "It's very pretty and peaceful, especially on a night like tonight."

Paul laughed. "It wouldn't be the first time, would it?"

Christine held onto Kyle's arm as they followed their friends down the stairs to the first floor of the dance hall. They were suddenly surrounded by a combination of two groups sticking mostly to their own class, the wealthy men dressed in fine clothing and their ladies in flowing gowns, and the common men and their wives, who were dressed humbly in their Sunday best but had splurged to buy a ticket to a rare Shakespeare performance. Spread out through the large room, the actors and entertainers still in costume, were engaged in conversations with many of the spectators. Two tables offered hors d'oeuvres, with a punch-bowl on the center of the table. For the men who preferred stronger drink, a bar was set up at the far end of the floor. It only took a second for Sam and Helen to spot it and walk quickly toward it, followed closely by Paul and Edith. Christine paused a few feet from the staircase and said, "Edith, Helen, we're going to wait outside." She had no interest in mingling within the crowd and running into Travis and his wife.

"No, you're not. I'm buying you a drink!" Helen said loudly, getting the attention of many in the room.

It only took a moment for Lee and Regina Bannister to approach Kyle. They had been waiting close to the bottom of the stairs. Lee was dressed in a gray suit with a white shirt underneath a buttoned gray vest, with a gray bow tie. His short brown hair was combed neatly, and his thick mustache was trimmed precisely. Lee appeared to be the successful businessman he was, and beside him was Regina. She wore a flowing peach-colored gown with an array of flowery white lace and flowered embroidery. Her hair was up in a carefully designed bun. Regina was stunning, as usual.

"Hi, uh, Kyle," Lee said slowly, obviously curious about the attractive woman holding Kyle's arm. "So, where's Annie? You know, your wife?" Lee raised his eyebrows, waiting for an answer.

"Uh, she's at home," Kyle answered uneasily. Christine let go of his arm. "I'm just here for the weekend like I told you earlier today. This is Christine Knapp, by the way. She's friends with my friends, who are getting something to drink," he said with a nod toward the bar. "Christine, this is my brother- and sister-in-law, Lee and Regina Bannister."

Christine looked at Lee and Regina with a touch of surprise and smiled awkwardly. "Hello," she said pleasantly, "I don't know your brother-in-law. I was only holding his arm for him to escort me out of here so a certain individual wouldn't talk to me," she explained, recognizing the awkwardness of the situation.

Regina raised her eyes brows curiously, but it was Lee who spoke with an implication that hid none of his displeasure, "You came here with her on Annie's birthday? What the hell's wrong with you, Kyle?"

"Oh, no! It *is* her birthday, isn't it?" Kyle asked as a wave of alarm and shame swept over him like an unstoppable tsunami. He closed his eyes, his disappointment with himself evident in his expression. Of all the days of the year, none was more sacred to Annie than her birthday. He had been frustrated by the hours of hauling hay, the heat, and his discontent that he had been in a hurry to leave and then angry about their fight, and he had forgotten about her birthday. "Crap! Well, she'll forgive me for a lot of things, but maybe not for forgetting her birthday." He shook his head, disheartened by his failure to remember this most important of days. He put his attention back on Lee and Regina. "Anyway, I came here with a group of friends. You know Sam and Paul? They're over there getting a drink. So, how'd you like the play?" he asked to change the subject, his countenance suddenly solemn.

Regina ignored Kyle and looked curiously at Christine. "So, Miss Knapp, I have not seen you around here before. Are you new to the area or related to any families I might know?"

Christine shook her head. "No. I have no family here."

Lee asked quickly, like a lion pouncing on a field mouse, "How do you survive? I notice your gown is quite beautiful and costly, isn't it? How does a woman without a family afford such extravagant garb?" He did not hide his indignation at seeing her with his sister's husband.

Kyle answered for her. "She's an entertainer. She's well-known, and the most popular girl at Bella's Dance Hall."

Christine closed her eyes and sighed inwardly. She was filled with shame as she witnessed the revulsion cross their faces.

"Oh," was all Regina said, unimpressed.

Lee looked at Kyle sharply. "I'll bet she is the most popular! Does Annie know you're going to places like that on her birthday, Kyle? I assure you, she will."

"Places like what, the dance hall?" Kyle answered, suddenly irritated. "There's nothing going on there except dancing. There is no crime in that, is there? You ought to check the place out yourself, Lee, before you condemn it!"

Regina responded to Kyle with her eyes burning into him, "Um, no! And shame on you for even suggesting such a thing! I am disappointed in you, Kyle. It's Annie's birthday, for Pete's sake! You should be home with your family, not here with her!"

Kyle shook his head and held up his hands. "It's not what you think." Regina's words cut him deeper then she would ever know.

Lee spoke again. "Well, that's amazing, because it looks a little suspicious to me. First, you wanted to borrow money to buy the Green Toad Saloon this morning, and tonight you're here with your friend hanging on your arm instead of being home with Annie. I haven't gotten where I am in life because I'm stupid, Kyle," he said condescendingly, his eyes turning hard.

"That's debatable," Albert Bannister said jokingly as he and his wife Mellissa stepped to Lee's side. Albert handed Lee a glass of wine. "What am I missing?" he asked, looking at Kyle. Albert was dressed in a brown suit with a matching vest over a white shirt, but he had no bow tie around his thick neck. Albert was a big man, with bushy dark hair that fell over his ears. He had a thick beard about two inches long, and a well-trimmed mustache. His countenance was joyful and light-hearted, as was his wife's.

Mellissa Bannister handed Regina a glass of wine as

well. She was a heavyset woman with dark brown hair pulled back into a bun, an intricate ivory comb holding it in place. She was in her early forties, and her age showed around her joy-filled eyes. Mellissa was dressed in a light-green gown over a medium bustle, with white lace and white sequins that sparkled in the light. Her dress might have sparkled, but not as brightly as her friendly personality. She looked at Kyle and his pretty friend with a smile and then became aware of the tension between them and Lee. "Hello. I'm Mellissa Bannister, Kyle's sister-in-law, and this is my husband Albert," she said, holding out a hand toward Christine.

Christine looked at Mellissa with an unspoken appreciation for treating her like a real person rather than a whore, which was the way Lee was making her feel. Christine smiled slightly, intentionally ignoring Lee. "Nice to meet you. My name is Christine Knapp," she said with a slight smile and quick handshake.

Mellissa's genuine acceptance and kindness were evident as she asked, "Did you enjoy the play as much as we did?"

Christine smiled softly as she nodded. "Very much."

Lee spoke suddenly, "I'm sorry to interrupt, but this is one of Kyle's girlfriends, Albert. In fact, she's the most popular entertainer in that new dance hall over on Rose Street, Kyle says. He was good enough to bring his plaything out of the back room to the play tonight so she could play dress up and pretend to be a respectable lady while Annie is celebrating her birthday alone at home. Isn't that about right... I'm sorry, what's your professional name again, Rosie Two-Lips?" he asked Christine sarcastically.

Christine could feel her face reddening, a combination of humiliation and anger disrupting her normally calm.

Tears indicating her fluctuating emotions blurred her vision, and she shook her head slightly as she looked at Lee with disgust. She was shocked and shaken by his hostile words that she could not think of anything to say. She had never in her life been spoken to in such a belittling way. Her response was purely reactive and came out bitterly, "Go to hell! My name doesn't really matter, does it?" Tears of humiliation and anger spilled down her cheeks as she turned back to Mellissa and said shortly, "It was nice to meet *you*." She walked quickly toward the front door to leave the building.

Lee answered with an unconcerned shrug as she walked away, "No, it certainly doesn't matter unless the doctor needs to know what disease Kyle needs a cure for!" he called as she walked out the door.

"Who is she, and why are you with her?" Regina asked Kyle abruptly.

"Christine! Wait up!" Kyle looked at Lee angrily. "What is wrong with you? You had no right to treat her like that!"

"Yeah, I did," Lee said simply. "You're married to my sister, and that's all the reason I need. I get the feeling that you're more than interested in that whore. You can count on me to talk to my sister about it, too!"

Kyle shook his head as he stepped backward toward the door. "Tell your sister whatever the hell you want, but Christine's nothing like what you think." He turned around and walked away.

Lee spoke irritably. "Go on after your whore, but you had better beware, Kyle: none of us will take it kindly if you hurt our sister, especially me!"

Kyle stopped and turned around to face Lee. "Are you threatening me in front of all these people, Lee?" he asked in disbelief.

Lee shook his head slowly. "No, I'm warning you. Go home!"

Kyle left the building to go find Christine.

Albert asked with concern, "What is this all about?"

Mellissa Bannister stated pointedly, "I don't know what this is about, but I thought you were very rude to her. I don't know anything about her, but I do know she's not a prostitute. I can tell that much."

Regina said simply, "I have no idea who or what she is, but she has no business being with Kyle."

"That's my point," Lee told Mellissa respectfully. "I don't need to know who she is. All I need to know is that she was with Annie's husband! He's been acting a little strange lately, so no, I don't need to be nice."

Travis McKnight put a hand on Lee's shoulder as he stepped up behind them. He asked quietly, "Who was that guy with that pretty girl you were talking to? Not family, I hope."

Lee looked at Travis curiously, "My brother-in-law, why?" he asked shortly.

Travis raised his eyebrows questionably. "Er...I hate to tell you this, but that girl is the bestselling whore at that new dance hall in town. I'd tell your sister to become a nun. He's probably going to have syphilis three times over and then some by the morning. That's her reputation, anyway."

Albert Bannister narrowed his eyes in growing anger. "Really?"

Travis shrugged innocently and spoke through a laugh. "Two-dollar whores don't buy dresses like hers without getting around, right?"

Albert looked at Lee. "Do you want to join me in having a private talk with Kyle in the back room of my shop before he leaves town?" Albert asked, his eyes displaying controlled anger. There was no question about his intent, and no man would stand in his way of him getting his brother-in-law straightened up and refocused on his own family before he went home to Albert's baby sister.

Lee nodded with the same look in his eyes. "Yeah, I'd love to. I'm also going to write Annie a letter tonight and have James run it out to her in the morning. I want her to know exactly what's going on, and what he wanted money for this weekend. I don't think he should be running around like an unmarried gent."

Mellissa Bannister asked, "What if he's telling the truth? Don't you think it's wise to maybe *not* assume the worst before you talk to him, and maybe *not* jump to conclusions beforehand, boys?"

Regina Bannister said with an affectionate smirk at her sister-in-law, "Mellissa, you always think the best of people, but we both know Annie and Kyle have been having trouble. I think Kyle is deciding he wants more than Annie can offer. It's his own stupidity, but I really think that's what we witnessed this evening."

Mellissa sighed. "I hope not, Regina. He has such a beautiful family to go home to. There's always hope when you see the brighter side of people, even if they are making bad decisions. And Lord, I hope Kyle isn't."

16

It was a hot evening, but the light western breeze felt good on her skin compared to the stifling heat inside of the building. Christine had no desire to wait for her friends, so she began walking down the boardwalk back toward Rose Street. She was angry, and had never been more humiliated by strangers than she had just been standing next to Kyle. She was an upstanding citizen, with morals just as high or higher than the pompous Bannister woman who had looked down upon Christine like she was louse-infested street trash. What bothered Christine even more was knowing that Lee Bannister, one of the most influential men in the entire county, thought she was nothing more than a diseased whore. Even more harrowing was that Kyle had allowed Lee and the others to believe she was a whore by admitting she was an entertainer—which wasn't untrue, but clarification needed to be made. She was a dancer, and sang ballads for her income. By no means could she be considered a whore. She had never sold her principles for money. In fact, if they wanted to cast stones, they might be surprised to learn that she had only been with one man in her life, and that man was her husband Richard.

Christine had read the story of Romeo and Juliet of course, and many of Shakespeare's other works as well. However, reading the written page and seeing it performed in period clothing with swords and backdrops had put the story in perspective and brought it to life right in front of her. She had not expected to become so emotional, but the sincerity Romeo had displayed when he thought Juliet was dead was reminiscent of her own emotions when Richard was killed.

Of course, her husband had died for no reason other than accidentally spilling another man's drink in a Denver saloon. He had been stabbed seventeen times and bled to death before Christine had the chance to say goodbye. She had fallen to her knees, too weak to stand, and wailed over his blood-soaked body with all emotion Romeo had displayed and more.

She could not hold back her tears as the memories of her sorrow at losing the last of her family were resurrected. She had lost her best friend, her security, and her only love when she lost her husband. They experienced the misery of loss when their daughter died from influenza only a few weeks before Richard died. It was Richard's strength, built upon his faith, that had helped her get through burying their only child in an unmarked grave and the horror of riding away from her.

There was no comprehending the depth of sorrow one experienced when they lost a child, except to feel alone in a world that no longer matters. Richard, in his own sorrow, could look at her with his gentle eyes and remind her that it wasn't the end. They would be with their daughter again when their own lives came to an end, a promise from the

Lord. The loss of their child could not be healed, but there was a hope for the future and a sense of peace, despite the sorrow knowing precisely where their baby was. She was not lost, she was in Heaven. Richard's faith had brought her strength, and she had known she could manage through life with him at her side. But then, while celebrating the milestone of reaching Denver, Richard was killed. In the matter of an hour, her world came to an end. No longer did a farm in the new land of Oregon sound appealing. No longer did their team of oxen matter to her. No longer did she want to live. Like Juliet, she at the time had felt like there was nothing left to live for. She remembered all too well how it had felt to be utterly hopeless.

That had been three years ago, and Christine consistently thanked the Lord for Bella and the opportunity to dance and sing to make a good living. For a moment, she thought Travis McKnight might be the man God would bless her with, but as it turned out, God had only protected her from him. She had seen Marshal Matt Bannister on the sidewalk once, and as she passed him, her eyes had held his like an invisible force bound them together for a moment. His slight smile and nod had sent butterflies through her stomach like a teenager's first infatuation. She had been hoping to meet him this evening, but he was out of town. If she'd had any hope of one day meeting the marshal, after tonight, it was hopeless. It wouldn't matter if they ever met now because his family was convinced that she was nothing more than a common whore.

With all that in mind, Christine walked quickly through the beautiful evening without taking time to enjoy the full moon shining down on her or the cool, refreshing breeze that caressed her skin. The night was perfect in every way, but it did little to ease the hopelessness that filled her. If there had been a bright side to her evening, it was that she didn't have to speak to Travis McKnight. Even so, seeing him with his wife had been another dagger plunged into her heart.

"Christine!" Kyle called as he stepped out of the dance hall and jogged quickly toward her. "I'm sorry about that. They're my wife's brothers. I don't know why Lee's being such an ass. Maybe he—"

Christine cut him off quickly, "Maybe it's because you're with another woman on your wife's birthday?"

Kyle grinned sadly. "Yeah, probably. But even so, it's not like I'm committing adultery or anything."

"No, we're not!" she said pointedly.

"If you think tonight was bad, wait until I go home and apologize to my wife. She may not forgive me for this," he said with a nervous chuckle.

Christine glared at him without any amusement in her expression. "I'm sure she will be angry. I certainly would! And your brother in law is an ass! I'm nothing but your whore, right? That is what they implied. Let me just tell you something, Mister Lenning, I have never been more humiliated in my life by people I have just met! You introduced me as an entertainer, which makes it sound like I'm a whore! I don't know you, so maybe I shouldn't have asked to hold your arm. It was wrong to ask you to stay by my side. I knew you were married, and I shouldn't have done that. I knew Travis wasn't going to talk to me with his wife there anyway. Maybe I wanted to make him jealous. I don't know. But why didn't you tell me your wife's family was downstairs? You knew they were, so why didn't you mention it to me? If you had told me that, I wouldn't have been holding your arm!" she said bitterly, glaring at Kyle.

Kyle shrugged and sighed. "I didn't think it was a big

deal," he answered awkwardly. He had been taken back by her hard tone and the hostility in her eyes.

Her eyes widened, and she raised her voice. "You didn't think they'd notice a strange woman holding onto your arm? You're married to their sister, Kyle! Of course, they'd notice! And yes, it does matter! I'm not even mad at them. They didn't know any different, but you do! Or at least you should. I am not a whore, and I don't want to be thought of as one by anyone, especially your family members!" Tears of frustration filled her eyes, and she wiped them away with her hand.

Kyle spoke placatingly. "I know you're not..." He paused as an older couple left the dance hall with smiles on their faces. They were pleased with the play, and obviously with each other's company as they walked past.

"Then why didn't you say something?" she asked, and then spoke more heatedly. "I didn't come out tonight to get to know you, Mister Lenning. I wanted to see the play, yes, but I also wanted to ask you to introduce me to Matt. And now, even if I did meet him, he'd just think I'm nothing more than, well, as your brother-in-law put it a minute ago, your whore!"

A twinge of bitter jealousy shuddered through Kyle, but he forced it away with the remorseful thought of forgetting about Annie's birthday. It weighed heavily upon his heart that he would hurt Annie as deeply as he knew it would. "Matt's not exactly marriage material," he replied simply.

Christine continued with the same scornful tone and fire in her eyes, "A gentleman, Mister Lenning, would've protected my honor! I dance and sing for a living because I must! My morals are just as high as your two sisters-in-law's, one of whom looked at me like I was a filthy bedbug! I will tell you this much: if their husbands died like mine did, I bet they'd have to make a living on their own too. They might even have to do worse than me to survive, because this world isn't kind to women on their own. It may not seem respectable to some, but the Lord has blessed me with a profession I enjoy, and a place to live as well. Your relatives can look down on me all they want, but as a Christian lady, I am grateful to be where I am!"

Kyle took a deep breath. "I apologize for Lee. Trust me, he's not usually that way. And I'll make sure they all know the truth about you, including Matt. So, was that why your crying during the play? Because your husband died?" Kyle asked.

She nodded. "Yes. Now, if you'll excuse me, I'm going home."

"I thought you couldn't go back without your friends?"

She responded uncaringly, "Let them know I went back. Have a good evening, Mister Lenning."

"I can't let you walk back alone. Let me go tell Paul and Sam, and then I'll walk you back."

Christine frowned, displeased when she looked past Kyle to the dance hall door as Edith and Helen stepped outside with their gentlemen. Edith spoke to Helen when she saw Christine. "See, I told you she was going home."

"Whew! For being so warm out, it's a lot cooler out here than in there!" Helen said, wiping her forehead with her arm. She walked toward Christine and said, "The way you were bawling in there, I thought you'd left us already."

"I am. I was leaving when Mister Lenning stopped me. I'm sorry, ladies, but I've had enough fun for one night."

Edith quickly stepped over to Christine and put an arm around her to lead her away from the others. "No, no, no," Edith said as they stepped away. Helen quickly appeared at Christine's other side as they walked away from the men.

"Excuse us, we need some girl time," Helen said looking back toward the men with a short laugh as they stepped away.

Paul questioned Kyle irritably, "What did you say to her to make her want to go home? We're supposed to go make a fire at the falls. Hopefully, you didn't screw that up for us. What did you do, ask her to marry you already? Tell her your plans for her?"

"No, nothing like that!" Kyle answered, agitation evident in his voice. "Lee and Albert ambushed us inside and made a big deal about her being with me. They thought she was a whore."

"Oh. That might do it." Paul nodded. "Did you tell them she's not? I know Edith has mentioned to me quite a few times that Christine is a devout Christian. They were told to get Christine drunk tonight, but Edith doubts they can. That's probably what they're talking about now."

Sam offered, "She may be pretty, but she's a bit of a stick-in-the-mud. She's not the same kind of Christian as you, that's for sure. You're fun to drink with, but she takes that religious stuff too seriously. As much as I enjoy drinking with you, if she goes back home, you're not coming with us either." He tapped Kyle on the stomach. "You understand that, I hope. But the first thing we must do is get something to drink, right?"

Kyle could feel his shame growing. Sam's words cut him deeper than the wound to his already conscience-stricken conviction that he was a fool. He shook his head, disgusted with himself. The word "Christian" defined a follower of Jesus, but it didn't define the commitment of the individual. Jesus had told a parable about that very subject in the Bible, "The sheep and the goats," about sheep who followed Him and goats who didn't.

Kyle knew Christine was a sheep who put the Lord first in her life, but he was guilty of compromising his faith for weekends of drunkenness and gambling occasionally. He never spoke of the Lord while he was with his friends, and buried any conviction he felt until he was home. In June, he had sworn he would not do it again, but here he was a month later in Branson, about to go drink and having fun with his friends for the second night in a row. After Sam's statement about *his* type of Christian, Kyle had to ask himself if he was a sheep or a goat. Did the Lord really matter to him, or was he simply going through the motions to play a part he really didn't want to play?

He knew all too well that being a Christian, if he was to call himself one, meant being fully submitted, committed, and obedient to the Lord of Heaven and Earth. Sam's words cut him deep because he *was* a Christian. He just hadn't been living like one since Reverend Ash had belittled him in front of the congregation for going to Branson to drink and gamble one Sunday afternoon at a church picnic.

It might not have been intentional, but the words condemned Kyle's chosen activities, and he was offended. He had not been to church since, and he refused to serve the Lord because of the boldness of the reverend's words, but even more so the thoughtless manner in which he had spoken openly for all to hear. It had shamed him, and for that, he wanted nothing to do with the church anymore. But the truth remained when it was brought to light: was he a sheep or a goat? The question could only be answered by his decision to serve the Lord or not.

Adding to Sam's convicting words, an hour before, he'd had high expectations of winning Christine's heart like he had Annie's years ago. He was sure she was the other half who would make him complete, because no one else had ever made him feel the way she had when he met her. Then, moments later, he had witnessed her heartbreaking departure from a favored man's courting.

It was beyond coincidence that they would be paired by fate to go see the classic love story of Romeo and Juliet. Was it a coincidence that Romeo had a love of his own named Rosaline, but when he first saw Juliet, he knew she was his true love? Romeo understood that Juliet was the one God had made to complete him, and only him. All the emotions Romeo had expressed were the emotions he was feeling.

Kyle didn't believe in coincidence, and his hopes had risen with each moment that they were being pressed together by fate...until now.

It hadn't taken much, really; only to be reminded that it was Annie's birthday and he was out drinking with friends rather than home with his family. If he had been reminded or remembered that it was her birthday, he would not have come to Branson. Annie, his beloved wife, was probably crying herself to sleep thinking he didn't care about her after their fight the day before. Oh, it was true he hated the ranch work sometimes, but the thought of losing Annie became very sobering now that he realized what a fool he was for acting the way he had.

Worse, somehow, in some almost obsessive way, he had latched onto Christine as a hope for his future. He had been tired, hot, angry, and had wanted to get away for a while when he fought with Annie, but now that he realized he had forgotten her birthday and that being alone would wound her to the core, he feared losing her for good. Annie was a Bannister, and she acted more like one of her brothers than a lady. Because of that, yes meant yes and no meant no. If she told him to leave their home, there would be no going back.

He had been foolish enough to speak openly of divorcing her and starting a new life as a saloon owner, and in the heat of the moment had spoken of marrying Christine. He had always been an emotional person, but the truth was, he had been acting like a fool. The emotions seemed real at the time, but now that losing his wife and children could be very real, it scared him. If Annie was done with him and wanted a divorce, he would find out very quickly the life he dreamed of wasn't so fulfilling after all. He would miss the daily moments of waking up to Annie's humor, their children's laughter, and the life he knew so well on the ranch. The work was tedious and labor-intensive, but he suddenly realized how lucky he was to have his family. If Annie was willing to forgive him and welcome him home, he swore he would not complain again.

Kyle had looked forward to going to Premro Island after the play with the three ladies to build a fire beside the waterfall and spend some time drinking and reminiscing with his friends. It would be very much like the old times when he and his friends were younger and roamed through the quiet streets of Branson like roaring lions. He had thought it was a perfect summer's night to sit down beside Christine next to a romantic fire and listen to the waterfall. Now, thanks to Lee and Regina, Christine was going home rather than to Premro Island, and oddly enough, Kyle was okay with that. He already felt like a fool, and thought he'd better go to the stable to get his horse and head back toward home. It would be a long and dark ride to Willow Falls, but it seemed like the right thing to do would be to apologize to Annie. He felt like a piece of garbage for all that he'd done, and it was eating at him from the inside out. For the first time ever, he would prefer to go home and try to save his failing marriage instead of going to the Green Toad to drink and gamble his money away.

Kyle sighed and spoke to his friends. "Guys, I messed up. I forgot today is Annie's birthday."

Sam laughed. "Hell, what difference does it make now? You're going to be divorced by the morning anyway after forgetting that! Maybe you better come drink with us whether Christine comes or not. Who knows when we'll get to see you again? I mean, after tonight, Annie may never let you come to town again!"

Kyle frowned and nodded. "Oh, that's if she'll keep me around. If not, you'll see me more than you want to, most likely. After our fight yesterday, and now missing her birthday, she may never forgive me. You guys go enjoy your ladies. I think I am going to go on home."

Paul asked mockingly, "Wait, what happened to your big plans with Christine? Why are you acting upset about missing Annie's birthday when you were going to divorce her and marry Christine just a few hours ago?"

Kyle paused momentarily and looked sad, then answered as honestly as he knew how. "I was mad." He shrugged. "I don't know what the hell I was thinking, but I don't want to lose my family. You're right—I love Annie too much to let her go, and I know forgetting about her birthday hurt her. I have never forgotten her birthday before, and I can't believe I did tonight. Damn it!"

Sam tried to be empathetic, but couldn't resist saying with a smirk, "Well, it was bound to happen. You're married!" He laughed.

Kyle ignored Sam's attempt at a joke.

Paul smiled and shook his head at Sam's words. He said with a friendly slap on Kyle's shoulder, "Well, it's too late to ride back home tonight anyway, so you might as well come with us." He then hollered out to the ladies, "Hey, let's go! We're not going to be the only ones down there on a night like this, and we still need to go get something to drink."

"We're coming. Aren't we, Christine?" Helen said loudly.

"Well...okay," Christine reluctantly agreed, just loud enough for the boys to hear.

"Perfect," Paul said. "Now you have to come with us to keep her busy. So, you're not going to marry her now, huh?"

Sam laughed.

Kyle smiled slightly. "No. I don't think she's my type anyway. She likes guys like Matt, apparently. Besides, I really think I ought to go home and talk to Annie."

Paul shook his head with a smile. "No. You need to get drunk and have a few laughs like we used to out on the island before you go home. In reality, I'm glad to have you back, but like Sam said, we may never see you again after tonight."

Kyle smiled slowly. "I shouldn't, because I'm already in enough trouble. But Lee let me try a shot of a new Tennessee whiskey they sell at the Monarch Lounge, and it's pretty dang good. It's strong stuff, but I think I will buy a bottle of that and take what I don't drink home with me tomorrow."

17

Premro Island was a large basalt land mass that separated the Modoc River as it dropped in elevation just outside of Branson's city limits. The island was surrounded on both sides by channels of fast-moving water that hurtled down the natural chutes over a series of turbulent waterfalls and rapids. The force of the current created a perfect power source for water wheels to power the equipment of the Premro and Sons Milling Works on the wider eastern edge of the island named after its owner. On either side of the river, companies had installed their own water wheels, including Seven Timber Harvester Lumber Mill, a small flour mill, and others that took advantage of the natural power source.

A heavy wooden bridge had been built from Branson across the narrow channel to the island, and there was another bridge on the far side of the island across the wider chute to the Seven Timber Harvester Company and other businesses before the road went on up into the Blue Mountains.

The main attraction wasn't the narrow twenty-foot-wide

rapids that fired past the island, but rather the waterfall on the south side of the island by the harvester company. The waterfall didn't fall straight down but roared down a steep incline as the whitewater dropped sixty feet in a short distance where the river came out of the Blue Mountains and entered the Jessup Valley. The two courses of water came together in a deep pool on the western side of the island.

That was where the three men took their ladies to enjoy a bonfire. The stars were bright and the air was warm, although there was a light breeze. In the moonlight, the whitewater of the falls was clearly visible, and the moon reflecting off the large pool of water was beautiful to see.

The island was ten feet above the river, with a steep rock face all the way around the island that dropped straight into the rapids. The only place the island narrowed was where the two river forks met at the pool. There the island tapered and allowed easier access to the water's edge.

For Christine, it would be a pleasantly beautiful place to spend a lovely evening if she were alone. However, her present company was ruining what could have been a beautiful night. Helen and Sam couldn't seem to keep their hands off each other, and every time she looked at them, they were kissing more passionately than the time before. Edith and Paul were holding each other in the firelight. All four of them were drinking either from the two one-gallon kegs of beer they had acquired or from a bottle of liquor they had also bought. Although they were all getting intoxicated, it was Kyle who made Christine most uncomfortable. He had been drinking heavily from a bottle of whiskey he had bought for himself. He stared at Christine with a strange expression on his face and stood closer to her than she was comfortable with. She feared he would put his arm around her or try to kiss her, so she had moved across the fire from him to be closer to Edith. Even so, he held his half-empty bottle and just stared at her like a statue, motionless except for the swaying like a sapling in a gentle breeze. Christine became more uncomfortable the longer Kyle just stood and stared at her.

"Don't..." Kyle began softly, which got everyone's attention.

"Don't what?" Sam asked.

His eyes never left Christine. "Don't waste your love on someone who doesn't value it," he said, slurring his words.

"What?" Sam laughed. "What are you talking about?"

"Christine!" Kyle snapped abruptly. His eyes were still locked onto her like she was the only person there.

She looked at him, startled by his sudden harsh tone and the look that was growing in his eyes. "Yes?" she answered, and stepped closer to Edith and Paul.

"Don't waste your love on someone who doesn't love you. Matt doesn't love you!" Kyle said slowly, hostility evident in his voice.

The others laughed, but Christine felt a growing anxiousness that she couldn't control. "I know that," she told him as nicely as she could.

Kyle ignored the laughter and glared at her. "Did my heart love till now? I swear it. I never saw true beauty until this night," he said with a swaying head.

Sam bent over and laughed so hard the drink of beer he just swallowed came back up and out through his nose. Helen leaned on his shoulder, laughing heavily at the combination of Sam's reaction and Kyle's words.

Paul stepped forward with a small smile. "What are you talking about? Give me that bottle; you've had enough."

Helen said through her high-pitched laugh, "He's quoting Shakespeare!" She laughed harder.

"Hark!" Kyle smiled at the knowledge that Helen and Sam were laughing at him. He pulled the bottle of whiskey from Paul's hand and held it away from him like a raised sword. "It's thy drink!" he hollered.

Paul nodded. "'Thy' means 'your.' If you're going to speak old English, speak it right."

Kyle looked at him with a touch of indignation in his eyes from being corrected. His head tilted as he stared at Paul. "It rhymes."

Helen laughed so hard she bent over like Sam had.

"Rhyming or not, it's not proper. Now, come on, Kyle, you're acting weird. That's enough drinking for tonight," Paul said, reaching for the bottle again.

Kyle hollered, "Nay. Nay! I say, naay! I bite my thumb at you! Nay!" Kyle put the bottom of his thumb against his top teeth and cast his arm toward Paul.

Paul laughed despite himself and shook his head. Christine smiled too, even though she was regretting that she had come out to the island with her friends.

"I have to pee!" Helen laughed so hard she could barely speak. She grabbed Edith and began pulling her toward a thick area of brush. "Come help me," she said, laughing hysterically. Edith called for Christine to go with them.

Christine happily agreed to join them and walked quickly away from the fire and the men. She heard Kyle yell, "Christine, wait! I never knew true love until this night. Don't leave!"

"She's just going to the privy," Paul offered. "Besides that, you already have a beautiful wife, so leave Christine alone, buddy. You're making a fool of yourself."

"Naaay!" Kyle yelled, imitating a goat. "Thou insolent

swine! How darest one so weak come against-est me?" Kyle's eyes suddenly grew darker and turned serious. "My wife!" Kyle exclaimed, then stared at Paul with dark, unfocused eyes.

"What?" Paul asked, growing frustrated with his intoxicated friend. He could tell by the look in Kyle's eyes that he was not only drunk but on the verge of becoming violent. He had that angry glare building in his eyes. Paul had seen that look a few times over the years, but only when Kyle drank too much whiskey. "What about your wife, Kyle?"

"Me wife's a rotten sow. Sooww!" he yelled loudly with an intoxicated grin. "Sooww!" He laughed.

"Annie's one of the neatest women in the world. You shouldn't talk about your wife like that."

"What's it to you?" Kyle turned aggressive in a matter of seconds. "You love her or something?"

"Kyle, you're being ridic—"

"You can have her!" Kyle interrupted with a smirk. "Taketh the wencheth, you pricketh!" he yelled with a laugh. He took another slug of his whiskey. "Aye, I missed her birthday," he said softly, regret showing in his eyes.

Paul had been growing more uneasy. The romantic night he had hoped to enjoy with Edith was turning into a babysitting session for his drunk friend. He seldom got to see Edith on a Saturday night, and he didn't have any intention of having it ruined by Kyle and his foolish drinking. Kyle normally drank beer and a few shots of whiskey perhaps, but tonight Kyle had bought a bottle of straight Tennessee whiskey from the Monarch Lounge. To drown his guilt in, Paul figured, because it was uncommon for Kyle to drink this way. For a moment, he hoped Kyle was calming down and would sit down and be quiet.

Then Kyle narrowed his eyes and smirked with the same

alcohol-induced expression he'd had a moment before. "Sir Pricketh!" he yelled. "Pricketh! I bite my thumb at you!" he said again, and again flicked his thumb across his teeth toward Paul, then laughed.

"I wish you would," Paul replied mostly to himself. "Kyle, why don't you sit down by the fire and relax for a bit?"

"Fire be damned!" Kyle yelled, and then kicked the fire toward Paul with his boot.

Paul jumped back, alarmed, and cursed as a flurry of red coals and a few larger pieces of burning wood flew toward him. He brushed the coals off his chest, obscenities flying from his mouth. "For crying out loud! What are you trying to do, start a fire?" Paul exclaimed loudly. He kicked the burning pieces of wood that had landed in the dry grass over the edge of the rock face to the water below and stomped out the coals that were burning in the sparse grass.

Sam laughed when he saw Kyle stand there swaying with a goofy smirk on his face, watching Paul.

"Are you stupid?" Paul yelled at Kyle. "You could've set this whole island on fire, including the mill! Now sit down and shut up! You're making a complete ass of yourself! No one is enjoying you being here tonight! Not me, not Sam, not anyone! I mean, look! Edith and Christine would rather go watch a girl pee than talk to you! Now sit down and shut up for a while!" He turned to Sam. "It isn't funny! Don't encourage him."

Sam laughed harder. "I'm trying not to, but tomorrow you'll laugh about it too!"

Kyle smirked as he glared at Paul, the intoxicated aggression clearly showing in his eyes. His head bobbed from left to right as he slurred, "Tis no less, I tell ye, for the bawdy hand of the dial is now upon the *prick* of noon." He glared at Paul. "Pricketh!"

"You're starting to piss me off," Paul said seriously.

Kyle's eyes hardened, and his smirk slowly changed to a deformed grimace. "Do something about it. Come make me sit down, why don't ya? Ye who wants thy wife, come make me cow down." Kyle's eyes were filled with a burning hate that only the bitterness of whiskey could bring about.

Paul sighed. "You're too drunk to stand, and you think I couldn't knock you down?" he asked with a frustrated smile. "Keep it up, and I will."

Kyle glared at him. "I'm here. I'll whip you here or..." he paused for a moment and frowned. "You need to get the fire going. It's burning out."

Sam laughed. "That's because you kicked it, you idiot! Maybe you should go get some firewood."

Kyle's eyes grew heavy as he stared blankly at Sam. "I'm not—"

"No!" Paul interrupted quickly. "The fool will walk off the ledge and break his leg or something, then we'll be stuck with him while he heals because Annie sure as hell isn't going to take him back! When Edith gets back, she and I will go gather some more wood. In the meantime, why don't you go sit over there somewhere and pass out or something," he said to Kyle.

Kyle shook his head. "I have to pee," he said, and set his bottle down and began to unbutton his pants.

"Don't piss in the fire!" Paul yelled, but it was too late, Kyle began relieving himself in the fire. Sam bent over, once again laughing hysterically. Paul, however, stepped forward and pushed Kyle away from the fire. Kyle stumbled back and fell to his back while still urinating, mostly on himself. "I told you not to pee in the fire!" Paul yelled angrily.

Kyle turned to his side to finish urinating. "Thee still have to pee," Kyle muttered as he finished.

Sam had sat down on the ground and had tears running from his eyes. Paul stood above his friends with a smile as he looked at Kyle. "I'm never going to let him forget about this! You know that, right? He pissed all over himself. I'm pretty sure Annie won't be too impressed by that." He laughed.

Kyle sat upright, fully exposed, and held out his hand for Paul to help him up.

Paul shook his head with a chuckle. "I'm not touching your pissy hand! Just stay there and relax for a while. Button up your pants though, huh? The girls should be back shortly."

Kyle chuckled and looked up at Paul. "I'm waiting for your woman. She's what, two bits? I have two bits in my coin purse," he said.

Paul's smile faded. "Don't talk about Edith like that! I'm warning you, friend or not, I will bust your mouth open if you ever say that again. Do you understand me?" he snarled.

Kyle laughed and then yelled, "Edith, come forth!" He continued to laugh as he struggled to reach into his pocket and grab his coin bag. "See, I have some change right here." He looked up at Paul and asked, "How much is she? Two bits, you say?" He guffawed at his own cleverness.

From the bushes, Edith yelled back, "I'm coming!" It was followed by some talking among the ladies that the men couldn't hear, followed by their laughter from the darkness of the bushes.

Kyle sat exposed on the ground, holding some change in his hand with a big grin on his face. He was looking at Paul. "See, I just jingle my change, and she comes running!" He started laughing again.

Without saying a word, Paul dove on top of Kyle, forcing him to his back. He moved to straddle Kyle's stomach and swung his right fist toward Kyle's face, but it barely grazed his cheek. "I told you to shut your damn mouth!" he said as he pulled his arm back to hit Kyle again. His arm was caught by Sam.

"Get off him, Paul!" Sam exclaimed as he pulled Paul away from Kyle. "You two are friends, damn it. Now stop it!" he yelled as he threw Paul to the ground. Kyle had kept laughing through the scuffle.

Paul stood up quickly, anger burning in his eyes. "I told him I'd bust his mouth if he didn't shut up!" He pointed his finger at Kyle and spoke heatedly. "Now button your damn pants and shut your mouth! Don't ever talk about Edith like that again!" He turned to Sam and added, "You'd do the same thing if he spoke about Helen like that!"

"Maybe, but he's so drunk he doesn't know what he's doing. Why hit him? He won't remember it tomorrow."

"Better yet!" Paul exclaimed.

Sam laughed. "Go find the girls, and keep them over there until Kyle's dressed. I'll take care of him." He looked down at Kyle with a large smile. "Let me help you up, you crazy bastard. Button your pants, for crying out loud! What would Annie say?"

"Tis Annie's birthday and thy's not there," he said with an obviously heavy heart.

Sam frowned. "You should be there, Tybalt. That's who you're acting like you know—Tybalt."

"Tybalt's a fish! A fish!" he yelled. He added with a scowl toward Paul, "Just like Pricketh is a fish!"

18

"Edith, come forth!" a voice cried out from the fire about thirty yards away.

"I'm coming!" Edith called back loudly as she stood with the two other ladies. "Well, do you think he loves me? He apparently can't stand being without me," she asked Christine with an expectant smile.

Christine rolled her eyes skeptically. "I think that was my so-called date calling you, Edith. Mister Kyle Lenning must've given up on me finally."

Edith and Helen both laughed. Edith added, "You can keep him. He started off so nice, but that man can't hold his liquor. At least Paul doesn't overdo his drinking—I can say that for him. He's a hardworking man who might just make a good family man. What do you think, Christine? You were married to a good man. Do you think Paul's a good man?"

Christine shrugged thoughtfully. "He seems like a good man. He definitely is falling for you, that's easy to see."

"Really? Do you think he'll ask me to marry him someday?"

Christine smiled gently in the moonlight. "Yes, he will.

You are far too beautiful and good-hearted for him not to. But if I could offer just a bit of advice?"

"Of course."

"If you marry him, do it because you love him, not just to have a place to go when the dancing's over. Eventually, all three of us will be replaced by younger and prettier girls; we all know that. But don't rush into marriage because of it. Make sure you love him before you say, 'I do.' Marriage can be hard and hopeless if you don't love him."

Helen interrupted, "How would you know? You were married to the love of your life. I don't think it matters. It's still better than going back to whoring when we're too old to dance, so I'm making sure Sam marries me. And if I'm not pregnant yet, I sure hope to be before too long. I might take Sam for a little walk into the bushes before we go home."

Edith gasped. "Helen, you can't do that! You heard Bella. What if you get pregnant?"

"That's the whole idea, Edith. I want to get pregnant so Sam will marry me. And don't act like you haven't thought of doing the same thing! I know you would if you loved Paul like I do Sam. I know Sam will marry me, so why not get out of the business while I can?"

"What if he doesn't marry you?" Christine asked.

"He will!"

"But what if he doesn't? Have you considered what you'd do then?"

Edith spoke for Helen, "He will. Sam would marry her even without her being pregnant."

"Then why hasn't he?" Christine asked simply. "What you're doing is wrong. If he loves you, he will ask you to marry him when he is ready to. You shouldn't have to trap him into it with a baby. That's not right. Why not wait for him to ask for your hand?"

Helen frowned. "Christine, you are the most beautiful girl in the world, I think, and so does everyone else who sees you. You make more money than any other girl ever has in Bella's history. Trust me, you won't have to worry about being replaced by a younger and prettier girl for years. But I'm not you. I'm not the prettiest girl, and so far this month, I've made the least money of all of us dancers. How long do you think Bella will let that go on until she brings in a prettier dancer than me? Think about it. Maybe the reason she has been so willing to allow me to see Sam so much lately is that she knows my time dancing is coming to an end," Helen said, moisture appearing in her eyes. "This is my chance, and I'm taking it."

"If he loves you, he will not let you go back to selling yourself. He would want all of you. Besides, Bella would never let you go without telling you in advance. At least, she never has before, to my knowledge. All I'm saying is marry him, but do it the right way. Wait for him to ask you to marry him. That's how Richard proposed to me. Helen, you have time. If you get pregnant, and for some reason he doesn't marry you, then Bella will have no choice but to let you go, and it would be a whole lot harder to find a husband with another man's baby in your arms.

"Don't try to trap him into marriage before he is ready to ask you. That's unfair to him and you. You'd only be cheating yourself out of perhaps the best day and year of your life. Let me ask you...would you rather have him get down on his knee with a ring and surprise you with a loving request for your hand for life, or would you rather walk up to him and say, 'Hey, hog, we're going to have a piglet, so make room in the hog shed?'"

Helen laughed. "Thanks for calling me a hog, Christine."

"It has nothing to do with you being a hog. It has everything to do with your approach to marriage. Do it right, Helen. Wait until marriage to give yourself to him. That's my advice."

"Well," Helen said, smiling as she shook her head, "I don't want to be compared to a sow, so maybe you're right. Besides, it is my dream that he would ask me to marry him. I guess if he loves me, he will, yeah?"

"As long as you're not giving yourself away for free, yes. But if you're giving your body away without a wedding ring, there is nothing sacred about it. Marriage is supposed to be a sacred union. Wait for that wedding day, and you'll be thankful you did, I promise you. Don't hog-tie him like a spoiled sow, okay? You're worth so much more than that," Christine told her sincerely.

Helen nodded as she thought about it. "Okay, I won't hog-tie him into marriage." She chuckled despite her sincerity. She continued with a smile, "You know, you should consider Kyle. He seems interested in you, even though he's calling for Edith right now. At least he's honest: he just wants to leave his wife and kids for you!"

"Funny. No thanks," Christine said simply.

Edith added with a smile, "You'd at least meet his brother-in-law, the one you wanted to meet if you hooked up with Kyle."

"Hmm... Yeah and he'll be convinced that I'm a home-wrecking whore, too. No, the Lord will bring Matt into my life somehow if He wants that to happen, but I'll pass on Mister Lenning."

"Hello?" Paul called hesitantly from behind some brush. "I came to find my beautiful queen, if you're all decent."

Edith snickered with delight. "Excuse me, ladies," she said and walked toward Paul. "Did you miss me already?"

Paul scoffed dramatically. "Being left with that idiot over there, you bet I missed you!" He took her in his arms and kissed her. "Yeah, I missed you."

Helen took Christine by the hand and said, "Let's go find my man and leave these two young lovers alone for a while." As they stepped past Edith and Paul, Helen said sarcastically, "Remember, it isn't nice to hog-tie him, sow!"

"What's that mean?" Paul asked Edith.

Edith shook her head with a short laugh. "Nothing. So, am I really your beautiful queen?"

"Yeah, I think you are," Paul said and kissed her again.

When Helen walked out of the brush and into the firelight, the only person she could see was Kyle. He was standing by the fire, swaying back and forth holding his whiskey bottle in his hand. He was beyond laughter and giddiness. Now Kyle's expression was empty of any emotion except a fine line between a need for sleep and rage. His eyes lit up, and he smirked when he saw Christine following Helen. "Christine!" he shouted.

"Where's Sam?" Helen asked.

"Sam who? Christine!" he called again. He stared at her with his mouth open and his head weaving from side to side.

"Oh, Romeo, my sweet Romeo," Helen called, "Where art thou, my sweet Romeo?"

Sam answered from the bank of the river. "Down here behind a bush, so throw me some paper!" he said, and then laughed heartedly.

Helen laughed and stepped near the steep edge to look over it. Sam was standing at the edge of the water about ten feet down on the rock bank buttoning up his pants. "I want to come down there."

"There's a trail and some steps carved in the bank over

there, but be careful, because it's hard to see them at night. I'll come up and help you. I'd hate to see you fall and get hurt."

"Can I make it down in my dress or do I need to take it off?" she asked flirtatiously.

Sam chuckled. "If you don't want it ruined, you might want to take it off. It's a beautiful night for a midnight swim."

Helen giggled and asked Christine to unbutton the back of her dress.

"Are you insane?" Christine asked, surprised by Helen's request. "Didn't we just talk about being a hog?"

"I'm going swimming in my camisole, so hurry up," Helen stated.

Christine sighed with disappointment and reluctantly unbuttoned the back of Helen's dress. When she was finished, Helen walked over to the edge. She let her dress fall off her shoulders, revealing her camisole and bloomers. Kyle, who had been watching in silence with unfocused eyes, began to laugh as his eyes widened. "Take it off!" he yelled. "I've got money, take it off!"

"Shut up, Kyle," Sam said calmly. "Take my hand, and I'll help you down," he added to Helen and began to walk down the steep edge carefully.

"I'm going swimming too," Kyle said and took another drink of his whiskey. "Wait up. I'll come with you."

"No, you won't! Stay up here with Christine for a while," Sam suggested.

Kyle looked at Christine. "Do ya want me to help you take your dress off? We're going swimming."

Christine watched Sam gently guide Helen down the bank, leaving her alone with Kyle. "No, thank you," she said trying to ignore him.

Kyle spoke in a demanding tone with no hint of humor in his heavy eyes, "Come on, let's go swim. It's what we came here for, isn't it? To skinny-dip in the moonlight? You shouldn't be so shy. I've got money. Money!" he yelled unexpectedly and leaned toward Christine with his empty hands cupped together like he was holding water out to her to drink. He shouted with a drunken slur to his voice, "I've got mon-ney! Do you want some mon-ney? Come earn some mon-ney in the river with me. One dolla! One dolla! Three? Three dolla! Three dolla!" He began laughing loudly, then reached down to grab his bottle of whiskey and took another drink.

"Edith!" Christine yelled toward the brush. "Get out here, please."

"Edith!" Kyle called through his laughter. "I've got a dolla! Dolla, whaaa? Dolla Whaaa!" he said in a high-pitched voice, then laughed uncontrollably for a minute.

He regained his composure a bit. "You're a whaaa too. How much are ya, one dolla whaaa? Two?" He again said "Whaaa" in a high-pitched voice.

"Edith, get out here now, please!" she called loudly. She was discouraged to hear Sam and Helen laughing at Kyle's nonsense at her expense. "Will you leave me alone, please?" she asked Kyle bluntly.

"How many dollas for a kiss, whaaa?" Kyle asked, licking his lips disgustingly and letting saliva drip from his tongue and lips. He began laughing again.

"I don't think your wife would appreciate that, Mister Lenning." There was no humor in her voice. She was repulsed by what she was seeing.

"I said we're going swimming!" His tone turned demanding, almost threatening as he glared at her with very unkind eyes. Her response had enraged him.

Christine prayed silently as his expression sent a wave of fear down her spine. Despite that, she refused to submit any ground whatsoever. "Then go, but leave me alone! I don't want to talk to you."

"You will talk to me, whaaa!" He began to laugh over his pronunciation of "whore" in a high-pitched voice again. "How much? Edith's two bits, you're what? Half a bit? Half-bit whaaa! Half-bit." He bent over laughing hysterically again.

"Edith!" Christine yelled angrily.

"Coming," Edith replied, nearing the fire. "What do you want?" she asked, irritated about being disturbed. Paul was right behind her.

"You all left me alone with him!" she said, pointing at Kyle. "And I'm ready to go! I won't tolerate being called a whore by a drunk! Take me home *now!*"

"Wait a minute," Edith said softly. "Where's Helen?"

"Down there with Sam! And this drunk thinks we're going skinny-dipping together! I'm done. You guys can take me home or I can go alone, but either way, I am going back to the dance hall right now!"

Paul sighed heavily in disappointment. "Kyle, what is your problem tonight?" he asked impatiently.

Kyle smirked and took another sip of his whiskey, then smiled slowly at Paul. "I want to swim." He tossed his bottle down and ran toward the edge of the bank Sam and Helen had climbed down.

"Don't!" Paul yelled urgently as Kyle dove head-first over the edge. From below, Sam watched Kyle fall ten feet toward the water's edge, but in his drunken stupor, he had dived from the wrong end of the bank. Kyle's extended arms buckled and he landed head-first on a rock next to the river, the deep hollow *thunk* of his skull cracking under the full force of his weight upon impact echoing across the water. His body slid off the rock and he landed in the water on his back, quickly beginning to sink as the current pulled him away.

"Kyle!" Sam screamed and went into the river to pull his friend out. Paul ran down the bank to help Sam get Kyle out of the water. Sam grabbed Kyle's torso and was dragging him toward the bank when Paul took Kyle's hands, and together they laid him on the bank.

"Oh, lord! Please let him be okay!" Paul said through his fear. "Edith, go get help! Go get it now!"

Helen asked, "Is he dead?"

Edith stood on top of the bank staring at them. "Who?"

"You!" Paul yelled bitterly. "Go get some help now!"

"Who? Who should I get?" she asked helplessly, beginning to panic.

"The doctor! The sheriff. Anyone, just go!" Paul said through the tears that were building in his eyes.

Kyle bled heavily from the top of his head. His breathing was shallow as he opened his eyes halfway and looked at his friend Sam. "Go get Annie, please. Get Annie. I need to go home." He tried to sit up, but he couldn't move. "I can't..." He smiled, then fear began to take over his expression. "Get Annie, please! My head hurts. Get my wife. I need Annie." He closed his eyes as his breathing slowed.

"He's not breathing! Oh, my lord, help him," Sam shouted. "Kyle! Come on, man. Stay awake, brother, please!"

"Kyle! Come on, breathe!" Paul yelled.

"He's breathing, he's breathing, but he needs the doctor now!" Sam looked up the bank toward the two girls. Edith and Christine were standing together and watching helplessly. "Get help now!" he screamed.

"I don't know where the doctor is," Edith said, and sank to her knees, sobbing helplessly.

Paul stood up, "I'll go! Stay with him," he said to Sam and Helen. "Did you hear me, Kyle? I'm going to get help, okay? You just hold on," he urged, and ran up the bank and across the island as fast as he could.

He hardly noticed Christine on her knees holding Edith and praying to the Lord above for Kyle.

Helen knelt beside Kyle and spoke in an intentionally upbeat tone, "Do you want me to have Christine come down here and talk to you about tomorrow night's plans? I think sure she likes you, but you have to get better first, right?"

Kyle opened his eyes enough to see her. A tear slid out, but it went undetected in the water that dripped from his face. "Jesus forgive me," he said as another tear fell. "I'm sorry. Annie... Just tell Annie I'm sorry. I love her. It's her... birthday," he whispered, and closed his eyes as exhaustion took over.

"Kyle! I need you to stay awake. Paul's getting help, okay?" Sam paused to look at Kyle in the moonlight. "I don't think he's breathing," he said through his own deep breaths. "Damn you, Kyle, wake up! Wake up! Don't you do this to me, you son of a bitch! Damn, Kyle, you're so stupid!" Sam yelled, and began to cry. His old friend Kyle Lenning had passed away in his arms.

Christine Knapp, still on her knees holding Edith in her arms, burst into tears.

19

It was late when Regina Bannister shook her husband Lee awake. "Lee, someone is at the door."

"Huh...what?" he asked, irritated about being woken up. He heard the knocking. "What time is it?" he asked as he sat up in bed and turned the kerosene lamp beside his bed up a bit to light the room. He checked his pocket watch, which was beside the bed, and frowned. "It's almost two in the morning. Who in the world's knocking on the door at this time of night?" He put on a pair of pants and pulled on a shirt that he didn't bother to button, then went to his dresser drawer and pulled out his old Navy Colt revolver and checked the cylinders to make sure it was loaded. He paused at the bedroom door and looked back at his wife. "Stay here."

"Be careful," she called as he left the room.

Lee went downstairs with a dim lantern in one hand and his revolver in the other. He set the lantern down on a table and asked, "Who is it?"

"Um, Lee, it's Tim Wright. I'm afraid I'm here on official business."

"Tim?" Lee asked, and unlocked the door and opened it. "What are you doing here? It better be important. Well, come on in," he said, inviting Tim and his deputy Mark Thiesen inside. Lee turned the lamp up and then moved to another one to turn it up as well. "What's wrong?" he asked.

Tim was uncomfortable. "I'm sorry to tell you this, but I didn't know who else to go to. Your brother-in-law Kyle was killed tonight over on Premro Island."

"Oh, my lord!" Regina gasped from the stairway behind Lee. She came down quickly to stand by her husband.

"Are you sure?" Lee asked as he put his arm around Regina.

Tim nodded. "I saw him myself. It's him."

"How?" Lee asked, shocked by the news.

Tim took a deep breath before explaining. "He was apparently on the island drinking with some friends, and at some point, he dove into the river and drowned. That's what his friends say, anyway. He dove in, hit his head on a rock, and drowned."

Lee frowned. "Who were his friends?"

"Sam Troyer and Paul Johnson. There were some courtesans from the new dance hall there too."

Regina said, "The same people he was with earlier, then. Tell me, was that girl there that he was with at the play? The very attractive woman in a green dress?"

Tim nodded. "Her name is Christine Knapp, and yes, she was with Kyle tonight. The other two women who were there tonight aren't important since they were with Sam and Paul, but Christine was with Kyle."

"Who is she?" Regina asked with no emotion in her voice.

"She's the premiere dancer at that Bella's Dance Hall, which moved into town a month or so ago. I can only imagine Kyle met her there through his friends, who are courting two of the dancers. I saw Kyle there last night when I was making my rounds, and he was paying a lot of attention to Christine. I was there on official business, just so you know," he explained to keep his reputation clean.

Lee said to no one in particular, "We need to tell Annie. Does she know, Tim?"

He shook his head. "You're the first we've told. I could send Mark to Willow Falls in the morning to tell her if you'd like. I was kind of leaving that up to you."

Regina spoke softly, "That's something *we* need to do, Lee. Not a stranger."

Lee nodded in agreement. "I hate to do that. I suppose Albert and I will ride out to Willow Falls in the morning."

"Mellissa and me too. Annie will need her brothers, but she'll need her sisters-in-law more. My heart is broken for her and those children."

Lee took a deep breath. "Tim, thanks for telling me. I need you to go inform Albert and tell him we will pick him and Mellissa up at sunrise. Tell him we have to go inform our sister of the bad news."

"I'll go tell him. I'm sorry, Lee and Regina. I really am."

Lee nodded sadly. "Me too. I'm afraid I wasn't very nice to him tonight. He was already upset with me for turning him down for a loan earlier today. I imagine he was more so tonight."

"A loan for what? Is Annie having financial troubles?" Regina asked.

"No. He wanted to buy the Green Toad Saloon, and I wouldn't help him with that. He said Annie didn't know about him buying it, so I figured it was a spur-of-the-moment decision without a business plan."

"Oh," Regina responded thoughtfully.

Tim spoke carefully. "I heard from his friend Paul tonight that Kyle was talking about buying that saloon and divorcing your sister to start a new life with that Christine girl. I'm not one to gossip, but it may be important," he said with a shrug.

Lee shook his head somberly. "I don't think it matters anymore. Well, thanks for coming by, Tim. Tell Albert and Mellissa we'll be there early. Thank you, Tim."

"You're welcome, but again, you have my condolences. And tell your sister I am sorry."

"By the way, where is his body? Does my uncle Solomon have it?" Lee asked. His uncle Solomon Fasana was the local mortician, and the owner of the Fasana Funeral Parlor and Furniture Store.

"Yes, he came and got Kyle's body already."

"Good. Did you notify Kyle's parents yet?"

"No, I came here first. I didn't know what you wanted me to do. This is technically Matt's jurisdiction since Premro Island's outside of city limits, but he's not here, so it falls to me," Sheriff Wright explained.

"You better go tell his parents too. Let them know that Annie is making the funeral arrangements, not them. I'm not sure if she'll want him buried in Willow Falls or here, but either way, she has the final say. Let them know that for me."

Tim nodded at the gun in Lee's hand and said, "You know, I know it's a bad time and all, but I have never seen you hold a weapon before, Lee."

Lee smirked. "It shouldn't be too surprising, Tim. I used it all during the Snake War, and fought my way through the battle of Coffee Creek with it. I used to be pretty good with it. I imagine I still am when I need to be."

"That was a long time ago. I'd think you'd have a newer model by now," Tim commented.

Lee nodded. "I do, but this old revolver and I go back a long way. We've been through some close, bloody battles together, and to be quite honest, this particular weapon has become a natural extension of my arm. I don't miss with it."

"I understand. Well, goodnight to you, Miss Regina, and again, I am sorry," he said with a tip of his hat.

Lee closed and locked the door, then looked at Regina and shook his head sadly. She wrapped her arms around him comfortingly.

"Poor Annie," she said. "She is going to be so broken," she said, tears softly falling from her eyes.

Lee nodded. "Yeah. Let's go try to get some sleep, my dear. Tomorrow's going to be a long, hard day."

"I am so sad," she whimpered and began to sob lightly against his chest.

Lee held her gently. "I know."

20

Christine Knapp hadn't slept at all. It had been a terrible night, and it ended horribly with the accidental death of Kyle Lenning. It had been a nightmare to witness his death, but it was made even worse when Sheriff Tim Wright came to investigate and asked his many questions.

They had gotten back to the dance hall around two in the morning, and she had spent the rest of the night weeping and praying for Kyle's wife and children. She understood what Kyle's wife would be going through all too well, and it broke Christine's heart to know another family would be forever changed by the actions of someone under the influence of alcohol.

Kyle's family would need prayer, and a lot of it. Christine had already decided to send some money to the grieving family out of her savings anonymously to help with any expenses his family would face.

Christine was propped upright against the headboard of her bed, dressed in her bloomers and camisole with the Bible on her lap. She had read 1st Corinthians and found some solace in the scriptures to ease her unsettled soul.

A knock on her room door brought her out of her thoughts. "Come in," she called.

When the door opened, it was one of the younger dancers named Rebecca. She told her, "Miss Christine, Miss Bella wants you downstairs."

"Okay, thank you, Rebecca."

Ten minutes later, Christine, wearing a robe over her bloomers, walked into Bella's office and sat down. A moment later, Helen and Edith, both hungover, walked tiredly into the office and sat down as well.

Bella was fully dressed as usual and looked very stern as she sat behind her desk with a cup of coffee. "It's just after ten o'clock in the morning. Do any of you know what the gossip in town is?"

"No," Helen said uncaringly. She wasn't feeling nearly as good as she had the night before.

Bella looked sternly at Helen. "Let me enlighten you. I went to the bakery this morning, and Fiona asked me about Christine's relationship with Mister Lenning. It seems that someone is spreading the rumor that Christine and Kyle got into a lover's quarrel because he wouldn't leave his wife for her."

"What?" Christine snapped.

"And, rumor has it that a witness has come forward saying they witnessed Christine and him fighting at the edge of the bank and she pushed him over! That is what the sheriff told Fiona this morning! There is a possibility that they will charge Christine with manslaughter, if not murder, if they can prove it! As corrupt as they all are around here, they will find a way to do that!"

Christine scoffed. "That's not true!"

Edith spoke hurriedly, "That's bull! They can't prove

anything. We were all there, including Kyle's two best friends. They couldn't prove anything if they tried."

Bella looked at the girls, irritated. "I don't think you understand. The Lenning family has been in this town for a long time. Kyle married Annie Bannister, and she owns the Big Z Ranch over in Willow Falls. Her brothers are Lee, Albert, and Matt Bannister, and those three are a powerful force, not only in this community but in this county. Trust me, if they want Christine to be arrested and thrown in prison or...hung, it won't matter how innocent she is. If they want it, they will get it. Where there is corruption, it pays for a way. If they want her hung today, she'll be hung today! There is no help in this county if one of the good ole boys is wronged. The most powerful people in this entire county are known as the Branson Elite Seven. The Bannister brothers, Lee and Albert, are two of the Elite Seven. How powerful are they? They convinced the federal government to commission Matt Bannister to be a U.S. Marshal and built his office. These guys are dangerously unlimited, and now have a U. S. Marshal in their pocket, as well as Sheriff Wright."

Helen spoke tiredly. "That doesn't matter. Sam and Paul will tell the truth. They are his best friends. The Bannisters should believe them."

Bella shook her head. "There's more. Christine humiliated Travis McKnight here the other night. As you know, Travis manages the lumber mill and is a powerful man in his own right. His two best friends are Josh Slater and Sheriff Tim Wright. Your two special suitors, Sam and Paul, work for Travis, and he might fire them if they go against the grain. Don't think for a moment that they can't set those two boys up for some kind of a crime if they wanted to." She paused, then added, "These lies are being spread to save

Kyle's reputation because he's part of the Bannister family and vilify ours, especially Christine's."

"But we're witnesses!" Edith exclaimed, incensed.

"Honey, it won't matter. They can buy better witnesses than you'll ever be. We live in a corrupt world with corrupt officials, and the judge and jury will do as they're told. Unfortunately for us, Kyle Lenning was family to some of the most important men in the community, and they'll do anything to protect his reputation. And that puke Travis McKnight is friends with every one of them. I can promise you he is feeding that fire to get even with Christine for embarrassing him."

Christine sat quietly, resting her head on the palm of her hand, and a tear rolled down her cheek. After a moment of silence, she murmured, "I have nothing to say. I have always tried to do what was honorable and right, and this is what happens. My reputation's dirt and I've done nothing to deserve it."

Bella spoke determinedly. "Well, I can promise you this: if the sheriff wants to follow that route, we will fight him every step of the way!"

Edith patted Christine's leg. "You'll be fine. Remember, you're the one who is always talking about God."

Christine smiled sadly. "I know, and the Lord will help me through this somehow. I mean, they may not charge me with anything. It is just rumors."

Helen spoke to Christine. "Well, you always say, 'Walk by faith and not by sight.' Just because it looks bad doesn't mean it is."

Christine glanced at Helen. "So, you *are* listening when I talk about the Lord. Good, I'll keep doing it then. By the way, I needed to hear that, so thank you."

"You're the one who always says it!" Helen exclaimed.

"Yeah, but sometimes I need to hear it too."

Bella spoke seriously. "One more bit of bad news. The marshal is out of town. He is over in Sweethome, Idaho, searching for a man who killed a passel of people, including a woman. When he comes back to town, be prepared for all hell to break loose. I have a feeling the Elites are going to let him do all the dirty work to get justice for his sister, and I have no idea what that might entail."

Christine frowned and shrugged. "Well, as Helen said, as a Christian, I walk by faith and not by sight. I suppose that means I will get to meet the marshal after all, even if he thinks I'm his brother-in-law's whore rather than an honorable lady." She sighed. "I am never leaving this building with a man again."

Bella replied to Christine's words. "Beauty attracts all kinds of pukes and beasts, but it also attracts honorable men. You just need to recognize them from the trash. You'll find your Romeo. Just make sure he's a good man and not a Travis McKnight in disguise."

"That's the problem. Sometimes it's a very good disguise."

21

It had been a very hard day for Annie Lenning and her children. Her oldest son, eight-year-old, Ira, and six-year-old daughter, Catherine were both devastated. Erika, her four-year-old, was too young to comprehend what all the crying was about. The three children had left no time for Annie to grieve throughout the day. It was getting late and growing dark outside when she went to lie down with her son, Ira, while he slowly fell asleep. Annie couldn't sleep, and she didn't intend to as she carefully stood up from Ira's bed, kissed his cheek softly, and then went downstairs to her parlor, where much of her family sat quietly together.

Usually when her family got together, it was a celebration with much laughter and multiple conversations going on at once. But on this evening, the tragic loss of her husband left a void not only in the room but in the hearts of everyone in the house. It meant a lot to have her brothers, sisters-in-law, and friends come by her house to stay with and help her today. The whole Willow Falls community had come out to the Big Z throughout the day to offer their condolences and had brought more food, prayers, and well-wishes than she could hardly stand. The food they brought had fed her family, and for that, she was more grateful then she could express. She had never experienced such an over-whelming sense of friendship and love. It had brought a sense of comfort during the worst day of her life.

She walked into her parlor and flicked the back of Albert's head as she walked by. He was talking quietly to their brother Steven.

"Watch it," Albert said to her as a threat.

"Hush it," she replied. "Well, the kids are finally asleep," she said, sitting down on a large milk can beside the front door.

"Annie, sit down here," Lee said, standing up from a soft armchair facing the davenport.

"No, I've been lying down with Ira for an hour, so it will do me good to sit here. Actually, I think I'm going to go get some fresh air and be alone for a bit." She stood up and slipped into her moccasins by the door.

"Would you like some company?" Mellissa Bannister asked.

Annie shook her head. "No, I'd like to be alone."

She stepped out into the warm July night air, which felt cooler than inside her home. The stars were bright, and the night was silent as she walked toward the barn. She had not had a moment to herself since that morning when her little girl Erika woke her up by kicking her in the back. Annie had lain awake, waiting for the morning sun begin to rise. When it did, she got up and made a fire to make some coffee, and a bit later made breakfast for her family. There were morning chores to do, and it was just after feeding the livestock that she'd seen Lee's carriage pull up to her house unexpectedly.

Lee, Regina, Albert, and Mellissa all got out to inform her about Kyle. She had not been alone since.

Being outside in the solitude and the quiet vastness of the country, Annie could take a deep breath and exhale as her emotions came to the surface and tears once again began to burn in her eyes. She looked up at the stars and focused on the Big Dipper, which seemed to be almost directly overhead. "Lord, I don't even know where to start. You are my God, and I will trust you. But...Ira is so broken. How am I supposed to tell him his father was drunk and fooling around with another woman? A whore, at that. I don't know when he started to become unhappy ,or when he started whoring around, but it hurts worse knowing he did that than it does to know he's gone."

She began to sob as she leaned against a hay wagon parked by the barn. "Jesus, I am hurting so much. He might've been a worthless husband, but he was *my* worthless husband, and I loved him. I feel so guilty for thinking about getting a divorce. On the other hand, I'd like to beat him senseless! How dare he pay for a whore on the side? I am embarrassed, humiliated, torn, broken, angry, furious, and incredibly...sad. I don't even know what I'm feeling, I just want to explode and beat him and then hug him, because I wish he was here. I love him, Lord. I wish I never would've said the things I did to him."

She paused to take a deep breath and wipe her eyes, but it failed to stop her tears. "Help me, Jesus, to raise our children without him. And help my children to get through this. Help them to do that. In Jesus' name, Amen."

She wiped the tears from her face, walked into the barn, and closed the door behind her. She turned up an oil lamp hanging from a heavy post that was barely lit, then stepped over to a saddle set over a sawhorse by the tack room and sat on it. The smell of leather, fresh cut hay, and manure filled her senses, but it was a comforting mixed fragrance that she had grown to love over the years of living on the Big Z Ranch.

It was nice to sit alone with her own thoughts, without her children pulling at her sleeves or someone else asking if she needed anything. She needed solitude and quiet to be able to simply unwind and relax enough to find out how she really did feel. Many things hurt—a toothache perhaps, or a sore back or knee. The ranch wasn't the place for weaklings, and Annie could take a hard day's aches and pains, but nothing in her life had prepared her for the blow she had received that morning. Kyle, her beloved Kyle, was dead. It was still unbelievable to her that he would never come home again.

Twenty minutes later, the barn door opened and Adam Bannister stepped quietly inside. "Annie, I thought I might find you in here."

Annie stepped off the saddle and walked over and hugged him. As soon as his big arms went around her, she began sobbing.

For a moment, he just held her and let her cry without saying a word, then, "I'm sorry, Annie."

She let him go and wiped her eyes. "Thanks. It seems like 'I'm sorry' is all I've heard today. I'm already tired of hearing it, Adam. And I have to go to Branson tomorrow to make funeral arrangements with Uncle Solomon and Kyle's parents. I got a wire today from his father, who set that meeting up. He wants Kyle buried in Branson and not here in the family plot."

Adam frowned. "It doesn't really matter, does it? I mean, it doesn't matter where you bury his body. He's not there anyway."

Annie gave him a serious glare. "I know that! But maybe my children would like to go to their father's grave sometimes. It might help them cope with his absence. I don't know. How did you cope with it when Mom died? Did you go to her grave and visit with her or anything?"

Adam nodded thoughtfully. "Yeah, I suppose I did."

"Then he needs to be buried here, and that's final. My children come first, not his parents."

"Is someone going with you?" he asked.

"Uncle Charlie and Aunt Mary. Probably everyone else will show up too. Do you want to go?" she asked, sounding hopeful. "My kids and I could use some strength when I haven't got any more, Adam. I'm not going to get through this very well."

"You're a strong lady. It'll be hard, but you'll get through it okay." Adam was trying to encourage her.

Annie gave him a slight smile, although her eyes were full of tears. She shook her head as she spoke. "No, I don't think I will. I always told him I didn't need him, but I did. I never told him that I needed him to need me. I never told him I needed him to love me." She shrugged as she continued, "One of the last things I did tell him was I didn't need a lazy-ass husband."

A tear slipped quietly down her cheek from her eyes. "I wish I had never said that, or other things. I was mad and embarrassed. I didn't think he'd never come home again. If I could go back just for a minute, I would tell him I love him. I would tell him I need him. Not to clean the pig stall, like I always told him, but to be my husband.

"Yeah. Damn it, Kyle! I needed him to be there for me like a husband is supposed to be. I needed him to be a father! I needed him to want me, and not some damn prostitute!" She looked up at Adam as she admitted weakly, "He was cheating on me." She began to sob into her hands.

Adam frowned and put a big arm around her lovingly. "Little sis, you and the kids will get through this. We're all here to make sure of that. As far as the prostitute goes, he just doesn't seem like the kind of guy who would do that to his wife and kids."

Annie wiped her eyes and glanced at him hopelessly as she sniffled. "I know, but Lee and Albert saw him with her at a play. She was with him when he died."

"Annie, you know him better than I do. Honestly, do you think that's him?"

Annie grimaced. "Do I think that's him? What's that even mean, Adam? Of course, it's him, Uncle Solomon identified his body!"

Adam chuckled quietly. "No, I mean do you think it's in his character to cheat on you?"

Annie frowned. "I don't know. He's always gone to Branson, and I never worried about it, because I knew he wouldn't. He loved me too much to do that, and I knew it. But we've been fighting for a while now, and things aren't quite like the way they were before. We were talking about getting a divorce, so he wasn't too happily married when he left here. I don't know anymore, Adam. He might have bought more affection than I can give during hay season. All I know is Lee and Albert saw him with her, and she was with him when he died, like I said." She exhaled heavily. "Anyway, maybe I don't want him buried near me when I die after all."

Adam shrugged. "I don't think you have to decide tonight. Sleep on it, and see how you feel in the morning."

Annie nodded. "Do you ever go to Mom's grave? Do you

ever go sit on the bench and talk to her or Grandma and Grandpa?"

Adam shook his head. "No."

"Me either."

Adam took a deep breath. "You didn't know Mom. She was a very sweet lady who loved us all very much. We were her life, and she really wanted a baby girl." Adam's eyes misted over as he finished, "She had one, and she got to hold you while she died. She loved you, and she would be so proud of who you turned out to be. I wish she could meet all of her grandchildren. Maybe she will someday in Heaven. I don't go hang out at her grave because like I said a few minutes ago, she's not there. She's in Heaven, and happier there than she ever was here. Does it matter if you bury Kyle here or in Branson? It might, that's up to you. Something to think about though is, you're still young. What, twenty-eight? The chances are you will get married again, and probably be married for a whole lot longer than you were to Kyle. It's just a thought, but would you rather have him sharing a family plot with you or a husband of forty years?"

"I don't have a husband of forty years, and I am not thinking about getting married twenty-four hours after my husband died either. I know you're just trying to help some-how, but your timing's not very good, Adam."

He smiled and shook his head. "I'm just trying to point out something that you might regret forty or fifty years from now."

Annie frowned. "I wonder if I could worry about that forty or fifty years down the road and not right now? What do you think?"

Adam nodded. "Probably."

"Can we get back to talking about planning his funeral

again? So, would you like to come along with us for some moral support? I'll need my brothers to get through this."

"Matt just left for Sweethome, Idaho a few days ago, so he won't be there."

"He was missing for fifteen years of my life, you weren't. I'm used to him not being here."

Adam nodded. "Of course, I'll be there."

22

The funeral of Kyle Lenning was held in the church Kyle had been raised in, the Branson Baptist Church. The plans were made at the Fasana Funeral Parlor and Furniture Store that was owned by Solomon Fasana, Annie's uncle. It was easily decided that the funeral would be held at the church, but where his body was to be buried was a tougher challenge to compromise on. Kyle's parents sincerely wanted his body buried near their home since he was their only child and all they had. They were getting older and did not want to travel sixteen miles to Willow Falls every time they wanted to be near their son. Their desperation to have his final resting place near them came as a surprise to Annie. She had wanted to bury him in Willow Falls so her children could go to their father's grave if it helped them through the process of mourning. Kyle's parents nearly begged Annie to allow them to bury him in Branson, and Adam's words from the night before came to mind. Kyle wasn't in the funeral parlor, nor would he be buried in Branson or Willow Falls. His body would be, but Kyle was a Christian. He had been drunk when he died, but he was still a Christian and saved by the grace of Jesus Christ. By the very definition of grace, and knowing Kyle's heart for the Lord in the past, she took comfort in knowing he was in Heaven despite his recent actions. Annie remembered when little Catherine had wandered away from her in the hardware store one time. Annie had let her wander, but never took her eyes off her. There were boxes of nails, stacks of jars, and cooking pots that could fall on her, and other hazards that could become dangerous at a moment's notice if Catherine pulled on the wrong rope or climbed on the wrong shelf that wasn't secured to the wall. Despite the dangers, Annie allowed her to walk around, but when Catherine went near the door leading to the busy street, Annie picked her up and carried her back to the safety of the counter where her father was making a purchase. In the same way, the Lord had allowed Kyle to wander away from him, but never let him go. Kyle had made his choices, and because of his own foolishness, he had paid the ultimate cost with his needless death. He would lose his life with his family, and would not walk his two daughters down the aisle on their wedding days, or watch Ira become a man, but he never lost his salvation through the grace of Jesus Christ. Of that, Annie was sure. Not because Kyle was such a Godly man at the time of his death, but simply because of the promises of the Bible and the grace of Jesus Christ.

The truth was, he would not care where he was buried or who was sitting by his grave talking to a piece of granite with his name on it. He wouldn't know or care who obsessed over the condition of his grave or who urinated on it. For him, the Earth no longer mattered and he was joyfully waiting for his loved ones to join him in the Lord's presence to experience Heaven with him. If Kyle's parents wanted to obsess over a piece of stone, Annie would let them. She had children to raise and would teach them that their father was in Heaven, not in the ground.

"Fine," Annie had said. "We can bury him here in Branson. It's not like he's really there anyway."

"Are you sure, Annie?" Mary Fasana asked her niece.

Annie smiled and looked at her aunt sincerely. "I really am. It's okay."

AFTER THE FUNERAL, there was a reception in the Branson Community Hall. It was the only place large enough to accommodate the many people who came to the funeral and reception. The Branson Community Hall was built as a community dance and meeting hall that was owned by the city and rented out for various events, including funeral receptions. Kyle had attended *Romeo and Juliet* there.

Lee Bannister, like everyone else, was downstairs with family and friends, enjoying the food and iced tea supplied by the Monarch Restaurant. He was talking to his Uncle Luther and a few other men about the building they were standing in. "We had to change the name of this building because it was confusing people to have the Branson Dance Hall and the new Bella's Dance Hall over on Rose Street. The problem we had in the city council was finding a name for this place. We couldn't seem to agree on one." He smiled. "I wanted to buy it, change the name to the Monarch Hall, and open it—after some upgrades, of course. The rest of the city council didn't want to sell it." He shrugged. "I don't know why they won't. It doesn't bring in much income for the city."

Sheriff Tim Wright suggested, "They should've named it the No Whores Here Dance Hall. That might've ended the confusion." He chuckled.

Lee shook his head. "It's not metropolitan enough, Tim. Respectful is what we were shooting for on the city council, so we changed the name from the Branson Dance Hall to the Branson Community Hall."

"Oh, just raise your price a bit, and I'm sure they will sell it," Tim suggested.

"No," Luther said slowly. "They don't want Lee to own more of the city than the city does."

Lee smiled. "I'll build my own hall in a year or two. I really like the sound of the Monarch Hall. It would double as an opera house. We don't have one of those, and that play we went to would have been better in a real theater. Don't you think?"

Tim agreed with a nod as he watched Annie walk toward them. Her sadness was plain to see, even though she tried to smile at the people who gave her their condolences and quick hugs as she passed them. "Lee and Uncle Luther, the kids and I will be leaving pretty quick with Uncle Charlie and Aunt Mary. We're going to go back home. I just wanted to give you two a hug before we leave."

Luther shook his head sadly and said, "Get over here, kid." He held her in his big arms for a few minutes. "Love you, girl. You'll be all right, yeah?" he asked as he looked into her eyes.

She smiled slightly and wiped her eyes. "I will be."

Tim spoke as Annie broke from her uncle's arms. "Annie, again, I am so sorry about your husband."

"Thank you," she replied and turned her attention to Lee. She gave him a hug in silence. She just held him. "Love you, brother," she said as she stepped out of his arms.

"Love you, too. If you need anything at all, don't hesitate to ask, okay?"

Annie smiled. "You've done enough, and thank you."

"Excuse me, Annie," Kyle's best friend Sam Troyer said nervously.

"What are you doing here?" Tim asked sharply. His friendliness left upon seeing them.

Paul Johnson answered before Sam could, "It's our friend's funeral." He didn't sound pleased to see the sheriff either.

Annie turned to look at the two men with no emotion on her face except a hint of contempt. She had seen them at the funeral but had intentionally avoided them. She had nothing to say to the two so-called friends who allowed her husband to cheat on her and kill himself with his alcohol consumption. As far as she knew, these two men encouraged him to live the kind of free and easy lifestyle they lived.

Sam continued speaking directly to her. "Annie, you have no idea how sorry we are. He was our lifelong friend you know, and—"

Annie could not help herself. Her pent-up rage came to the surface, and her moist eyes turned hostile. "Yes, I know! So, tell me Sam, are you and Paul here to apologize for running wild with my husband? For going to a play with your ladyfriends and setting my husband up with one your whores? For getting him drunk and having a great time without one thought of his wife and children until he falls off a cliff and dies? Now you have the gall to stand here and apologize like it's going to mean something to me? You're sorry for yourselves because Kyle won't be coming around anymore and buying your drinks!

"Don't stand here and pretend you were his friends! A friend would have told him to go home to his family, not gone to a play and then to the island to drink and have an orgy in the firelight! With my husband? You two make me sick! Now get away from me, because you're not welcome here. And don't ever talk to me again!" Her eyes blazed at them dangerously.

Sam was dumbfounded. He froze momentarily with his mouth open, unable to speak after listening to Annie's scathing words, which had been spoken too loud not to be overheard by everyone in the room. "Uh…"

"Sam," Lee said calmly, "I need you and Paul to leave, please."

Paul scoffed and shook his head in disbelief. "Let's go," he said to Sam and took a step toward the door. Sam hesitated and turned back to Annie. He held up his hands as a shield toward Lee. "Give me just one minute. Annie, I don't know what you've heard because there's a lot of rumors going around that are not true, but Kyle never cheated on you."

Sheriff Wright spoke in a threatening tone. "That's enough, Sam. She already asked you to leave. Let's go," he said, and tried to guide him outside by grabbing Sam's arm.

Paul urged Sam, "She isn't going to believe you. Let's just go."

"Let me go!" Sam pulled away from the sheriff defiantly. "Don't touch me, you piece of…"

"I'm warning you to leave right now! Not another word or you know what's going to happen…" Sheriff Wright's unspoken threat caused Sam to pause for a moment before he looked at the sheriff and said, "Go to hell! Does anyone know the kind of crap you're doing around here? You stay the hell away from Helen, you sick son of a bitch! You can arrest me, but you stay away from her!"

"One more word and it's done!" the sheriff said coldly. His expression showed his growing animosity, along with a slight touch of anxiety hidden within his eyes, like a trapped rat.

Sam took a deep breath and sighed. He looked at Annie with an angry expression. When he saw she was taken aback by the confrontation with the sheriff, his expression softened. "Annie, there's more to the story than you know." He looked at the sheriff with disgust and changed his direction. "I can tell you with all honesty and God as my witness that Kyle never to my knowledge cheated on you. There was no orgy or anything of the sort that night."

"Hmm." Tim cleared his throat noticeably.

"Who's the girl, then?" Annie asked pointedly, "and why was she all over my husband? Lee saw them, so it isn't a damn rumor!"

"Her name's Christine, and she's just a dancer at the dance hall. There was nothing going on between them other than going to the play."

"Really?" Tim asked. "I saw them there too, and they looked pretty comfortable, in my opinion. And she was pretty upset out on the island."

Sam looked at Tim strangely and shook his head. "You're such a..."

"Actually," Tim said quickly, "I'll see you two outside. We can go to my office and discuss some unanswered questions about another investigation I am doing that's best not discussed in present company. So, Annie, take care my dear, and Lee, I will talk to you soon. Let's go, Sam."

Lee nodded.

"Annie, honestly," Sam tried to say, but Annie interrupted.

"I really don't care what you have to say, Sam. I just don't," she said with finality and began to walk away

Sam continued as he fought to break away from the sheriff again, "I don't know what you heard, but he never cheated on you, not one time in all the years I knew him, ever! He loved you too much for that! I don't know what you've heard about Christine, but the truth is she is our friend, and she had no interest in Kyle. She isn't a whore, she was just avoiding another man at the play, and that's the only reason she held onto Kyle's arm that night.

"She was only there because she thought Kyle might introduce her to Matt, but he isn't in town. Oh, it's true Kyle was drinking too much and being an ass that night and saying things he didn't mean, and things he has never said before. But I think that's because you two had been in a fight. Annie, all Kyle wanted while he was laying there dying was you. He wanted you, that's all." He paused as a tear slipped out of his eyes. "And that's all I wanted to tell you. He was my friend, and I love him too. But he wanted me to tell you he loved you and he's sorry most of all."

Sheriff Wright wrapped an arm around Sam's neck and squeezed it while he began to drag Sam backward toward the door. "Let's go!"

Paul yelled at the sheriff, "Let him go! We're leaving, okay? No one's going to ruin your party, just let him go!"

"Let him go, Tim!" Annie called. She raised her voice when he didn't. "Tim, I said let him go!"

Sheriff Wright paused. "Annie, you don't want this street trash in here looking for a free meal and..."

Paul scoffed in disgust. "You're one to talk!" he said to the sheriff. He turned to Annie. "What Sam said is true. Kyle died Sam's arms, so he knows what Kyle's last words were. He wanted you. It's my personal impression that he was sorry for being here in town with us. He had been acting weird the whole time he was here, but in hindsight, I believe it was the fear of losing you that made him act uncharacteristically. He loved you, and wanted me to go get you. You're all he asked for, not a doctor, not a drink, not anything except for you. And he asked Jesus to forgive him too, but he was sorry."

Annie stood in the middle of the floor and bit her lip as hard as she could so as not to cry, but her eyes filled with water and her breathing became heavy. "He never cheated on me?"

Paul answered irritably, "Not by a mile! You were his life, Annie. In case you're ever wondering, his last words were to tell you he was sorry for missing your birthday. It bothered him that he wasn't with you, and I know that because he mentioned it a few times during the night." He shrugged emotionally as he squeezed his lips together to fight his own tears. "That's why he was drinking so heavily. He had forgotten it was your birthday, and it bothered him a lot. He wasn't going anywhere except back home to ask you to forgive him, I am sure. You were all he ever wanted all these years."

"So, this Christine meant nothing to him?" she asked.

Paul gave a short chuckle. "No. After your argument, he was upset, and maybe it seemed like his world was beginning to fall apart. In desperation, I think he tried to grab onto anything that seemed to bring some stability to it, like the Green Toad Saloon. He didn't know Christine, and to be honest, she couldn't stand him. Like I said, you were the only person who mattered to him." He saw Kyle's three children standing near their mother and added, "You and them. He loved you all more than anything."

Annie closed her eyes with the relief of a burden that had nagged at her heart for the three days since his death. "Thank you," she said weakly.

Mellissa walked up beside her and gave her a hug, and Annie began to sob. "You're going to be okay," Mellissa said.

"I didn't tell him I loved him when he left," Annie said into Mellissa's shoulder.

"He knew," Mellissa said gently. "He knew."

Sam spoke sincerely. "Annie, he's always known that. Again, I am so sorry we couldn't stop him. It just happened so fast. Much love to you and your family," he said, and began walking toward the door to follow the sheriff outside. At the door, he paused to speak to Annie's friend Rory Jackson as she stood with her father and Charlie and Mary Ziegler. "Miss Jackson, I am almost nine years too late, but I want to apologize for being rude and out of line with you at Kyle and Annie's wedding."

The sorrow on Rory's face was obvious since Kyle was a part of her family too. She smiled slightly and nodded her appreciation. "Thank you. You're forgiven."

Sam nodded and stepped toward the door under the watching eyes of many of Annie's family and friends. He stopped when he heard Annie call his name. He turned around to look at her. She stood with Mellissa in the middle of the room. "Yeah?"

"Thank you."

Sam smiled sadly, turned back around, and followed Paul outside wordlessly.

Annie looked at Mellissa and said, "He never cheated on me after all."

Mellissa smiled. "I never thought he would. I met that Christine girl, and I don't know what it was about her, but you could tell she wasn't that way. I liked her, and I think you would too."

Annie shook her head with a grimace. "Don't push it. However, Paul did say she couldn't stand Kyle, so I guess we have that in common sometimes," Annie said in a feeble attempt at a joke. She smiled sadly, but it was a smile.

"Are you going to be okay?" Mellissa asked.

Annie nodded as she looked around at her family and friends. "Yeah. I think so. I'll be all right. It's unfortunate we left on bad terms and said the things we did, but it's comforting to know that he knew I loved him and to know he loved me. I can live with knowing that. Now, when I get to Heaven, I'm going to slap the heavenly snot out of him for dying on my birthday , but until then I'll just get stronger so it hurts him all the more when I do!"

She laughed at her own joke, then took a deep breath and sighed as she looked around at the people who had come to say their goodbyes to Kyle. "Thank you, everyone, for coming. You'll never know how much I appreciate it. Now, if you'll excuse me, I have to go home and focus on building a horse company."

The End

EPILOGUE

Branson, Oregon
Three weeks later

CHRISTINE KNAPP WAS SCARED. During the weeks since Kyle Lenning's death, the Branson sheriff had changed his official verdict from accidental death to homicide, and Christine was the prime suspect. His report had been written with excerpts from her statements and those of her friends. The rest of the statements were either falsified or blatant lies.

As for witnesses, there seemed to be more eyewitnesses than there had been people on the island when the accident happened. She was being set up to take an unjustified fall, and there wasn't a reasonable explanation for it until the sheriff came by Bella's Dance Hall to talk privately. Tim Wright sat smugly in Bella's chair behind her desk, staring at Bella and Christine, confident that he had every outcome covered and had gained full control to bend them to his desire. He addressed Bella first and gave her a simple choice:

either pay him three hundred dollars a month, or he'd ruin her business.

First, he would arrest all three of her employees who were present at Kyle's death and prosecute them to the full extent of the law. But the consequences of not paying him what he wanted didn't end there. He promised to submit a formal complaint to the city council along with documentation of the many crimes, acts of lewdness, and resident complaints against her business in the past two months. None of it was true, but that didn't matter. He had the means and witnesses to make it all appear real, and the so-called evidence appeared to be overwhelming. The city council would lean toward whatever the sheriff asked, since his best friend Josh Slater was on the council, as were Josh's father and sister. It was a family monopoly on a board of seven, and with the vote of Kyle's brother-in-law Lee, it would be a sure thing.

They were powerful enough to petition the U.S. Government to make Matt Bannister a U.S. Marshal in a matter of months, so there was no doubt that Sheriff Tim Wright was in good standing and could easily manipulate the law to do his will whenever he wanted to. He could have them raise Bella's license fee substantially or close her down. He could run her out of town, or fabricate charges against her or her husband and arrest them. He was backed by the most corrupt city government Bella had ever seen, and there was no way that she could see to stop him.

Bella put up a fight, but the simple fact was that Tim had covered his bases well and made up a convincing file with witnesses to back up his every claim. Tim could sit behind Bella's desk and blackmail her confidently, and Bella had no choice but to pay the money or lose everything she had, including the lives of three of her ladies. If it wasn't for the threat against Christine, Edith, and Helen, Bella might have told Tim to go to hell, but because of that threat, she agreed to comply with his terms. Once Bella agreed, Tim asked her to leave the room and go get his first monthly payment while he talked to Christine in private. Tears of fierce anger burned in Bella's eyes as she let go of Christine's hand and left her office like an excused child given a humiliating chore to do.

Tim Wright leaned back in the chair, put his hands behind his head, and crossed his feet on top of Bella's desk. Once he was comfortable, he smiled at Christine like a child eyeing a rare chocolate candy his mother was purchasing. He took a deep breath and spoke through his smile. "Christine, I want you to know that I have discovered enough evidence to put you and your two friends in prison for years. Murder is a very serious offense—"

"We didn't murder anyone, and you know it!" Christine stated sharply. The fear that pounded within her heart was quickly becoming panic, and she could barely control it. She was terrified to know the reason he was talking to her in private, shutting out Bella and her two friends. He had not even asked to see Edith or Helen, and it was becoming clear that they were merely innocent pawns to get what he wanted.

"Oh, I know," Tim said. "But that doesn't change the fact that you don't stand a chance in hell of proving your innocence against all of my witnesses. I have covered every possible angle, and you will lose if you try to fight me in a court of law. Even worse, your two friends will rot in prison all because you wanted to fight me rather than just do as I say." He shrugged. "I have enough evidence to arrest you and your friends right now, so...shall we make a deal, or do you want me to proceed with a criminal case?"

His offer to Christine wasn't as monetary as Bella's. She would be required you to "work" for the sheriff in a Monarch Hotel room every other Saturday night, or whenever she was summoned to host him or one of his special friends who paid him a good price to be with her. In other words, he was blackmailing her into becoming his private prostitute or face years, if not life, in the Oregon State Hospital where the female offenders served their prison terms for the murder of Kyle Lenning.

Christine was given no choice but to submit to his demands. She too would have told him to go to hell, had it not been the threat against her friends, who were as innocent as her. He wrote a date on a piece of paper and handed it to her, directing her to meet him at the Monarch Hotel at eight o'clock that evening.

The first Saturday night she was supposed to go to meet him at the Monarch Hotel, her desperation to get out of the nightmare led her to lie and sent a message to Tim earlier in the day needing to cancel because she was beginning her menstrual cycle. It wasn't true, but it saved her from prostituting herself for a few days if nothing else. That had been the week before, and today she had gotten a message telling her to be at the Monarch Hotel at eight o'clock tonight with no excuses.

If she didn't show up, she would be arrested immediately and charged with murder. It was now one o'clock in the afternoon, and she just opened another envelope addressed to her. It was from Travis McKnight.

It read:

You'll earn every dollar I ever paid tonight, my love. See you later, beautiful.

- Travis and friends

. . .

THERE WAS no way out of it, but she was desperate for any escape she could find. She had money, over two thousand dollars saved up in the bank. She could disappear on a stagecoach to anywhere but here, but the sheriff made it very clear if she ran, it wouldn't be him that tracked her down but the deadly U.S. Marshal Matt Bannister, who was already hungry to get hold of the person who had killed a member of his family. The sheriff made it clear that Matt would not have any mercy on her.

Every option she thought of only led to further discouragement, and the desperation of between being forced to choose between prison or prostitution mounted. Neither option was more appealing than the other, but there was no way out of choosing.

The only thing she could think of doing was praying to the Lord for a way out of this dreadful and evil blackmail scheme she was being victimized by. She had been praying from the beginning, and yet, nothing had changed. The situation had only grown more desperate, and time was growing shorter. Her values, integrity, self-respect, and all that she was were only seven hours away from being stolen by the highest bidder. It scared her to death, and there was nothing Bella or any of her friends could do about it.

They had tried every avenue for help, and they all had come to a dead end. Bella even considered closing the dance hall and moving on to protect Christine from the wickedness of this town, but the arrest warrant would follow her and her two friends wherever they went. The corruption of Branson knew no bounds, and when one of the good ole boys wanted to play, the rules were changed to play their way.

Christine's personal creed had always been "Walk by faith, not by sight," but this time a situation had come up where the sight was overwhelming and closing in quickly. As each second ticked away on her large mantel clock, the walls of "sight" closed in on her. She knew all too well that when prostitutes were used up, they were thrown away like a dirty rag.

The question that ran through her mind was, would the sheriff release her from the shackles of his slavery when he was through with her, or would he have her arrested and sentenced to prison just so he'd never have to see at her again? She was not a slave per se, but she knew she was no longer free either. She was owned by Tim Wright, and was only hours from being bought and sold with no say as to whom or how many times. She would get nothing from it, except an unwanted child perhaps, or a disease she'd never be able to get rid of.

It made her sick to her stomach just thinking about it, and she ran to her washbowl on the vanity, leaned over it, and vomited. Her nerves and panic felt like they were going to make her heart explode and kill her where she stood. In a way, she hoped her heart *would* explode and end her nightmare before it became reality.

A knock on the door pulled her from her thoughts and the bowl of vomit she was holding in her hands. She wiped her mouth with a rag, and then the tears from her eyes. "Yes?" she asked.

It was the young dancer, Rebecca. "Miss Christine, there's a man here to see you," she said nervously.

Christine closed her eyes as a sinking feeling swept through her. "Who is it?" she asked, although she was afraid to find out.

"The marshal, Matt Bannister. He wants to talk to you downstairs," Rebecca replied, sounding very worried.

A glimmer of hope shot through Christine. If she was

arrested by the marshal, she wouldn't be able to go to the Monarch Hotel tonight. Who was she kidding? The Monarch Hotel belonged to Matt's brother, and they were a tight-knit group of friends. Perhaps the marshal just wanted to get a look at her to see how much he wanted to bid for the night. She was accused of killing his brother in law. What other reason would he want to talk to her? Whatever the purpose of his visit, it wouldn't be good.

"Tell him I'll be down in a minute," she said. She felt like vomiting again, but instead went to her bed and got down on her knees and prayed for what seemed to be the ten-thousandth time, but this time the need was desperate. "Lord, please help me! You know I had nothing to do with Kyle's death, but I'm going to..." She began to sob, and her body shook. "I'm going to be sent to prison if you don't help me. I didn't do anything wrong, Jesus. I am scared to death, and the marshal is downstairs waiting. Lord, I am so afraid!"

She breathed in sharply before continuing as if in a panic, "I don't want... I'm afraid he'll drag me out of here to the hotel, and I don't want to be...a prostitute. Oh Lord, help me! I don't have the strength to continue doing this. If I refuse to give myself away like a prostitute, I'll go to prison. So will Edith and Helen, and they've done nothing to deserve it. All I ask is that I'm the one who suffers, not anyone else, if it must be. Jesus, I am scared to death, and the marshal scares me more than anything. He's a cold man, and I don't know what he'll do now that he thinks I killed Mister Lenning.

"Jesus, I am asking you to be with me and give me the strength to face the marshal and... I don't know, just help me, please. I trust you, despite the fear that's tearing me up from the inside out. I can't keep anything down, I'm so scared of what's going to happen."

She paused to take a needed breath. "The Bible says I'm your daughter. Oh, God, protect me like your daughter. If I am arrested tonight, let it be because it's your will and not because of the wickedness of this town's men. I have no alternative but to trust you, Jesus, and that's all I know. Be with me, and I pray you'll protect me somehow. In Jesus' name, Amen."

She opened her eyes slowly and wiped away the tears, then took a deep breath and got up to put on a dress. She looked at herself in the mirror and ran her brush through her long, straight hair until she looked presentable. She took a deep breath and exhaled to calm her nerves. "Okay, Lord, let's go face the marshal."

MATT BANNISTER STOOD in the entrance of the new Dance Hall, looking at the hardwood dance floor surrounded by tables and chairs, a bar, and a stage at the far end of the building. Other than the young girl who answered the door for him, the dance hall seemed empty. He waited patiently with his gun belt on and carried a folder in his hand. He was dressed in dark pants and a tan button-up shirt, and had his U.S. Marshal's badge pinned to the left breast. His sleeves were rolled up almost to his elbows. His long dark hair was in a ponytail, and his beard and mustache were neatly trimmed. He had hung his brown hat on a hook in the entry. He walked into the ballroom and stood alone in the center of the dance floor. His wait seemed longer than he was expecting, but then he heard from behind him, "May I help you?"

Matt turned around and froze momentarily as his eyes beheld the most beautiful woman he'd ever seen. It was the same woman he had been scrutinized by as she walked past his office two months before. He could not take his eyes off her then, and he found it difficult to do so now. Her thick black hair was long, falling to her lower back, and her soft oval face was matched only by her beautiful brown eyes. She was simply stunning in a white dress with black-piped seams and ruffles. For a minute, he was speechless, and his eyes refused to leave hers. The one thing he noticed was that she no longer had the bright and lively fire in her eyes like she'd had when he'd first seen her. Now they were dull, hopeless, and hardening. "Um, I'm waiting for a Miss Christine Knapp," he said.

"I'm Christine," she said with no emotion on her face. Any hopes of impressing or even meeting the handsome marshal were gone. She knew he had no interest in her other than that which the law could prosecute or the sheriff might broker.

"Oh," Matt said awkwardly. "I'm Matt Bannister, the U.S. Marshal here in town—"

"I know who you are," she interrupted him rudely. "How can I help you?" Her response had been sharp and angry.

"Is there someplace we could talk in private? I have some questions I would like to ask you."

Christine looked around the empty dance hall and raised her arms with a shrug. "No one's here. Isn't this private enough?"

Matt eyed her, slightly irritated by her rudeness. "I would prefer a smaller enclosure, like an office perhaps?"

"Not my bedroom?" she asked scornfully.

Matt frowned. She had appeared before to be far more dignified than a prostitute. His disappointment showed in his voice, "No, that won't be necessary. An office with a desk and a chair, perhaps, would be more appropriate. We could go to my office if you don't have one here."

"We have an office. Follow me. So, what is this all about, Marshal? Are you going to be at the Monarch Hotel tonight too?" she asked bitterly.

Matt frowned, unaware of any events happening at the hotel that evening. "No, I don't intend to be. Why do you ask? Are you singing there tonight? I understand you're quite a singer."

"No, I haven't felt like singing much lately," she said as she opened the office door and waited for Matt to enter. "So, what *is* this all about? Go ahead and sit behind the desk. Bella's out shopping. Are you here to arrest me, or is this a proposition?"

Matt took a seat behind the big desk and laid the file down and opened it, ignoring her questions. "Please have a seat," he said, and waited for her to sit down in one of the chairs facing the desk. He could see she held great animosity toward him, but he couldn't understand why. "Miss Knapp, I just wanted to ask you if you knew my brother-in-law, Kyle Lenning? I understand you were with him the night he died?"

Christine sighed. "No, I didn't know him, and you already know I was there with my friends when he died. I didn't push Kyle over the edge, and I didn't kill your brother-in-law! I know it doesn't matter, but just for the record, I had nothing to do with his death."

Matt looked at her, plainly irritated by her rudeness. "You're right, I do know that. I'm afraid I was over in Sweethome, Idaho when this happened, but I read the file prepared by Sheriff Wright—"

Christine interrupted quickly, "The sheriff made up that whole damn story in front of you." She waved her hand at the sheriff's report that was on the desk.

Matt ignored her and continued, "It paints a pretty good

picture of what happened that night, and it looks to me like you're the cause of Kyle's demise. I don't think any jury in the world would acquit you, the way it's written here."

The fear she felt came to the surface, and she began to sob into her hands.

"Do you have anything to say about it?" he asked, watching her carefully.

Christine dropped her hands to her lap and spoke urgently through her tears. "I swear to you on the Lord's word that I had nothing to do with him jumping off that bank! He was drunk and dove off the bank with his own two feet into the river. Everybody who was there said the same thing, but the sheriff lied!

"But I'm sure you already know that or you wouldn't be here. So why *are* you here? Now that you've seen me, you can go back and make your damn deal, okay? I'll be there tonight, so please leave!" she yelled in a desperate combination of fear and anger that didn't go unnoticed. She replaced her hands over her face and wept bitterly.

Matt leaned forward in the chair, resting his hands on the desk and watching at her closely without saying a word for a moment. He frowned and asked softly, "Tell me, why would he go to all the trouble to lie about this?"

Christine lifted her head to glare at Matt through her reddened eyes, then shouted angrily through her tears, "Why are you doing this to me? Why? For crying out loud, just arrest me if you want to, or take me to the hotel, but stop playing games! Please! Maybe I'd be better off if I just killed myself." She began sobbing into her hands again. She muttered the words, "Lord, I can't do this anymore," in a high-pitched, weak voice.

Matt frowned and felt his own eyes grow moist at the torment that visibly ate at Christine's soul. "Miss Knapp, I'm afraid I don't understand what you're talking about. Please tell me why he'd lie. What's his motivation?" Matt asked quietly.

"To blackmail us!" she exclaimed as she wiped her eyes. "He's blackmailing Bella and...me," she said as another tear fell from her eyes.

"How so?" Matt asked, his eyes hardening.

She reached into a hidden pocket of her dress, pulled out a calling card, and handed it to Matt. "It came about an hour ago."

Matt read the typed card. "Travis...McKnight?"

"How'd you guess?" she asked with disgust.

Matt nodded. "Miss Knapp... May I call you Christine?"

She nodded.

"Christine, last spring, when I first came here and opened my office, Kyle stopped by the office and introduced me to his two friends Sam and Paul. Over the months, I've seen them from time and time and said hello. They seem like good men to me, hardworking and honest men. I've been meaning to talk to them since I've been back, but I wanted to talk to you first. My sister told me that at Kyle's funeral reception, Sam and Paul mentioned rumors that weren't true, and that there seemed to be some level of hostility between them and the sheriff. Do you know what the source is? I mean, your two friends, according to this report, are romantically tied to those guys. Is that true, and what's happening there? I must tell you, I read this report when I got back a few days ago and it didn't add up for me.

"I found it odd for a sheriff who barely does his own job to spend all his energy doing mine, and then he didn't want to give the file to me. When there was a couple murdered and their bodies burned in a cabin up in the mountains, he showed no interest in solving that case." He shrugged. "So on my way over here, I went to talk to a man named Andrew O'Riley, who is listed as a credible eye-witness. It didn't take too much pressure for him to admit that he owed the sheriff some money and his testimony was his payment." He paused to swallow, then pointed a finger at her as he spoke. "This whole report about Kyle really is a lie, isn't it?" He didn't mention that Annie had told him Sam said Christine was with Kyle because she had hoped to meet him.

Christine's eyes held Matt's, hope creeping onto her face. "You believe me?" she asked skeptically.

Matt nodded. "Now, I'm asking you, what does he want from you ladies here, and what did he say would happen if you refused?"

Christine began to cry again with her face buried in her hands. She was relieved and gratified to finally hear someone with some sort of power say he believed her.

Matt asked again, "What does he want?"

Christine looked at Matt with the tears smeared across her face. "He said I would go to prison for killing Mister Lenning if I...didn't show up at the Monarch Hotel tonight. I am not a whore, Marshal Bannister. I swear I'm not. I've never been with anyone other than my husband! I sing, and I dance, but that's all I do! I am scared to death to go tonight, but I don't have a choice. I don't want to go to prison either," she said weakly as she began to cry again.

Matt looked back at the note from Travis and asked her, "If I may ask, how do you know Travis? This note seems a bit personal, if you will."

Christine sighed and wiped away her tears silently as an expression of disgust crossed her face. "He lied to me. He said his wife had passed away a year ago." She paused and then looked at Matt in the eyes. "We were courting until I found out about his wife."

Matt frowned. "Just so you know, he lied to me too. I came in here a month or two ago, and he said you were a prostitute and had given three of his employees syphilis."

Christine gasped in disbelief. "That bastard! Well, that's interesting, because he told me *you* had syphilis! I remember you coming in here, and he told me you left because he told you we weren't prostitutes. He said you preferred prostitutes, and even forced yourself on women who weren't."

Matt smirked but had an irritated look in his eyes. "Even with syphilis, huh?"

She shrugged. "He said you hated women."

Matt nodded as he thought back to that night. He had come with the intent of meeting Christine, but Travis had lied to him. Travis had then lied to Christine about him, all in a deceptive ploy to keep her for himself. Matt could feel his jaw tighten, angered by the very idea of it.

He took a deep breath. "Christine...Miss, I'll tell you right now that you don't have to go anywhere tonight or any other night. I will go in your place, and I promise you will never be bothered by Sheriff Wright or Travis again. If you are, if he tries to intimidate you, just come to my office and tell me. That's an open invitation for anything at any time. My door will always be open. Okay?"

She looked at him in disbelief. "You'll help me?"

Matt nodded, "Of course. From this moment on, you are free from any threats he has made. The sheriff's a little porcelain snarling tiger paperweight, meaning he might put on a good front, but he's weak. Just so you know, I will personally take care of him and Travis and anyone else who's involved in this, and I probably won't be very nice about it. I don't have syphilis, by the way, nor do I..." He paused to shake his head in irritation. "I prefer to remain celibate for my wife someday. I'm a Christian, Christine. I'll help any prostitute on the street as much as I can, but I'm not a customer. He lied to you about that, too."

She smiled as she stared at Matt. "I know. Kyle said you weren't like that at all. He said you were a Christian."

Matt looked down at the file uncomfortably. "Kyle was a good man. So, I must ask, is the sheriff trying to set up hotel dates for your friends, too? What was the hostility between the guys and the sheriff all about at the funeral, do you know?"

Christine shook her head. "No, just me. The sheriff threatened to prosecute my friends Edith and Helen if I refused to be his...personal prostitute. That was why the guys were upset. If they mentioned it to anyone, they would lose the ladies they love. Trust me, the sheriff had his bases covered. He is blackmailing Bella for three hundred dollars a month too, or he will make another file up to ruin her business, and we three will be arrested if she doesn't pay. I had a choice..." She paused and swallowed. "Life in prison with my two friends, or...show up whenever he sent for me."

"His own high-priced lady of the evening, huh?"

She nodded. "I suppose so. Do understand, Marshal—"

"Matt. Call me Matt," he said with a warm smile.

"Matt. Well, do understand I have never been with any man other than my husband. I'm a Christian and believe sex comes after marriage too, so I was horrified. The only reason I would even consider showing up is because of my two friends and Bella. She saved my life and has treated me like a daughter. Bella only wants the best for all of us, and Helen and Edith are very close to getting married and starting a whole new life. I couldn't live with myself if they were sent to prison because of me. I had no choice."

Matt nodded. "I understand. Where is your husband now, if I might ask?"

Christine frowned. "Heaven. He was stabbed in Denver. We were coming west when he was killed. That is how I came across Bella. She heard about it, and came to offer me a job dancing. I have high morals, Matt. I really do."

Matt smiled as he looked at her. "I have no doubt about that." He stood up from the desk. "If you don't mind me saying so, in the future stay away from Travis, Sheriff Wright, and if by chance their third wheel, a man named Josh Slater, shows up, stay away from him too. They are a tight little bunch that I have come to call the three trolls for a good reason. They are not good men."

"Trust me, I will never talk to any of them again if I can help it! But thank you. I just can't believe it. I have been praying so long for a miracle," she said with an unbelieving sense of joy that lit her eyes and face with an unnatural glow, or so it seemed to Matt as he watched her with a smile. The beautiful young lady he had seen in an ostrich hat with bright, cheerful eyes had just come to life in front of him.

"The Lord protects His own. I suppose that's why the Bible says to walk by faith and not by sight, huh?"

She looked at him, stunned that he'd repeat the words she had clung to all this time. She smiled through the tears that filled her eyes again. "Yes. That's what I have been telling myself all along," She looked upwards and said, "Thank you, Jesus, thank you!" She began to weep again with relief.

Matt stepped forward and knelt in front of her, and he touched her arm. "Miss Christine, my new friend, you have a good night and get some rest. Premro Island is in my juris-diction, and that means all of this," he reached behind him and grabbed the file off the desk and held it up in front of her, "is garbage. You and your friends have nothing to fear anymore."

"Thank you!" she whispered, and then lurched forward to hug him. "Thank you!"

"It is my pleasure." He found himself holding her, and not understanding the sensation he was feeling. He had just met and started a new relationship with an attractive lady from Sweethome, Idaho named Felisha Conway.

He broke the hug and stood up. "I will see myself out."

"Please," she said, grabbing his arm. "Come back one of these nights and dance with me. It would honor me."

Matt smiled. "One of these nights, I might just do that. Until then, feel free to come by my office anytime. Even just to talk."

"I will. And thank you again. May God bless you, Marshal Bannister."

He smiled. "Matt. If we're going to be friends, you have to call me Matt. And God already has blessed me, Christine. Far more than I deserve."

"Me too," Christine said with a smile. "He just waited until the last moment. I am so thankful. Thank you, Matt. I owe you so much for helping me."

Matt shook his head. "You don't owe me anything. It's my pleasure. The Lord sometimes does wait until the last moment to help us. I guess that's why we are supposed to be faithful enough to live by faith and not by sight." He smiled. "It was nice to meet you, Christine."

Christine stood and looked at Matt awkwardly in thought. "Bible verses are nice to quote, but it's easy to forget that we have to live them, huh?"

Matt nodded. "You know it. I tell people all the time to read their Bible and build a deeper relationship with the Lord, but those Bible verses people quote mean nothing if you don't believe in them enough to live them, even when it's hard to do. I'll see you later tonight and let you know how it went with Sheriff Wright and Travis."

Christine smiled. "Thanks to you, I'll be dancing until midnight. If you want to talk, you can come by afterward when it's quieter, or you can come dance with me."

"To be honest, I'm not much of a dancer, but I'll see you later tonight."

MATT LOITERED in the hallway of the fourth floor of the Monarch Hotel, looking at his pocket watch every few seconds, it seemed, as he waited for it to be eight o'clock exactly. He had checked with the front desk clerk, and the only room rented on the fourth floor was engaged by Tim Wright. At eight o'clock, Matt knocked lightly on the door, clenched his teeth, and gripped his Winchester rifle tighter when he heard multiple men's laughter from inside of the room.

When the door opened, Tim Wright had an expectant smile on his face and a drink in his hand. He said, "Come on in, sweet... Matt?"

Matt kicked Tim Wright in the testicles with his right foot as hard as he could. Tim immediately bent over in agony, and Matt stepped forward and brought his rifle butt down on Tim's head as hard as he could. Tim reeled out of control and fell on his back beside the bed, then rolled onto his side in a fetal position and passed out. He still moaned painfully, but it sounded more like short grunts since he couldn't catch his breath from the blow to his groin.

Travis McKnight was standing close to Matt's right side, holding a glass of brandy. "What the hell?" he demanded as he listened to his friend Tim sounding like he was choking on his own blood.

Matt, in a continuous motion, stepped to his side and rammed the rifle's butt into Travis's forehead. The blow sent Travis across the room and down to his back with an open a gash on his forehead that began to bleed profusely. He laid there stunned by the blow and held his forehead. Matt then turned to look at Josh Slater with hard eyes.

Josh remained seated in a decorative chair in the corner of the elegant room. He was watching him with concern in his eyes but tried to hide it with a fake coy smile. "Don't even think about touching me, Matt. I'm far above you, and you know it."

Sheriff Tim Wright came to, sat up, and looked at Matt over the bed. He demanded through the pain in his groin, "What the hell is your problem, Matt? You just about split my head open! I didn't do anything to you!"

"What's my problem, you sick son of a bitch?" Matt switched his attention from Josh back to Tim. "You falsified a report to blackmail an innocent girl to become your whore! What kind of a man does that? You don't deserve to wear that badge, you sick bastard!"

Tim stood up slowly, using the bed to help him, then bent over to put his hands on his knees to recover from the kick to his testicles. Blood dripped from the back of his head to the floor. "She killed your brother in law."

"No, she didn't!" Matt shouted. "I checked your story out, and you're a liar. A straight-up lie to blackmail and intimidate innocent people is all it is! Trust me, I will bring this up to the city council and petition for your immediate removal as sheriff!"

Josh Slater smirked arrogantly from his chair and then chuckled. "Matt, I am on the board, and so is my father and sister, so for all practical purposes, Tim isn't going anywhere. But I do suggest you calm down. Tim investigated a crime, and the evidence says she's guilty. She's choosing—how should I say it?—community service rather than a conviction, and *that's* just the way it is. Now I suggest you send her up here like we planned before you get on my bad side."

Matt looked at Josh Slater with a sigh and lowered his head. "Maybe you're right, Josh. I should probably apologize to you gentlemen for this great misunderstanding," he said calmly, sounding nearly apologetic. He stepped toward Josh and laid his rifle on top of a vanity set against the wall. He continued in the same apologetic tone, "Sometimes I just don't see the whole picture and react—how should I say it?—unreasonably. I don't want to get on your bad side, Josh, because I know how important you and your family are in this town, and I ought to respect you for that."

Josh relaxed and smirked before putting on a more serious face. "Thank you for that. But you interrupted our party and bloodied my friends, and that's not a good start to your marshal's career. We city leaders didn't go out of our way to get you that badge and pay for your office to get this kind of crap in return. But now that we're on the same page, maybe you can make up for it by going down and bringing that young lady up here. I didn't rent this room for nothing, you know what I mean?"

"In the meantime, while these two go get cleaned up, if not doctored up, I'll be here waiting for her. You kind of did me a favor by hurting those two, if you know what I mean?" he said with a chuckle.

Matt nodded slowly and casually stepped closer to him. "I really ought to respect you for being who you are around here, but you know what? I don't!" His face hardened as he stepped forward and grabbed Josh with both hands by his suit vest, pulled him up out of his chair, and then slammed him against the wall and held him there with his eyes burning into those of the son of William T. Slater, the Silver King of Branson and the city's mayor.

Josh was surprised by the speed and ease with which Matt had moved to slam him against the wall. He stared into Matt's cold face and demanded in a shaken voice, "Let me go, Matt. I'm warning you—"

"You're warning me?" Matt asked sounding amused.

Josh nodded toward Matt's rifle on the vanity. "Your back's turned to your rifle," he pointed out in desperation.

Matt smirked. "There's no bullet in the chamber, and I'd have my sidearm out and firing as soon as I heard either one those two grab it. Besides, they can't see so well with all that blood in their eyes, now, can they? The only troll not bleeding so far is you."

Fear crossed Josh's face, and his voice became higher-pitched as he said, "You'll be doing yourself a favor by letting me go. My family and I made you, and we can destroy you. If you want to stay a marshal in this town, you'd better let me go right now. I'm not telling you again!"

Matt released his grip on him.

"Now, go get that girl and bring her here—"

Matt threw a hard right elbow that connected with Josh's cheek and sent him to the floor holding his cheekbone in shock as he looked back up at him. The marshal moved his left leg forward and followed it with a hard kick to Josh's face that rolled him onto his back. He reached down with his left hand, grabbed Josh's vest again, lifted his head up, and threw a fist into Josh's face, then hit him again. When blood was smeared across Josh's face and his cheek had begun swelling from the elbow, Matt let him go and he dropped to the floor.

The crotch of Josh's gray suit pants darkened as he urinated. Matt stood up and looked at Tim, who now pressed a bloody towel to his head as he sat on the edge of the bed watching Matt. Travis was still on the floor holding his hands over his forehead. Matt looked back down at Josh and said, "You don't look so far above me after all, Josh. You might want to remember that."

He stepped back to the middle of the room and looked at three hurting men. "How disappointing. I was expecting more of a fight from you three trolls. Here, put this under your head. You're getting blood all over Lee's floor," he said, tossing Travis a towel.

"You're going to pay for that!" Josh yelled bitterly as he turned onto his hands and knees to get up. He was horrified to have pissed his pants.

Matt stepped quickly to Josh and kicked him hard in the stomach. He fell to his back against the wall, holding his stomach. He'd had the wind knocked out of him and struggled to get a breath.

Matt shouted, "Don't threaten me! What are you going to do, piss on my boots? Where's your wife, Josh? Does she know you're waiting up here for another woman to force yourself on? A blackmailed woman who has been set up illegally by your so-called sheriff! Does your wife know that? You all make me sick!" he exclaimed sharply while turning around to face the other two. "And what about your wife, Travis? Does your wife know what a lowlife piece of slug shit you are?"

Travis sat against the wall in a puddle of blood, trying to stop his cut forehead from bleeding with the towel Matt had tossed him.

Matt stepped over to Travis and knelt in front of him. "You've been lying to Christine since she arrived here. And this note here..." He pulled out the note Christine had given him. "Should I hand it to your wife when I explain where that gash on your head came from? Would you like that?" he shouted, demanding an answer.

"No," Travis said quietly in response.

"Look right here in my eyes, Travis," Matt said and motioned to his eyes. When Travis looked up from the floor, Matt continued, "If you ever tell someone I have syphilis again or tell another lie about me, I will break your jaw. Do you understand me?"

"Yes," Travis affirmed, closing his eyes. His head throbbed, and he was nauseated.

"Good," Matt said. He suddenly threw a sharp right fist into Travis's nose, and it knocked Travis's head against the wall. He slid to the floor and lay on his side.

Matt stood up and turned toward Josh. "What about you, Josh? Do you think your pretty wife would like that?"

"No, she wouldn't!" he said through gritted teeth, looking at Matt with furious eyes.

"None of you had better ever speak to Christine Knapp again! Do you hear me? You all better leave her alone! Bella too, Tim. Do you hear me?" Matt asked, anger burning in his eyes. "Do you?" he yelled, and slapped Tim hard across the face to get him to answer.

"Yes!" Tim shouted painfully. "I hear you!"

"Good," Matt said pointedly to Tim. "I'm going to tell all three of you trolls something right now: if you try to sneak around my back somehow to scare her, I will bust you up much more than I already have. I'm warning you, I will hurt you bad! If you think you're hurting now, I promise you're not. Your days of intimidating, blackmailing, and harassing the citizens of this town and this county are over. I won't allow it! The corruption of this town is coming to an end, and it's coming to an end right now!"

Josh Slater lifted his head as he slowly stood up to sit down in the chair again. His eyes burned into Matt. His nose bled steadily, but it wasn't broken. "Your whole family's in on the corruption business around here! The only reason you became a marshal is because of us! You owe my father, and you owe me! Who the hell do you think you are to hit me? You'll be lucky to stay around here when I get through with you! We own you as much as we own that girl!"

Matt chuckled and shook his head at Josh's obstinance. He walked across the room toward where Josh just sat down on the chair and covered his face to block any forthcoming slaps like Tim had received. Instead, Matt unexpectedly kicked through the front left leg of the chair with a powerful downward blow, collapsing the chair out from under him. Josh fell to his hands and knees on the floor.

"Wake up, Josh! You are dreaming if you think you have any control over me. All three of you trolls are sitting here bleeding like abused pups, and there's only one of me! Do you really think your words scare me? Your threats are what, political? I don't make threats, gentlemen. I'm all about blood and pain. Remember, I'm the guy who killed the Dobson Gang when I was just a kid, and I've killed a lot of men who were a hell of a lot more terrifying than any of you since then.

"Weigh your options carefully before you threaten me because next time I won't be nice to any of you." He paused to look at the three men, then spoke harshly. "This is your only warning: leave her alone! And I better never hear of you trying to blackmail another girl again, not ever!"

"She's just a whore!" Tim stated from beside the bed.

"Are you really stupid enough to keep talking?" Matt asked, amazed. "If she was, you wouldn't have to make up lies to blackmail her!" he yelled fiercely. "I've seen a lot of sick things in my life, but you three have the least morality of the worst of all whores by far. You all disgust me, and trust me, if this happens again, I *will* punish you! The corruption stops tonight!"

He opened the door and paused before leaving with his rifle in hand. "You know, you're supposed to protect the people of this community. All of them, despite who they are or what they are. All three of you have positions of authority, and you're abusing them. I for one won't allow that to continue. I'm here to stay, whether you like me or not. You want to fight me? I'm game. If you want to get along, then earn my respect by being decent human beings. The choice is yours."

He paused and sighed. "By the way, Tim, I sure am glad it was you who rented this room. That makes you responsible for the damages. And I think it's going to be expensive, if you don't mind me saying." He chuckled as he stepped out into the hallway and closed the door behind him. He had been hoping for a tougher fight, but then again, an easy but thorough whipping leaves a deeper impression than a barely-won fight. They had been warned.

MATT WALKED into Bella's Dance Hall near midnight and stayed in the entry alcove to remain out of sight until the last dance auction was over. He didn't want to be noticed, but he had to stand in the doorway to find Christine. He saw her smile shine while she watched her friends being auctioned off, and their smiles growing as the price went up. Warmth grew within Matt as her joy for her friends heightened. She looked so innocent and adorable standing in the background and allowing her friends to be the center of attention. When the time came for Christine to be auctioned off for the last dance of the night, the crowd of men suddenly sprang to life to keep the price going up, but it was brought to an abrupt halt when Bella yelled, "Wait! Hold it, Ernie!" to the band leader, who doubled as the auctioneer.

When he paused, Bella told everyone, "I'm sorry, gentlemen, but this dance is on me" and walked toward the alcove. She smiled widely as she neared Matt and said, "My name is Bella, and I understand I owe you more than I can ever pay back. Thank you, Marshal Bannister. We'll talk later, but right now I need you to go dance with Christine, please. The band is waiting on you, and so is Christine."

Matt chuckled. "Ma'am, I'm afraid I can't conform to your rules. I might've made some enemies tonight, and I've got enough already that I won't be without my sidearm," he said with a nod toward the sign mentioning no weapons were allowed.

Bella scoffed, waved her hand, and took his arm to lead him through the door into the main dance hall. "If there's anyone in the world I don't mind breaking that rule, it's you. Now do me a favor and go have some fun with Christine. You'll find she's a very respectable young lady."

"I have no doubt," he said as he was led onto the floor by Bella.

Christine's eyes locked onto his, and she smiled appreciatively while she waited for Bella to escort him through the crowd to her. Bella took his left hand, and with her other hand reached for Christine's. Putting her hand into his, she held them there with her own as she said, 'Christine, may I introduce you to Marshal Matt Bannister? Matt, this is Miss Christine Knapp, a professional dancer and singer. May I be so bold as to encourage you two to dance and enjoy some time talking after we close?" She let go of their hands and said to Ernie, "Okay, Ernie, play something long and slow. It's a special night."

Christine was embarrassed, and smiled as she took Matt's other hand and held it as the band grabbed new music. "Forgive Bella's forwardness. She can be a little bold, but she has a heart of gold."

Matt smiled uneasily as an uncommon excitement like static electricity ran through him at the touch of her hands. "She seems very nice. Um, just so you know, I don't know how to dance very well."

"I guess I'll just have to teach you because you're not getting out of it now," she told him. She spoke sincerely as she looked into his eyes. "I was hoping you would show up in time to dance at least once. I'm glad you did."

Matt smiled uncomfortably as she let go of his right hand and placed her hand on his bicep. He placed his on her side lightly as the music began to play and they started to move slowly across the floor. "Me, too," he said.

They danced across the floor slowly to the rhythm of the band. Matt held her firmly but kept an appropriate distance. Even so, his eyes were drawn to hers. She smiled warmly. "You're not a bad dancer," she commented awkwardly.

He smiled at her compliment, feeling more at ease. "I haven't danced since I was what, fifteen? It's been awhile."

Her eyes shifted away from Matt, and her smile faded into what appeared to be a sad expression of deep thought. She kept her eyes toward the floor while they danced. After a few minutes, she looked up into his eyes and asked softly, "Can I tell you something?"

He nodded. "Of course," he said, knowing she was sincere because of the childlike honesty in her eyes.

"I..." she started hesitantly, then paused. "I've never felt safer in anyone's hands. Not even my husband's."

He tilted his head in question and then straightened it, a gentle smile growing on his lips. "Well, you're pretty safe."

She grinned and shook her head, not expecting him to answer her the way he had. She had been sincere. She had never spoken those words to anyone else she had ever danced with. She couldn't understand it, but being held by Matt's strong hands and with the gentle strength that she recognized in his eyes, she knew no one would ever hurt her in his presence. The only other man who had ever made feel that safe in this big world full of cruelty was her grandfather. Her husband Richard was a wonderful man, and she always felt safe with him, but he didn't have the strength to put a protective shield over her the way her grandfather and Matt did. It was a secure sensation, and oddly comfortable enough that she didn't want the dance to end. Her left hand moved behind his shoulder, and they danced a touch closer as the music continued. There were about twenty couples dancing to the same song, but for the ten minutes the band played, they noticed no one but each other and felt nothing but the warmth of their hands as they held each other.

It was easy to understand why Kyle might've been attracted to her. She was beautiful, and had an inviting warmth to her character that was both wholesome and adorable. However, Kyle was married, and that made all the difference between right and wrong. There were lines of morality a man should never cross, and the lines outside of a marital relationship should never be crossed. Those same lines applied to anyone in a relationship where loyalty was supposed to define the very words "committed relationship."

Like the one Matt had started a week before when he was in Sweethome, Idaho with a beautiful single mother named Felisha Conway. He had devoted himself to Felisha, and now, dancing with a lady he had just met, he could feel himself growing quite fond of Christine. It was an attraction that he had to force away and keep locked up tight as his thoughts went to Felisha and the friendship he had built with her.

He frowned because the realization of being attracted to Christine weighed heavily upon his heart.

She noticed his subtle change of countenance. "Is something wrong? If what I said bothers you, I'm sorry. I didn't mean to."

He shook his head. "No, it's fine," he said as the dance came to its end. He reluctantly let her hands go, and then stood where he was staring into her eyes without the words to say goodbye.

"Marshal Bannister, you dance just fine," she offered, a compliment from a professional dancer. "I think you must've learned how to dance very well back when you were fifteen. I have never felt safer, and that's a nice feeling. Thank you for everything."

He nodded slowly and smiled sadly. "You're welcome. You have nothing to fear from the sheriff or his two trolls anymore. If they ever bother you again, and I don't care what they threaten, please tell me. I can't protect you if you don't trust me enough to come tell me. Okay?"

Christine frowned with disappointment when the conversation turned professional rather than personal. "I promise, I will."

Matt nodded. He seemed quite uncomfortable, and perhaps even troubled in his thoughts. "Thank you for the dance. I enjoyed it, but I better get going."

"You don't want to stay after and visit for a bit? I would like to say thank you for all you've done for me."

Matt smiled. "You already have."

Bella walked onto the dancefloor and hooked Matt's arm into hers. "I sure am glad you're staying after for a few minutes so we can get to know you a little bit, Matt. You know, it looked to me like you have a natural grace in your steps. That's a rare thing in most mining towns. Most men just stomp their feet and end up nearly tripping my ladies with their drunken steps. You don't drink, do you?"

"I do not."

"I don't either, nor do my girls when they're dancing. Christine doesn't drink at all since she's a faithful Christian lady. The only reason she's with us is because of what happened in Denver, which I'm sure she's already told you about. It was very sad, but she's come a long way since then. Not to change the subject, but I heard you beat those pukes up pretty good for us. Thank you!"

Matt frowned. "How did you hear about that so soon?"

Bella gave a loud, hearty laugh. "Branson's not so big that it takes any time for gossip to get around here," she said as she led him to a table near the emptying bar.

"I suppose not."

Edith and Helen led Sam and Paul over to join Bella and Christine to visit with Matt. Helen quickly introduced herself and wrapped her arms around him unexpectedly. "I know you don't know me, but I want to thank you! Oh my gosh, you just saved our lives, and I don't know how to say thank you, except, thank you!"

Matt smiled pleasantly. "You're welcome. It's what I'm here for."

Edith asked, "Marshal, I want to thank you too. What you've done is an answered prayer, and I haven't prayed so hard in years. Can I be so bold as to ask you for a favor? I left home under bad circumstances. Is it possible that I could get you to write to the sheriff of my home town and see if he knows where my brother and sisters are? My parents want nothing to do with me, but my siblings might. I'd like to connect with them if I could get their address. Can I get your help with that? I heard from the lady who mends our dresses, Missus Lesko, that you did that for her daughter, who I heard you just brought back here from Sweethome."

Matt nodded. "I'd be glad to. Come by my office on Monday and give me all the information you have, and I'll send a letter for you."

Edith smiled joyfully as she wrapped her arm around Paul. "I'll be there, thank you. You have no idea how much that means to me."

"I might. I didn't see my family for a long time either, and to be honest, I wasn't so sure they'd accept me back. But they did, and I hope yours will too. Besides, I saw the reunion between Abby Lesko and her parents, and that's all the thanks I need. It was a powerful moment. Yes, I'd be happy to help you out if I can."

Sam Troyer reached over to shake Matt's hand. "Matt, I don't know how to say thank you for what you did. I wanted to kill that bastard, so thank you!"

Matt shook his hand. "You're welcome."

Paul stuck his hand out as well. "We owe you!"

Matt shook his hand too. "No, you don't. It was my pleasure. And you won't have any more trouble with them, I promise."

Helen spoke excitedly. "It sure is a beautiful night outside! You should take Christine for a walk and enjoy it. She's been hiding in here for a long time now. It would do her good to get out into the fresh air."

Bella frowned since the idea had not occurred to her.

"Why don't you two go for a walk and get to know each other? I think that's a good idea."

Christine looked at Matt uncomfortably, "We don't have to if you don't want to."

Matt smiled. He disliked being put on the spot like that. "I actually need to get going. It was nice to meet you all, though."

"What, are you kidding me?" Helen asked surprised. "Every man around here would love to take Christine out for a walk on a night like this. Are you courting someone else or something?" Helen asked bluntly.

Matt nodded slowly. "I am, actually. I met a lady in Sweethome when I went over there, and we are courting, I guess you could say." Matt noticed the disappointment in Christine's expression. He couldn't think of anything else to say in the uncomfortable silence that followed his statement. "Well, I must be going. Have a good night."

"I'll see you out," Christine said.

As they began to walk toward the door, Bella asked, "Matt, you didn't go to that play of *Romeo and Juliet*, did you?"

Matt turned to look at her and shook his head. "No. I was out of town."

"Have you ever read the play?"

Matt nodded. "I have, but it's been years."

"You should read it again, because you know, Matt, one of the saddest things in the world is being in a relationship with the wrong person when the right one comes along."

Matt looked at Bella for a few seconds before answering her. "I'll keep that in mind."

"You better, because you'd be a damn fool to give up the most perfect lady I have ever known. I'm not normally this bold, but you two have something special between you. I can see it, and so can my girls."

"That's true," Helen agreed quickly.

"Bella!" Christine exclaimed, shaking her head in embarrassment.

Bella raised her hands in surrender. "Okay. I'm just calling it as I see it. I apologize, Matt, if I embarrassed you, but before you say 'I do' to some other lady, get to know Christine. You'll be glad you did."

Matt smiled awkwardly. "I'll do that."

"Come on, I'll show you out," Christine said. She took Matt's arm and led him toward the door, her friends continuing to urge Matt to break it off with the other lady and get to know her. She stepped outside onto the empty front porch and closed the door behind her to end the embarrassing clamor. "I am so sorry about them. I really am. They just...I don't know." Christine was horrified to have been involved in such a high-pressure situation.

Matt laughed. "It's fine. Christine, it was nice to meet you, and thank you for the dance." He paused, leaving an uncomfortable silence between them. "I'll see you around." He went down the first three steps.

"Friends?" she asked suddenly.

He looked back up at her. "Absolutely. You're welcome anytime. Have a good night, Christine." He stepped off the porch slowly and walked up the street to go home.

Christine watched him walk away. Her heart was filled with sadness, and she wondered if she would ever find love again with an honest and good man. She had felt something for Matt, something deep down inside, but it was apparently for nothing. He had another lady in his life, and Christine was back where she had started her dancing career—heartbroken and alone.

Bella stepped outside and put an arm around her, and she too watched Matt walk away. She took a deep breath and said softly, "He'll be back. Until then, just be his friend."

"I don't know Bella. That lady must be something special to win his heart."

"Maybe, but not as special as you. How did you get to know your husband?"

"We were neighbors."

"I didn't ask how you met him, I asked how you got to know him?"

Christine smiled sadly. "We were friends. Best friends."

Bella nodded. "Start small. Be his friend. Go see him this week, and make yourself known. His lady friend lives in Idaho, and those long-distance relationships seldom work out. She'll have to move here to be with him. Until then, go be yourself and shine. He's a good man. He'd be a good friend and a good...best friend. Now come on in and get some rest. It's been a long day."

Christine turned around to face Bella. "It's over, isn't it? The sheriff and Travis and all that fear?"

"It sure is, sweetheart."

There was a glimmer of a tear in her eyes as she asked, "Do you think I'll ever find a love like I had with Richard again?"

Bella smiled kindly. "No. It will be magical, exciting, and just as real, but more so."

"I don't see that happening," she said as she wiped her eyes.

"What is it you always say? 'Walk by faith, not by sight?' You never know what the future holds when the Lord is your shepherd. Be patient."

Neither of the two ladies noticed Matt stopping at the corner and turning back to look at Christine before he disappeared around the corner. He sighed as he remembered Annie's words from back in June about women watching him walk away if they were interested. A certain sadness filled him from the inside out since Christine's back was turned toward him while she spoke with Bella. She was probably giving Bella an earful for embarrassing her in front of a man she was not interested in. She certainly wasn't interested enough to go for a walk or to watch him walk away.

It didn't matter since he was committed to Felisha, and she would be moving to Branson soon enough. Yes, Felisha was coming to Branson, and he'd probably never see Christine again except for a casual wave on the street. He had done his job, and he had done it right. Christine had been thankful, and it made a difference in her life. He couldn't ask for more gratitude than that.

He turned the corner with a frown and walked toward his empty home.

WATCH FOR WOLVES OF WINDSOR RIDGE (MATT BANNISTER WESTERN 4)

Welcome to Windsor Ridge, where Adam Bannister is led by a huge wolf – straight into the blurred battle lines.

Nathan Peirce is hiding from an unjust bounty in Loveland, a small logging community in the treacherous Wallowa Mountains of Oregon. When the bank is robbed, Nathan is asked to join the local posse being led by their incompetent sheriff and a brooding stranger forced by the sheriff to help track the robbers.

Adam Bannister is elk hunting in the southern Wallowa's when he sees the largest wolf he's ever seen. Determined to hunt the wolf, he follows it over Windsor Ridge and into the direct path of the bank robbers and what's left of the doomed posse.

One man is a serial killer, another is one of the most wanted men in the west. A gang of bank robbers and the brother of the U.S. Marshal Matt Bannister, who finds himself in the middle of a battle between some of the best and worst of mankind.

Watch for Wolves of Windsor Ridge (Matt Bannister Western 4)

Sometimes, it's safer to trust a pack of wolves than a man.

AVAILABLE NOW

ABOUT THE AUTHOR

Ken Pratt and his wife, Cathy, have been married for 22 years and are blessed with five children and six grandchildren. They live on the Oregon Coast where they are raising the youngest of their children. Ken Pratt grew up in the small farming community of Dayton, Oregon.

Ken worked to make a living, but his passion has always been writing. Having a busy family, the only "free" time he had to write was late at night getting no more than five hours of sleep a night. He has penned several novels that are being published along with several children stories as well.

Made in the USA
Monee, IL
05 November 2020